GHOST TOWN

THE GENESIS EVENT

PART – 1: DESTRUCTION

By

Leif J. Erickson

Contents

Ghost Town – The Genesis Event Part I: Destruction

The small village of Whiterock had been left devastated. Ghost Town Labs, led by Doctor Victor Tesla, had concluded their tests—turning almost the entire population of 800 into ghosts. The ghosts had performed better than Doctor Tesla could have ever hoped—causing death and destruction wherever they went. The government-funded project that Victor had started so many years ago, had now been completed by his company, Ghost Town Labs. His former government had no idea the terrors he was about to unleash.

Ghost Town Labs had discovered that when people turned to ghosts they would move through four different classes of ghosts. First, was a spirit—someone who was unaware they were dead and very easy to move around and get rid of. Next, was the shadow—someone who knows they are dead, who will attempt to kill the living, and is more difficult to destroy. Apparitions are next—cunning, vengeful creatures that enjoy killing, can set traps, and are very hard to destroy. The final class—phantoms. Phantoms are almost impossible to kill as they can set traps, disappear in the blink of an eye, and will not stop killing for anything.

All people who are turned to ghosts, start at the spirit class. The way they develop further is based on how many people and other ghosts they take—merging the souls of the living and dead to make themselves stronger. To date, only one ghost has developed to the phantom class—Hannah Jones. Hannah, a former FBI agent until her untimely death in the labs beneath the forests of Whiterock, was carefully monitored by Doctor Tesla and his team as she grew and developed. Doctor Tesla now plans to show the world his power with what he's dubbed *The Genesis Event*.

Starting in Genesis, Minnesota, Ghost Town Labs plans to allow Hannah to ravage the metropolis—turning its millions of citizens into ghosts, all the while being carefully monitored by Ghost Town Labs and Doctor Tesla himself. Much planning went into picking Genesis as the testing grounds. Ghost Town Labs has complete control over the cities cellphone towers, radio and television linkups, internet, and landline phones. They have placed cameras all over the city to monitor what happens. The city has been sealed so that once Hannah is released, no one will be able to get out.

Doctor Tesla, always determined to have the best data available, has sent a number of Ghost Town Labs' employees into Genesis under the guises of normal working-class citizens to gather intelligence in real time. His daughter, Morgan Tesla, being the youngest of the employees at 25, had used fake documents to get into the Genesis Academy—the top year-round high school in Genesis. Erin Minot, a British super spy, has accepted a sales position at The Mall of Genesis—one of the largest malls in the world. Mackenzie Hanson, former FBI partner of Hannah Jones will be positioned in the Genesis First Bank and Trust. Mackenzie is always working for Ghost Town Labs. Maria Diego, Victor Tesla's lover, is working with city workers throughout the city. Ryan Minot, Erin's husband, and Jake Arnold, a mechanic for Ghost Town Labs, will be posing as city police.

Doctor Tesla chose these positions to have a good representation of what happens in the city and to see how the people of Genesis will react in and around his ghosts. Tesla is planning to show the world the power of his ghosts and he wants everyone to know the damage that can be done. In Doctor Tesla's mind, he must have reliable eyewitness accounts to what is happening in Genesis.

One of the many questions Doctor Tesla and Ghost Town Labs wants answered, is how fast it takes a normal population to discover the secrets of how to disperse a ghost—that is, to banish it from this plane of existence. Currently, Ghost Town Labs knows that fire and electricity will destroy any ghosts, if enough is used. They have developed E.P.D., or electro-plasma distorter bullets that can be loaded into normal guns and are quite effective on the ghosts.

From the tests in Whiterock, they know that without a working separator—the device they built, which is put underground and binds the soul to earth after the body has died—how Ghost Town Labs created their ghosts. The ghosts can only survive for up to twenty minutes. Ghost Town Labs has buried separators all over Genesis to ensure that no matter where in the town the ghosts are, they will stay until taken out.

The events that took place in Whiterock, as detailed in *'Ghost Town – The Whiterock Incident: Parts I II & III'*—are nothing compared to the destruction that Doctor Tesla and his team have planned for Genesis. As military troops are racing to Genesis to prevent the attack, a black, 1965 Cadillac Hearse with the most dangerous payload is heading toward the Colfax Gallery—an open-air mall with upscale shopping and dining in the heart of Genesis. Inside the hearse is a custom-made casket—the lid magnetically sealed with an electric field running throughout to ensure the Genesis Ghost, Hannah Jones, remains inside until the time is right. When the electric field is turned off and the lid opened—nothing will contain Hannah, nor be able to stop her from unleashing Doctor Victor Tesla's madness and destruction on an unsuspecting population...

Summer School Part I

Two girls crept through the hallways of the old brick school building. The air conditioning had been on the fritz so the red brick walls bore a sweaty look as the humidity of the air made sitting in the building almost unbearable. With as beautiful a summer day outside, no one could expect high school kids to pay attention to the boring lectures in the year- round school.

The girls reached their destination—the weight room door. The female in the lead, a twig-skinny, freckled teen with wild autumn-red hair dropping just past her neck and deep green eyes, paused outside the door and looked around. The girl scanned the hallway, making sure no one was paying attention. No one would have questioned the first girl entering the weight room wearing red baggy gym shorts with a plain white t-shirt that was tucked in—and sneakers with no socks showing.

Her companion would draw more attention in the weight room. A five-foot-ten-inch girl, who looked more like a woman trying to act younger than a teenager with her brunette hair in a sloppy ponytail, adventurous brown eyes, a mature body, and a thin face. Her makeup was already smudged from sweat and it wasn't even ten in the morning. The girl wore the required school uniform—a black pleated skirt that touched her knees, a purple pullover, a wide black belt, black platform boots that went up to her knees and she was dripping with accessories as she followed her friend into the workout room.

Once in the empty room, full of iron and reeking of sweat, the girls looked around with pause, like they were waiting for someone. The girl in the uniform looked at her watch as she sat on a weight machine. She looked to the other girl who motioned for her to be patient. The girl in the gym shorts laid down beneath a bench-press bar that was loaded with one-hundred and forty-five pounds of weight. She attempted to lift the bar, but she couldn't even move it. Her friend giggled as she struggled.

From the bowels of the old building, an air conditioning system wheezed, sputtered, and coughed to life. The fans barely moved any air—air that was no cooler than the air that was in the room—but the humming and knocking noise of the system was just what the girls had been waiting for.

The girl in the gym shorts quickly moved to the wall of the room, where a three-foot by three-foot air duct grate was easily slid off the wall. The girl motioned her friend into the air duct. Both girls disappeared from the weight room through the duct as the girl replaced the grate, leaving no trace of their trespass to the room.

The girls moved quickly on their hands and knees through the duct. They didn't need to move very far, less than fifty feet before they were at another grate—this one already open. The girls quickly went through and found themselves in a janitorial storage room. The grate opened toward the rear of the room, underneath a shelving structure that ran along the length of the wall. On the shelving unit were cleaning supplies, paper products and an inventory of spare parts for the school. The red-haired girl quickly rushed to the door, making sure that both the knob and the deadbolt were locked.

"It's locked," a male voice rang out behind them. "I already checked it myself."

The girls spun around to see a handsome, buff male standing behind them. He was big—six-foot tall and very well-muscled, in black gym shorts showing off his six-pack abs, broad chest, and massive arms. The boy was tan, and even though he stood without a shirt, there were beads of sweat running down his face and chest. The boy had a block head, with wavy brown hair that broke to his neckline all pushed back. With thin eyebrows and sharp features, the boy was the all-American handsome quarterback star of the school.

The twiggy girl smiled at the guy as he walked up to her, grabbed her hand, spun her around, and planted a deep kiss on her lips—holding her left hand in his right. He placed his left hand on her stomach before slowly running along her side, allowing it to rest a little too far below her waistline. The pair shared a sloppy but passionate kiss while the other girl continued to look around the room. The boy tried to untuck the girl's shirt, and that's when she stopped the kiss, pulling her head away but leaving her body in his grasp. She gave him a seductive smile and a wink as she turned from him.

"This is my boyfriend, Sam," the girl said. "He's the quarterback and the captain of the football team."

"He looks like it," the other girl said, smiling.

"Sam, that's Morgan Tesla," the girl said. "She's the one I was telling you about. Lived out in the country...some ghost town. But her dad got a job here in Genesis, so she's starting school."

"So, you're a country gal?" Sam asked, extending a hand to shake Morgan's.

"I am," Morgan said, shaking his.

"You tip cows and stuff?"

"Never."

"Chew tobbacy?"

"Never."

"You ever..."

"She's okay," the girl said, interrupting. "Don't mind him, the only thing he can think about is sex and football."

"You're gonna love that football thought when I have a full-ride scholarship to state next year. Four years there, then on to the big leagues."

"You want to play professional?" Morgan asked. "What team?"

"Doesn't matter, as long as I'm getting paid. That all I care about. So, Amber," Sam said, turning his attention back to his girlfriend, Amber Dean, "it's awfully hot. You should probably take your shirt off. You'd be much more comfortable."

"Not even ten and you're already trying to talk me out of my shirt," Amber smiled. "You know that you need to work harder than that, Sam."

"I don't mean to be that person," Morgan said, "but won't we get in trouble for cutting class?"

"Right now, we have a school wide study hall," Amber said. "The teachers don't keep a very close eye on us."

"What about if the janitor comes in here to get something?" Morgan asked. "We don't have to keep him silent somehow, do we?"

"Don't worry about it," Amber said. "We lock both the knob and the deadbolt. We switched out the original deadbolt with our own so they don't have a key for it. He'll cycle through his key ring...trying to find a master key to open it...give up, go to the office for a different set of keys, at which point we open the deadbolt and scram from the room. It's a nice setup."

"Sounds good," Morgan said.

Amber was about to continue when more people entered the room from the same grate that Amber had led Morgan through. First out were two boys like Sam—tall and muscular, with soft high school faces that had yet to fully mature. Both boys had let their hair grow too long, looking scruffy as neither had shaved in days. Both in gym shorts and plain t-shirts, gave a high five to Sam as they looked over Morgan like she was a piece of meat for them to devour.

Behind the boys was a haunting Latin beauty of medium height, with a curvy and developed body. She was darker skinned, with long, thick black hair that shimmered like it was from a shampoo commercial as it cascaded down to her lower back. Her spider-black eyes sparkled like a star in the night as her plumped lips were curved into a bright smile. The girl wore red and white short nylon running shorts, a black tank top that didn't touch the top of the shorts and black running shoes with no socks showing.

"Thank God Principal Ross suspended the dress code this week," the Latin said. "There's no way I could have worn one of those uniforms in this kind of heat."

"There were rules that we were supposed to follow," the boy with the glasses said. "At least six inches of inseam on shorts and no stomachs showing. You're violating both."

"Are you complaining?" the beauty asked as she posed for the boy.

"No." He smiled. "Just commenting. Who's the new chick that didn't get the dress-code memo?"

"Morgan Tesla," Amber said. "Morgan, the one with the glasses is Jack. The dopy looking one is Todd, and…"

"And I'm Isabella Corvus," Isabella said. "But call me Is."

"Is?" Morgan asked.

"Yes," Is said. "Is. You're the new farm girl, right? Let me give you a few pointers for surviving the Genesis Academy. The boys here are very easy to figure out and play with. Sam's the quarterback, Jack and Todd are the running backs, Amber's the cheerleader, and I'm the volleyball captain. We're all pretty laid back. No drinking or drugs during the season, and if you need homework or tests, you can buy any of them pretty cheap."

"Sounds like my old school," Morgan said, with a smile. "Except, back there we had only ten to fifteen kids in each grade. One hundred and fifty in my school, K through twelve, all in one building."

"Wow," Todd said. "This building is freshman through senior and we have over six hundred here. So, why did you move here? What town were you from?"

"Whiterock," Morgan said. "I'd been there for over ten years. My dad's a scientist and he'd been working on a research project out there. He went as far with his work as he could in the small town, so we had to move here so he could finish."

"Any siblings?" Sam asked. "What does your mom do?"

"Well…" Morgan looked down. "I had an older sister but both her and my mother passed away. I'm sorry, but I really can't talk about it. Just too painful."

"Sorry," Sam said. "What do you do for fun?"

"I helped dad with his work," Morgan said. "And I read a lot. I didn't have a lot of friends in Whiterock. I spent a lot of time with dad's girlfriend, Maria. She's pretty fun."

"Nice," Is said. "Any sports?"

"Never really took to any," Morgan said.

"I just got to say it," Jack said, looking Morgan over from head to toe. "You look older…like mid-twenties or something. How old are you?"

"I get that a lot," Morgan said. "I'm eighteen. I was held back."

The entire group looked at Morgan, all thinking she looked much older than a high school student. Morgan hoped they would believe the lie. She thought that with her school uniform, and the way she did her makeup and hair, her true age would be disguised. As Morgan looked over the group, she noticed Sam couldn't take his eyes off Amber. Amber knew it and was deliberately playing with her hair and posing with her chest out to drive him nuts.

"So, what do you guys do in this room?" Morgan asked, hoping to divert the conversation. "Nothing too extreme, I hope."

"We do," Sam said, as he grabbed Amber's hand.

Amber smiled and walked with Sam as they went around a storage shelf. Morgan could hear them kissing as she saw Amber's t-shirt hit the floor. Morgan raised an eyebrow as the pair moved themselves onto a pile of floor mats. She looked back to the others. Todd and Jack were already looking at a tablet computer with a certain intensity. Morgan tried to get a look at what they were watching but couldn't see the screen.

"Last year's football games," Is said. "They are already getting ready for the season. Watching games to see what went right and what went wrong."

"How far are those two going to go?" Morgan asked, pointing to Sam and Amber.

"You don't need to watch your hair," Is said, smiling, "if that's what you're worried about. They'll just make-out for the hour. They save the heavy stuff for after school. So, what should we do Morgan, watch old football games...or make out?"

Morgan's eyes got big as she looked over Is. Morgan was caught off guard by the comment. She had been paying attention to her watch, knowing that very soon Hannah would be released from the casket and there would be destruction in the area. Morgan looked back to Is, to see a giant smile across her face.

"Just messing with you, girl," Is said. "You gotta realize that I'm not the most serious person around."

Is moved to the back corner of the room and moved some boxes around to reveal a small duct grate which she quickly removed. Is pulled out a pill bottle and a bottle of Rum. She quickly took the cover off the pill bottle and took one of the small, round white pills— swallowing it with a giant swig of Rum from the bottle. She then offered a pill to Morgan.

"What is it?" Morgan asked.

"A synth," Is said. "We have a nerdy, science geek friend that makes them. She makes us these right here in the school."

"What does it do?"

"Makes you feel amazing," Is said. "It feels somewhat like X but you don't feel the need to listen to crappy techno music all night. It's really euphoric. The Rum enhances it. You'll feel great the rest of the day."

"I'd better not," Morgan said. "I've never really done anything like that before and I don't want my first experience to be in school. I'll take some of the Rum though."

Is handed the bottle to Morgan and she took a couple gulps from it. Morgan handed the bottle back to Is, who took another drink before putting both bottles back in the vent and returning all the boxes to hide the grate. Morgan noticed that Is's eyes were already dilating and she had a distant look on her face.

"So tell me, Morgan," Is said, as she made herself a chair from the items on the floor, "what do you think of Genesis and our school so far?"

"It's nice," Morgan said, sitting next to her. "The country has a certain charm but there's something to be said for excitement."

"What were the boys like out there?"

"Same as here," Morgan smiled. "Two things on the brain...sports and sex."

"Boys are so predictable," Is said.

"I thought Amber said you don't drink or do drugs during the season," Morgan said. "What's up with the stuff you're taking?"

"Practice doesn't start for another month," Is said. "This is the only way I can get through a day here. No one understands."

"Understands what?"

Is sighed a heavy sigh as she looked at Morgan. Morgan couldn't tell if Is was mad or upset at the question. Morgan worried that she may have crossed a line. Morgan didn't really care about these kids but she wanted to get a good handle on them before the incident occurred. She wanted to have good data to report to her father.

"My parents moved here from Spain before I was born," Is said. "I'm 100% Spanish. But when I was twelve, they divorced, and it's been hell ever since. Mom has a different boyfriend every month. Each a bigger loser than the last. Dad's been remarried twice, both were psycho women. My time living with them is split, and I never know where they are going to be or who's going to be with them. Right now, I'm with Mom, and we're living with this guy who's in the process of getting a divorce. Think about this...he has three kids living with him, plus his ex-wife...well, wife, they aren't fully divorced yet...living in his house, and then my mom and I move in. I can't stand him...or his son, who's a year younger than me. He thinks that we should be hooking up. I'm worried he's going to do something some night. He drinks a lot. No one around here understands. I just can't wait to turn eighteen in a couple months. Then I'm moving into a place of my own. I have a plan all mapped out."

"Sounds like a lot," Morgan said. "You open up to me pretty easily."

"You've been through stuff," Is said. "If you're mom and sister died young, you know the kind of pain I've been through. There are so many times I just want to get revenge."

Morgan looked at Is. Morgan knew what revenge was going to cost the city. Revenge is what drove Doctor Tesla to destroy a small town, and now revenge was going to destroy a city. Morgan knew that their former country needed to pay for the death of her family, but what Victor was going to do was going too far. As the girl's eyes met, there was an understanding of pain there. Morgan moved up and hugged Is. Is was confused but accepted the hug, squeezing tight as a tear rolled down her cheek.

"Thank you," Is said. "What's your pain?"

"My dad worked for the government," Morgan said, knowing she had to tell Is something. "Classified work. There were a lot of rules about what he could do and who he could talk to. The stress was unbelievable. Things happened and they were murdered. They tried to get Dad too, but he was already gone. He'd asked one of his most trusted friends to get my mom and sister out, but the friend was already paid off by the government. They never knew about me, which is how I was able to get out."

"That's horrible," Is said. "How could a country get away with something like that?"

"I don't know," Morgan said. "It was a strange setup. I don't know if they know where my father went, or why they stopped hunting us, but we've been in the small town for a long time."

Is hugged Morgan. It was a hug that lasted slightly too long, with Is slightly too close to Morgan. Morgan didn't know what it meant, but she felt a connection to this girl. She didn't want to see Is get hurt in the events of the day.

"You should live with us," Morgan said. "We have a spare bedroom that you could stay in. I think that would be a great plan. Dad wouldn't mind."

"Are you serious?" Is asked.

"Sure," Morgan said. "Stick with me, Is, and things will be okay."

"Thank you so much," Is said.

"What the hell is this?" Jack said, as he smacked the side of the tablet. "There's no internet."

"What?" Is asked as she pulled out her phone. "Damn. No service, phone, or net."

"Mine too," Todd said. "Even the Wi-Fi is down. I wonder what happened."

"Hang on," Is said.

Is walked to the door, picked up a phone receiver, and dialed a four-digit number. A strange look came across her face as she depressed the receiver latch a number of times before hanging the phone up.

"That's dead too," Is said. "The last time something like this happened was when a construction project accidentally cut a fiber-optic line. I'm sure that's what happened."

"What are we supposed to do then?" Jack asked.

"Two boys," Todd shrugged, "and two girls."

"Why the hell not," Is said, feeling the effects of the drug kicking into high gear. "Come on, Todd. Morgan, you down with this?"

Morgan looked like a deer caught in the headlights. She had heard and read about teenage behavior, but she didn't think she'd get caught in something like this. Morgan looked over the other kids and knew they were waiting for an answer. Morgan found it funny. She'd done so much, seen so much in her life, but basic romance and fooling around was something that she'd never had time for—although she'd always wanted to find someone. Morgan was pretty sure that this wouldn't lead all the way to sex but she was nervous about how far it might go.

As everyone was waiting for Morgan to answer, a spunky looking girl entered the room from the grate. She was petite, with bleach-blonde hair in a ponytail, pale skin, and darting blue eyes. The girl looked younger that the other kids, her body still developing, and an air of immaturity about her. She wore gray sweatpants, flip flops, and a black t-shirt with cartoon characters on the front. The girl pushed her black-rimmed glasses up as she looked around the room.

"Tiffany," Is said, with surprise on her voice, "what are you doing here?"

"Something big is going on, guys," Tiffany said, quickly, in a nervous voice. "I don't know the extent. Who are you?"

"This is Morgan Tesla," Is said. "Morgan, this is Tiffany, Jack's little sister and a friend of ours. She can do anything with computers. She's incredibly smart."

"She got the brains of the family," Jack said. "I got the brawn and the looks."

"Don't flatter yourself," Is said. "What's going on, Tiffany?"

"I was in the computer lab networking with some teams on the other side of town," Tiffany said. "Net and phones started dropping out everywhere. Television is out, too. The radio hasn't started talking about anything yet. I don't get it."

"I wonder what's going on," Jack asked.

"I don't know what's going on," Tiffany said. "I've never seen systems drop offline like this. Here's the head scratcher...this wasn't a single point event."

"What?" Jack asked. "A single point event?"

"If a server went down," Tiffany explained, "or a line was cut, everything on that server or line would drop off at once. What happened here is that systems started dropping...one by one. The only possibility is that someone was shutting them down. I don't know what's going on, but it's big...really big."

Summer School Part II

Only a half hour had passed since the networks dropped offline but it seemed like a lifetime to kids who were normally glued to their network devices. Todd and Tiffany had left the storage closet to try and find out what was going on. Sam and Amber were still fooling around in a different part of the closet while Is, Morgan and Jack were sitting together telling stories of the past. Over time, Morgan and Is realized they had much more in common than they first thought. Morgan was feeling a deep connection to this girl—already considering her a friend.

As the group was talking, Morgan was hoping that some kind of information would come in that would be useful to Ghost Town Labs. There had been no word from outside the closet. Morgan knew that the networks would not be turned on but it didn't stop the others from constantly checking to see if they could search the net again.

Morgan already had a plan for the rest of the day—to get Is to stay with her, offer her a job within Ghost Town Labs, and take her away from the pain of her family. Morgan knew that Is's family wouldn't be lasting through the day anyway, so Is would have nowhere to turn to. The only problem Morgan could foresee was explaining to Is that she was a part of the madness.

"So Is," Jack said, "things getting any better at the house?"

"Worse," Is said. "The loser's youngest daughter steals anything she can. I have to hide everything."

"What about Terry?"

"He's pushing as hard as ever," Is said. "I'm really worried that he's going to try something one night. I could see him doing it and his dad not caring at all. I've already told mom about it but she thinks that I just don't like living there. She thinks I'm trying to break them up. I swear if I catch that freak in my room again..."

"She caught him looking through her stuff," Jack explained to Morgan. "Her..."

"She gets it," interrupted Is. "They should have found something out, don't you think? I wonder what could be doing this. Maybe we should all head out and see if something is up."

"They'll be back," Jack said. "I wouldn't worry about it."

"And if they don't come back?" Is asked.

Jack was about to respond when a clicking noise came on over the intercom.

"Attention all students," a powerful male voice crackled over the intercom. "This is Principal Ross. All students are to stay where they are. Please close and lock all doors and remain calm. The school is entering a hard lockdown. No students are to be in the hallways. Stay in your rooms with the doors locked. Thank you."

The intercom went silent. The group looked at each other, no one knowing what to say. Sam and Amber, hair a mess and covered in sweat, emerged from the other side of the closet. They too were stunned by what they had heard. In the silence of the room, the group heard someone coming through the vents. They all waited with baited breath, relieved when Todd and Tiffany emerged into the closet.

"What's going on out there?" Is asked. "Why are we in lockdown?"

"Reports are conflicting," Tiffany said. "One report said something about a shooter at the Colfax Gallery in the downtown area. The other report mentioned an attack somewhere on Colfax Avenue. The similarities of the reports are that they are both in the downtown area, and that a lot of people have died."

There was an uneasy silence in the room. No one was quite sure what to say. Morgan knew that this was going to be one of the effects of releasing the ghosts—total misinformation. She knew that until the people accepted what was really going on there would be all sorts of wild stories and rumors floating about.

"What should we do?" Amber asked.

"What do you mean?" Sam asked.

"Are we supposed to stay in the school and die?" Amber said, sarcastically. "I for one don't like this place to begin with. I have no intention of dying within the walls of this building. If there is something going on in Genesis, we should cross the river and head to another town. We could be in Nicollet or Mendota Falls in less than an hour."

"Mendota Falls has a killer used-computer store," Tiffany said, excited. "I could spend hours in that place. Any kind of network device and all the parts you could imagine. Not to mention the guy that owns it is a fox."

"That's in the Northdale Mall," Is said. "Lots of nice clothing boutiques there. I could spend some time there."

"How would we get there?" Todd asked. "I'm not allowed to drive out of Genesis."

"Neither am I," Jack said.

"I can get three others with me," Sam said.

"I can take the rest," Morgan said.

"What's your ride?" Jack asked.

"Hummer," Morgan said. The entire group gave her a strange look. "Dad wanted to make sure I was in a vehicle that would be safe," Morgan explained.

"I'll ride with Morgan," Is said. "Tiffany, you come with us. Amber, I know you'll ride with Sam. Todd and Jack, you might as well ride with him too."

"Good," Sam said. "I'll lead the way. I parked in the back lot near the weight room. Meet me at the gas station across the street. I need to fuel up before we go."

Sam, Amber, Todd and Jack left the room through the grate, leaving the girls by themselves. Morgan had second thoughts about the plan, thinking how good it would have been to gather information about the school's reactions. Morgan wanted to see how the administration was going to handle the day. The lockdown was expected, but Morgan wanted to know what unexpected things they were going to try.

Morgan watched as Tiffany went to the other side of the closet and moved a box to reveal another grate—this one much smaller than the one they entered through. Tiffany easily slid through the grate, but Morgan had reservations about her and Is fitting.

"Don't worry," Is said. "The duct is big enough to fit through…if I can get through it, you can. This will take us right to our lockers, if you want to grab anything. Then we can slip out a side door to get to the parking lot."

Morgan nodded and moved to the grate. She had to wiggle a little to fit herself through the tight grate but was led into a larger duct. She was able to quickly move on her hands and knees along the grate, following the other girls. They moved through half the building before reaching the grate that entered into the locker area.

Tiffany opened the grate and cautiously stuck her head out to look around. When she was certain the coast was clear, she slipped out of the grate motioning for the others to follow. In the hallway the girls went to their lockers and grabbed backpacks, filling them with anything they thought they would need. Morgan didn't go to her locker—she didn't have anything in it anyway. Morgan kept looking down the empty hallway, hoping that a teacher wouldn't bust them.

"How do you plan on getting out of here?" Morgan asked. "The main door is next to the office and the other doors are also watched."

"There's one door that isn't," Tiffany said, as she entered the grate.

Through the grate again, Morgan followed as they took turns through the building. Morgan was impressed at how well these kids had the school mapped out. As they were moving along, Morgan felt something strange—she'd never had a high school experience like this, never had a boyfriend she snuck around with, never got to hang out with friends, and never snuck out around teachers. Morgan began to realize just how much this revenge had cost her.

Morgan remembered some of her education—all private, all by Ghost Town Labs. Most of her training came from the mind control—a way to make her an intelligent doctor before she was twelve years old. She'd never even had friends her own age. A tear welled up in Morgan's eye. She pushed the thought away, knowing what she'd be facing today.

Tiffany reached a grate and opened it. The girls found themselves in a large, dark room. Morgan struggled to see what was in the room. It was a deep, vast, open space, but the only lights were from illuminated exit signs and a small window slit on the door. As Morgan's eyes adjusted to the darkness of the room, she started to notice cars on the cement floor. The smell of fuel and burnt metal gave the room away—the auto shop.

"Only door not on a motion sensor," Tiffany said, as she opened a single-stall garage door.

"Move quickly," Is said, as she ushered Morgan and Tiffany out of the building. "Have to be quick on this."

Is pressed the button to close the garage door and rushed out, jumping over the safety sensors that stop the door from going down if tripped. The group stayed close to the edge of the building as they ran toward the parking lot. They were on the opposite side of the main office so they rushed around the back, taking no time to enjoy the bright, hot, sunny day. When the group could see the parking lot, Tiffany stopped them.

"Okay, Morgan," Tiffany said, in a hushed voice, "where's your car?"

"The black Hummer," Morgan said, pointing. "Fourth row, halfway down."

"Okay," Tiffany said. "On my mark, start running. Have the doors unlocked so we can get right in without waiting. Once we clear the building, don't turn and look back. There's enough girls in this school that they can't positively ID someone from their back."

"Will someone be watching?" Morgan asked.

"You never know," Is said.

"Get ready," Tiffany said, looking around. "Go!"

The three rushed from the building into the open lot. Morgan fumbled, trying to get the keys out of her pocket so she could unlock the doors. Is, an amazingly fast runner, was almost at the passenger door before Morgan hit the unlock button on her keychain. Morgan was impressed that she was running at almost full speed, yet both Is and Tiffany were able to beat her to the car.

Morgan got in, fired the truck up, and pulled out of the parking space. She could already see the gas station across the street and could see Sam filling his car with gas. Morgan pulled up to the stop sign at the edge of the lot and rolled through before pulling into the station and parking. Morgan and the girls got out and entered the convenience store.

"I need the restroom," Morgan said, as she entered the ladies room. "Just be a moment."

"Take your time," Is said. "No rush anymore."

Morgan smiled as she locked the door to the restroom. She already felt like Is was a close friend. Morgan wondered how she could get Is to understand about her role in Ghost Town Labs. Morgan knew it may require mind control, but she didn't want to do that. Morgan wanted something in her life to be natural—pure. She hoped a friendship with a person like Is would be it.

Morgan pulled out her cellphone and smiled at the fact that she still had service. Ghost Town Labs had put up private towers throughout the town so they could stay in touch. Morgan pulled up the text editor on her phone and quickly wrote down notes on how the people reacted to the lockdown and the stories that were already flying around. When Morgan was satisfied with the notes, she put her phone away and exited the bathroom.

"I don't know what I want," Jack said, as he looked over the coolers of drinks. "Soda, energy drink, or sports drink?"

"Just hurry up," Tiffany said, grabbing an energy drink. "He always takes so long to choose."

As Morgan watched her new friends, she couldn't help but notice the other people in the store. They were all about the same—middle class, most on their way to work, looking somewhat professional but not too high up the ladder, and mainly white—but there was something else there. Morgan could almost feel the tension in the air. It was almost electric—like the calm before a storm, but it was there. Morgan strolled around the store, hearing bits and pieces of conversations.

"My phone is out, too…"

"I heard that there's four shooters…"

"It's a government test. Bastards are testing on their own citizens…"

"I heard that 200 people have died…"

"Why isn't there anything on the news?"

"They bought the news…"

"Aliens…"

Morgan smiled at the conversations. It amused her how over-reactive people could be, especially when they didn't know at all what was really going on. Morgan noticed that the others were checking out, so she grabbed a Coke and a chocolate bar and got in line to pay for her items.

There was a woman in front of the kids—mid-forties, hair a mess, clothes wrinkled, and yelling at the cashier. A younger, college-aged man was confused by the hostilities.

"I damn told you to run my credit card," The lady yelled. "I need gas."

"I'm sorry, ma'am," the boy said. "The credit card machines are down. I can only do cash sales."

"I don't like the tone you're taking with me," the woman yelled. "I want to speak to the manager."

"I'm the shift manager," the boy said.

"Don't get smart with me," the lady said. "I need to fill with gas. You value your job, boy? Take this card and run it or I'm gonna have you fired."

"Lady," the clerk said, with a grin, "this is a jag-off minimum-wage job to get me through college. I don't give a damn if you go to the owners...they'll laugh at you too. The machines are down, I can't run your card, if you don't have cash, then I don't have gas."

"You worthless piece of trash," the lady screamed with fire in her eyes, spittle coming from her mouth. "I should come over this counter right now..."

"There a problem here?" a male voice rang out behind them.

The woman turned to see two cops walking toward her. Morgan smiled at the cops, Jake Arnold and Ryan Minot, also Ghost Town Labs' employees dressed in police officer uniforms. Morgan knew their job today would be the most fun—being on the police force, they would be the most likely to see some real action when the Genesis Event got into full swing. Jake winked at Morgan as he walked by her.

"There is a problem," the woman screamed. "He is discriminating against me and won't sell me gas."

"The credit card machine is down," the clerk explained. "I can't run her card. I'd be more than happy to sell her gas if she had cash to pay for it."

"Sounds pretty cut and dry," Jake said. "Why don't you move along, ma'am? There's nothing to be done here."

"This isn't over," the woman shouted. "I'm going to your management and to the city. You cops think you can harass us? Just 'cause you got a badge and a gun don't mean jack. You haven't heard the last of me."

The woman stormed out of the store. She got into her car, revved the engine, and sped out of the lot. The cops just shook their heads.

"Everyone alright here?" Jake asked.

"Fine," the clerk said. "Just want to get the line moving."

"Okay," Jake said, putting two bottles of Coke down on the counter. "This is all we need."

The clerk looked at Jake and Ryan. They'd just cut in front of ten people in line. Jake was handing him money. The clerk didn't know what to do. There were sneers from some of the people in line, but others didn't seem to mind. The clerk let the cops budge and took the money.

"Thank you," Jake said, as the clerk handed him his change.

The cops looked over the line as Jake winked at Morgan again. This time her friends saw it. As Jake walked past Morgan, he gave her a look and she gave him a look back. Morgan was glowing, but not for the reasons her friends thought.

"He was totally into you," Is said. "He was checking you out the entire time. Damn, something 'bout a hunk in a uniform...wouldn't mind him patting me down."

"He wasn't checking me out," Morgan said, with a smile.

"You're blushing," Tiffany said, pointing to Morgan's reddening cheeks. "You totally like him. He was pretty cute though, for an old guy."

"I don't like him," Morgan said, getting more defensive.

"I could get his number for you," Is said. "I bet he'd be willing."

"We're like, teenagers," Morgan said. "Best let him pass."

The kids continued to play with Morgan as they waited in line and paid for their items. Even though they were teasing her, Morgan was secretly loving it, having never had friendly banter like this before. She had never even thought about how kids acted when they hung out, but now that she was getting to experience it, she wanted more than ever to keep the experience going.

The fun lasted until they went outside, heading back for the vehicles. As they were walking through the parking lot, the group heard a noise above them. At first it was a strange thumping noise. As they looked up it didn't take too long before three black helicopters were flying overhead. They moved from the west to the east at top speed. There were no markings on the copters but Morgan knew, beyond a shadow of a doubt, whose choppers they were.

"What the hell is that?" Sam said, watching the choppers fly low overhead. "They have no markings, not even registration numbers on the side."

"Choppers aren't allowed to fly that low over residential areas," Jack said. "Something's wrong, there must be some sort of emergency situation that's causing them to break the rules But those aren't police choppers...not local ones anyway."

"You familiar with police choppers?" Morgan asked. "Been given a ride in a few?"

"Cute," Jack smiled back. "No. My uncle is on the force. I've been in the choppers, when they were on the ground."

"Think they could be feds?" Amber asked. "Remember when that one prisoner escaped and was in the area? The F.B.I. had black helicopters chasing him."

"But those had numbers on the sides," Tiffany said. "These were unmarked helicopters. I couldn't imagine who would be allowed to fly them around."

"Must have something to do with the event that's taken place," Morgan said. "You said both reports placed the event at the Colfax Gallery...what's that?"

"Colfax Avenue and Colfax gallery," Tiffany said. "Colfax Avenue is like the first street in Genesis or something. Maybe it was a trail that was used before the town was here. It's old and famous for some reason. Now Colfax Avenue is the main street through downtown. Lots of stuff there. Colfax Gallery is in the heart of downtown on Colfax Avenue. It has a bunch of shops and street vendors, and other stuff like that. It's where the rich, snobby people hang out."

"Are there lots of people who hang out there?" Morgan asked.

"There are," Todd said. "But we've never been there. There's lots of places in this area that are better to hang out at."

"Maybe we should go there to see what's going on?" Morgan asked.

The group was silent, staring at Morgan. None of them really wanted to see what was going on. If there was a shooter or an attack, they didn't want to be anywhere near it. Morgan could see by the looks on their faces that she had said the wrong thing. As she was about to speak, four police cruisers tore past the store, lights flashing and sirens blaring. Cars were pulling out of the way as the police rumbled by.

"On second thought," Morgan said, watching the police. "Let's head to Mendota Falls."

Summer School Part III

Morgan followed closely to Sam's black Chevy Impala even though the boy had a bit of a lead foot. Morgan noticed that they crossed paths with a number of police cars, but none of them seemed to be too concerned with a pair of cars speeding on city roads. Every police car they met appeared to be heading somewhere to the east–toward Colfax Avenue, with a purpose.

Morgan listened to Tiffany as Is talk about their lives and what was going on. She never realized how much she'd missed, and now she was beginning to realize just how much it bothered her. Just the friendship of these two girls would mean more than anything she'd done in her life. Morgan always had reservations about what her father was going to do, but now she was beginning to question if she should have done more to stop this.

"I don't know," Tiffany said, with a sigh. "It's like, whatever, you know? I'll do it but come on, turn me on a little. Don't expect me to come over, sneak into your room and then *bang*, I'm going down."

"Tiffany's learning the joy of boys," Is explained to Morgan. "She's been hanging with one and it's getting serious."

"Serious?" Morgan asked. "Like thinking marriage?"

"Oh, God no!" Tiffany exclaimed. "You are a small-town girl."

"He wants her to go all the way," Is said. "They've done about everything else up to that point."

"How old are you?" Morgan asked.

"I'm fifteen," Tiffany said. "This is my sophomore year. He's the same age as I am but he's had other girlfriends. He's my first boyfriend."

"I keep telling her to date Todd," Is said. "He's the right guy for her."

"If he asks me out, I'll say yes," Tiffany said. "But he has to go that far. Morgan, what kind of boys do you like? You had a lot of boyfriends on the farm?"

"I didn't date much," Morgan said. "I was busy helping dad with his work. None of the guys in my school were my type."

"What's your type?" Is asked. "No, wait, let me guess. You want a real tough guy...macho type. Someone who when he takes off his shirt, everyone's head turns. Rippling with muscle. He has to be bold and loud, am I right?"

"Not really," Morgan laughed. "I guess that my type would be someone smart, very smart, who I could have intellectual conversations with. Someone who loves nature too. I love going for hikes in the forest."

"That sounds like a good guy," Tiffany said.

Morgan was about to speak when a police car zipped past her, cutting her off as he weaved between the cars on the road. The traffic was heavy and moving slowly. Everyone seemed to be in a hurry to get where they were going, but with all the cars, things were getting backed up.

"Man alive," Morgan said. "Is traffic always like this?"

"Not normally," Is said. "I don't have a car, so I always take the bus. We go down this road and it's never like this. I wonder if this event is what has everyone on edge."

"Turn on the radio," Tiffany said. "See if they are talking about what happened."

Morgan turned on the radio but the station it was set on had nothing but static. Morgan had a confused look on her face.

"Strange," Morgan said. "That station was clear as a bell when I was driving to school this morning."

Morgan tried the other stations on her presets but all were static. She scanned through the stations but there was nothing there. Morgan switched it over to the AM frequency, but it was the same—all static.

"This thing have satellite radio?" Tiffany asked.

"It did, but I didn't renew the subscription," Morgan said. "What could cause all the stations to be out? I thought this area had a lot of radio stations."

"This area does," Is said. "They have a ton of stations. I heard one time that Genesis and the surrounding area has more radio stations per capita than anywhere else. Don't know if that's true, but I know there are a lot of stations. Could an attack take the stations out?"

"They would need to knock out every one of them," Tiffany said. "Unless they had some kind of scrambler device that messes up the airwaves. It's theoretically possible but I've never heard of anyone trying something like that. Not for an entire area anyway."

Morgan nodded her head as they pulled up to a stoplight that was just turning red. Sam could have easily made it through but there would have been no way for Morgan to follow. As the cross traffic started to move, Morgan couldn't help but notice a man who was crossing the street. He appeared to be in his mid-thirties wearing a gray, professional suit. His brown hair was messy and he was sweating profusely. The man was carrying a briefcase which he was swinging wildly as he shouted while walking between cars.

Anyone with a window down was rolling them up. Morgan took a close look at the man. She was looking for any sign that he was a ghost. Morgan had an arsenal of EPD guns and regular handguns in the truck with her, but she wasn't sure what Is and Tiffany would say if she pulled them out and started shooting.

As the man got closer, Morgan could tell that he was human, solid, and hadn't been changed. She breathed a sigh of relief. Morgan knew that she would have to confront a ghost today, and that she would have to explain to her new friends her role in what happened, but she didn't know how she was going to do that yet. As the man got even closer, Morgan rolled the window down an inch to attempt to hear what he was saying.

"GHOSTS!" the man yelled. "There are ghosts in Genesis!"

"Is he saying *ghosts*?" Tiffany asked. "Did I hear him right?"

"You did," Is said. "Roll your window up. There are all kinds of freaks in this city."

"But what if he did see a ghost?" Tiffany asked.

"No such thing," Is said. "This one night I was coming home from the library, right? I was walking 'cause the bus I needed didn't stop near the library. On the street I met a man and woman. Get this, the man was wearing black dancing tights, gray dress shoes, and no top. His hair was long and multicolored. The woman, who was pretty hot by the way, had red pumps and a white gymnastics leotard, that's it, for walking down the street. She had dyed her hair a silver color and she had about a bottle's worth of glitter in her hair and on her body."

"Maybe they were dancers coming back from a performance," Tiffany said.

"No way," Is replied. "They were in no shape to be dancers. She was skinny, with no muscle, and he had a gut and flabby arms. No way were they performers. See, the thing is, I've seen them before...that's how they dress. Weird stuff like that. I've seen the girl walking by herself and talking to no one. I don't dare ever make eye contact with them, but it's no different than this doofus...just some whack-job looking for attention."

"I don't know," Tiffany said. "He looks professional, like he has his stuff together."

As they were watching, the man realized that the girls had their window open. He rushed over to them as Morgan made sure her doors were locked.

"There are ghosts," the man wailed. "You have to get me out of here. The ghosts will kill us all."

"Light's green," Is said, as a car behind Morgan honked. "Dust this loser."

Morgan took off, watching the man yelling behind them. She raced along, trying to catch up with Sam in the other car. As they got closer to the Lowry Lift Bridge, Morgan noticed the increase in traffic accompanied by a slowdown in the speed. The cars around them were getting much more aggressive and Morgan was glad they were in the big Hummer.

As they rounded a corner they could see the lift bridge, but they also noticed that there was no traffic moving on it. Morgan didn't think that Ghost Town Labs could have moved this fast, but she wasn't sure if her father had changed any of the plans.

"What the hell is that?" Tiffany said, pointing to the other side of the bridge. "It looks like they're not letting people over the bridge."

"That looks like a checkpoint or something," Is said.

Morgan looked to the other side of the bridge and saw two Ghost Town Labs' Hummers and some barricades blocking both lanes coming in and both lanes going out. They weren't close enough to see who was by the trucks, but Morgan was certain it was Ghost Town Labs' women. As she got a better view of the Hummers, she saw the Ghost Town Labs symbol on the door.

"The traffic looks to be at a standstill," Morgan said.

"That's standard for 394 at any time during the day," Is said. "Hey, look, Sam is pulling into the park."

Morgan followed Sam's car into a small park area situated next to the river. The park had a small jungle gym, sand box, sand volleyball pit, basketball hoop, picnic area and a few docks that went into the river—one with a pontoon tied to it. Sam and Morgan found two of the last places to park—the parking was full of cars, with all of the occupants standing to one side of the park, looking at the bridge.

Sam, Amber, Todd, and Jack got out of the car and looked at the bridge as the others walked up to them. None of them were certain what they should do. Morgan wondered how much damage had already been done—wondered if any of these kids could survive the day. As the group met up near the water's edge, they all had their eyes on the bridge, which even though was full of cars, started to lift.

"What the hell is going on?" Jack shouted. "There are no boats coming. They can't lift the bridge with those cars sitting like that."

As the bridge continued to lift, they watched three cars that were halfway on and halfway off the bridge begin to tip. The occupants of the cars tried to rush out. A couple did but some of the others fell into the water, right as the cars fell in too. There was a hushed silence over the crowd. All traffic was at a standstill as many people were starting to turn their engines off.

A silence started to hang in the air as the bridge reached the top, cutting off all people on the wrong side of the bridge. There was a tension building in the air—an electricity that no one could figure out. The people on the bridge were looking down, not knowing what to do. In the horror that followed, someone from the bridge was either pushed in the confusion, or they jumped—either way, with the height they fell from, there was no way they could have survived.

"What do we do now?" Tiffany asked.

"We could take a different route out of town," Jack said, "but there are only two other bridges. You think we could have any better luck at the others?"

No one said anything—they didn't need to. They knew if it was like this here, it would be like this at each bridge. Morgan wondered how the other bridges were doing. She knew her father had chosen Genesis as the location because the city was completely surrounded by a river. The water flowed from the north, then branched into two channels before meeting up about twenty miles to the south. They were at the northern tip, where the river split in two.

There was one bridge at the north crossing, with road 394 following the east bank of the river north through many miles of suburban cities. Morgan was glad the bridge was raised because it meant that suburbanites couldn't cross into the city to see what was going on. She was sure that people would be curious and they would have enough test subjects in the city the way it was.

"Hell of a way to start your new lives here, eh Morgan?" Sam asked, still looking at the bridge. "This town is normally pretty laid-back."

"I just wonder why they raised the bridge," Tiffany said. "And who those people up there are. I see something on the door of those black Hummers but I can't make it out. It's not police or F.B.I."

"I've never seen anything like it either," Todd said. "Not a military symbol. Who else could be doing something like this?"

"Either way," Jack said, "we need to be getting out of here."

"What?" Tiffany asked.

"Look, we got reports of a shooting or an attack," Jack said, "and now they're sealing off the city. That's what this is. There is no other reason. Sure, people could try to swim across or take a boat or something, but for the most part, we are trapped here. How else are we supposed to get out...the airport? Yeah, all this shit going down, I'm sure we could walk right in there. What are we supposed to do?"

"There has to be something," Sam said. "I'm wondering if we shouldn't find our families. I'm sure they are worried about us as well. I think we should all go home."

"We all live within a few blocks of each other," Tiffany explained to Morgan. "On the northeast side of town. Where are you?"

"There's an apartment building on Hennepin and twenty-eighth," Morgan said.

"That's only two blocks from us," Jack said. "Mom has the day off, so she should be home if you'd want to stay with us until your dad gets back from work."

"She's not a baby, Jack," Tiffany said. "I think she could take care of herself."

"I was just offering," Jack said. "That way, if she was scared, she wouldn't have to admit it to anyone."

"I think we're all a little scared right now," Is said.

"Thanks for the offer," Morgan said. "I don't know, do you think we should head home now?"

"I don't think we're going anywhere," Amber said. "Not by car anyway...look."

The group turned and looked at the road. The traffic had come to a standstill. People were standing outside of their cars on 394, looking at the bridge. On the side street the park was on, all the traffic heading to 394 was backed up. They were blocked in at the park.

"I'm still not certain on the layout of the city," Morgan said, "but we can't be too far from our homes, can we?"

"We'd be looking at walking about twenty blocks," Tiffany said. "Give or take. The nice thing is that there are bike paths throughout the town. We could walk along the river for most of the way."

"My dad would kill me though if I left the car here," Sam said.

"Coach will kill us if he finds we ditched school," Todd said. "You think they're looking for us? This may have been a rash decision guys. We should head back to the school, just in case."

"No one there is looking for us," Is said. "I'm sure they dismissed everyone and the building is empty by now."

Morgan was listening to her friends talk, but she was paying more attention to the crowd of people in the park looking at the bridge. The group of people were starting to get agitated and mad. There were people who were yelling and others who were trying to move around in the mass of humanity. Morgan and the group of kids couldn't help but notice that four people broke out of the mass and moved between the kids and the river.

Two women and two men—all four wearing business professional attire of gray suits with white shirts. The men wore pleated pants, and the women wore tight skirts. They all looked to be in their mid-thirties and were very fit and healthy. One of the women kicked off her black pumps as she started to take off her jacket.

"Now honey," the bald man said, "what do you think you're doing?"

"I'm going for a swim," the blonde woman said, as she started to unbutton her shirt. "You can stay here for all I care, but we've been working all night and into the morning on that stupid project. Work that we wouldn't have had to do if you did your damn job right. My place is just a couple blocks from the river. I'm swimming and going to bed."

"You can't swim the river," the man said, trying to get the woman to keep her shirt on. "What, you just gonna leave your clothes here?"

"No," the woman said, pushing the man back and tossing her shirt into his face. "I know you don't have the balls to swim this, so you're going to bring them home for me. Come on, Tina, let's go."

The other woman paused, looking at her friend who was now in a matching red underwear set with dark pantyhose. The friend stripped down to her black underwear and the girls made their way toward the water's edge. The men tried in vain to talk them out of what they were about to do.

Many in the group had drawn their attention to two knockout women who were almost naked. The guys in the group with Morgan were fixated on the women—so much so, that no one was paying attention to what was going on across the river.

Morgan was the first person on that side of the river to look across, knowing what orders the Ghost Town Labs' women most likely had. Her fears were confirmed when she saw one of the women balancing a massive rifle over the hood of a hummer. The barrel, which looked large even across the river, was aimed directly at the woman in the red underwear who was knee deep in the water.

As Morgan turned to look at the woman it took a moment to process what had happened. In the blink of an eye, half the woman's head went flying backwards, blood splattering all over her friend as the woman in red dropped to her knees. It was almost a full second before the crack of the rifle assaulted Morgan's ear drums.

Dumbfounded, the girl looked at her friend as a crimson fountain gushed from the woman's head into the water. Before she could even move, a bullet ripped through her chest as another crack thundered from the rifle.

Morgan looked back across the river, just in time to see the Ghost Town Labs' woman pulling the .50 caliber rifle up. She knew they had strict instructions to make sure no one crossed the water. The women going to swim were a problem—they had to make sure no one else got any funny ideas.

The mass of humanity was almost a mob now, shouting horrible things across the river—things the intended targets could never hear anyway. The men who were with the women were cradling their bloody bodies. They were praying and hoping there would be something to do to bring them back, but there wasn't. Morgan knew the shooter wouldn't leave anything to chance. With a gun as big as the one she fired, the person was going to die no matter where the bullet hit.

"We need to go," Sam said. "Let's just run to Jack's place. It's the closest one."

"I agree," Jack said. "This is messed up."

"Why would they shoot her?" Tiffany asked, still in shock over what she'd just witnessed. "Why would someone shoot her? They can't do that, can they?"

"Whether they can or can't is irrelevant at this point," Is said. "They shot her. I agree, let's get the hell out of here. Morgan, you cool with leaving your ride here?"

Morgan didn't answer. She was paying attention to the crowd beginning to see what was happening to their town. One by one, the kids turned to look at what Morgan was staring at. Although Morgan had seen it before and she had full knowledge and awareness as to what was about to happen, it still frightened her and filled her with sadness. Standing above their limp bodies, still being held by their boyfriends, were the two girls—transparent ghosts, unaware of their condition or why the mass of humanity was starting to get hysterical.

Summer School Part IV

Morgan tried to process everything that was happening. She'd seen many events like this in the Ghost Town Labs' training facility underneath the forest of Whiterock—but seeing the real thing out in the open was different. These people weren't bums taken from the streets and brainwashed. They were real people who had no preparation or warning for what was about to happen.

The mass of people were reaching a fevered pitch. People were screaming, crying and praying. Some men were trying to hit the ghosts but their arms were passing through them. The group was starting to move as Morgan felt a hand give her arm a death grip.

Morgan looked to see that Jack already had Tiffany under his left arm while his right arm was out a forty-five degree angle—perfect for knocking people out of his way. Jack's first move was to protect his little sister. Tiffany was confused as he was carrying her like a football. Sam had Amber in his grasp while Todd was a pace behind. Is was grabbing Morgan, urging her to run with them.

Morgan and Is took off running, trying to catch up to the others. The football players had no problems keeping a very fast pace. Jack put Tiffany down once he was comfortable with their distance from the ghosts. Morgan pushed herself as hard as she could but she couldn't keep up with the athletes—especially in the school boots she was wearing. Is and Amber were able to keep up with the boys but Tiffany and Morgan were falling behind.

Jack looked back to see how much distance they'd made from the park and noticed how far behind the girls were. He slowed the boys, but kept them moving at a quick pace. Morgan had no time to look at where they were going—she was pushing with everything she had to keep up with the fit teens.

The group reached a busy intersection and had to wait for traffic to allow them to cross. Morgan was out of breath. She put her hands on her knees, body dripping with sweat as they waited. No one spoke—no one dared to speak after what they saw. The cars that were passing had no idea what was happening just blocks away.

The light turned, allowing the group to cross the street and continue on the bike path. Morgan tried to remember how many blocks they'd gone, but her mind was blank—consumed by the pain of the run. The guys were still pushing themselves strong, but the girls were starting to slow down when they ran off the bike path and onto city streets. After a block and a half of running, Morgan saw the guys rushing into a house.

Lead by Jack, who unlocked the door, the kids ran into a large, split-level gray house with an attached three-car garage. They had a perfect lawn with extensive landscaping and shrubbery all around the house. Morgan could tell from the house and the neighborhood that Jack and Tiffany were from a well-off family.

Morgan entered the house, feeling a rush of conditioned cool air assault her body. The temperature change between the hot and humid outside, and the cool and dry inside took Morgan's breath away. Morgan felt a sharp pain running along the side of her body. Something was pressing against her back.

Morgan realized her clothing was soaked with sweat as droplets of cold water tapped her face. She realized that Is was close to her, shaking her shoulder.

"Morgan, Morgan," Is called out, frantically. "Are you okay, Morgan?"

Morgan opened her eyes, with no recollection of closing them. She saw that she was on the floor of a highly decorated entryway. Is was kneeling next to her with a glass of water in her hand. Is lifted Morgan's head and helped her drink some of the water as Morgan's senses came back to her.

"You collapsed as we entered the house," Tiffany said. "You think you're okay?"

"I guess I'm not a distance runner," Morgan said, chest still heaving as she tried to catch her breath. "Sorry I won't be helping your cross country team out."

The group let out a weak laugh—anything humorous was needed after the horror they'd witnessed. None of them wanted to admit what happened, what they'd seen. Jack entered the entryway looking disappointed.

"Mom's not here," Jack said. "I know she was going to run some errands today. She shouldn't be out too long. I wouldn't worry about it." Jack chewed his lower lip as he talked. "She'll be back any minute. No reason to worry."

"You are soaked," Tiffany said, looking at Morgan's clothes. "Come on, you can raid my closet. I think I have something you can squeeze into. Not my skinny jeans or cammies, but we can find something."

"If we need to run like that again," Morgan said, as she started to stand, aided by Tiffany and Is. "I want some of your running shorts."

Morgan and Tiffany walked out of the entryway and down a half flight of stairs while the others walked up to the living room and took places on the black, Italian-leather chairs and sofas. The living room was full of dark colors, with a plush brown carpet, and rich-red mahoganies that gave the room a warm feeling. On one wall was a massive flat television, surrounded by an extensive collection of movies. Large windows let in light above the chairs and a bookshelf stood on the wall with the entrance door.

None of the kids wanted to talk first. They all looked at the floor, not making eye contact. Not a single person in the group was able to process what they had just seen. It was like something from a movie or a nightmare—they were not ready to deal with it.

Is felt the effects of the drug she had taken wearing off. The drug was one of the reasons she'd been so calm when the event took place. She wished she had more to take. Is knew that Jack's parents liked to host dinner parties and had a well-stocked cabinet of liquor. She debated asking Jack if she could take a bottle but she knew what his answer would be. Even if she offered him money or pleasure, his parents would punish him if booze went missing.

Tiffany entered the room and dropped onto the floor, having shed her sweatpants, wearing black volleyball shorts with her shirt. She stretched out on the floor like she was trying to get comfortable but no matter what position she tried, she couldn't find anything she liked. She finally settled with lying flat on her back, arms outright on the floor above her head.

"What did I miss?" Tiffany asked, breaking the silence.

"Nothing," Sam said. "What in the world did we see back there?"

"They were ghosts," Is said coldly. "Ghosts, just like the man at the stoplight said."

"Man at the stoplight?" Todd asked.

"At the stoplight there was a man," Is said. "He was walking, yelling something about ghosts. I guess he was right."

"There's no such thing as ghosts," Jack said.

"What did we see out there?" Amber asked, almost shouting.

"There's a perfectly logical answer to that," Jack said. "When mommy gets back she will explain everything. She always knows the right answer, right Tiffany?"

"Jack," Tiffany said, "everything will be okay."

"What are we going to do?" Is asked. "I mean, is there a way we could leave the city? That's what we should do—leave. But how?"

"I'm not going to try to swim for it," Sam said. "Not after what happened to those two women."

"What else is there?" Amber asked. "I say we should head for the airport, try to get in a plane that's leaving."

"What about our families?" Jack asked. "What about our parents?"

"We need to gather everyone up," Amber said.

"And how are we going to do that?" Jack yelled. "Call them? Oh, that's right, all the phones are down. Should we go to their work, one by one, and round them up? You saw the traffic out there. Not to mention, GHOSTS!"

Jack started to cry. The other's knew why. They all wanted to join him but he was always the most emotional out of the group. Tiffany got up, attempting to hug her brother. Jack pushed her away, trying to compose himself.

"I suppose you're all going to make fun of me again," Jack said. "Go ahead, call me a baby, call me a weakling, I deserve it."

"Not this time," Todd said.

"We just saw people get shot man," Sam said. "That's messed up, that's what that is. Let it out man just don't take it out on us, we're here for you."

Jack let his sister hug him as he wiped away the tears. No one wanted to admit it, but they were all as scared as Jack was. No one had any good ideas about what to do, but none of the group wanted to just sit in the house and wait for something to happen.

Morgan entered the room, hair still wet from a quick rinse in the shower. She was wearing black bike shorts that were tight and almost touching her knees with a baggy blue extra-large Genesis Academy Football shirt on top. The shirt hem went so far down it almost looked like a dress but Morgan was in the process of tying it up in the back.

"Hey," Jack said, "That's my shirt...and my shorts!"

"My stuff was too small for her," Tiffany said. "Even my workout clothes. We raided your clean clothes pile in the laundry room."

"You can't wear my shirt," Jack said in a firm tone. "Take it off."

Morgan stared at him confusedly. She was about to tie the shirt up so it would not look so billowy on her body and not drop so far down, but she shrugged and was about to lift the shirt off when Tiffany stopped her.

"Morgan," Tiffany said, with a smile, "my brother will do almost anything to get a girl out of her shirt. Just ignore him."

Morgan looked back to Jack who had a weird smile on his face. Morgan couldn't believe how much she loved that, even with all that had happened outside, these kids were playing around with her, teasing her, flirting with her and treating her like a friend. She wanted to hug all of them, hoping that the fun would last, but she knew that they still had a long day ahead of them. Morgan acted like she was going to tie her shirt high on her stomach, showing off a good deal of midriff, but then she tucked the shirt into the shorts as she sat next to Jack.

"No free shows today," Morgan said, as she looked into Jack's eyes and seductively bit her lower lip. "Not yet anyway, we'll see how the day goes."

Jack returned the smile with a wink. Even though Morgan could tell that he had had tears in his eyes, she felt a masculine power there. The wink shot through her like a bolt of lightning. His eyes were so powerful she could hardly resist him. The thoughts of the ghosts outside and all she was supposed to do today were being pushed aside for thoughts of her and these friends.

"We have to do something," Is said. "We cannot just sit here. Morgan, you have any ideas?"

Morgan thought about the question. She so badly wanted to have a youth, a childhood, with friends like these, but she knew that all their youth was over. After seeing people murdered right before your eyes then turning into ghosts, there was no innocence left in any of them.

In that instant, Morgan made a split decision. She still had a device on her that would prevent a ghost from attacking, and she knew the layout plans of the city. Ghost Town Labs had installed a pipe that ran on the river bottom, connecting a point within Genesis to a point outside the area. The pipe was protected from ghosts and no one should be guarding it this early in the morning. The pipe was added in case the ghosts couldn't be controlled and Ghost Town Labs' personnel needed a quick exit strategy. The only question was how to explain to the people who'd lived in Genesis their entire lives how she knew about it and they didn't.

"I did some research on the area before we moved here," Morgan said, thinking quickly. "A long time ago the city council was worried about the water supply as the area started to really take off and expand. This was like in the seventies or something. They built a tunnel underneath the city as a means to bring in water, but it's never been used. I think I know the location of the entrance of the tunnel and I have an idea of where it will lead to. We could get out of the town that way."

"And go where?" Sam asked. "How do we let our parents know we left and where to find us?"

"We're all close," Amber said. "We could each rush home and leave a note. Just let them know we got out and that we are okay."

"I don't know," Todd said. "I think we should stay here…maybe each go to our own house."

"I'm willing to go," Is said. "I don't need to tell anyone."

"We can leave a note for mom," Tiffany said. "Right Jack?"

"Are you going, Morgan?" Jack asked.

"Yes."

"Then I'll go too," Jack said.

"I agree with Todd," Amber said. "I think I should go home to be with my family."

"I'm staying with Amber," Sam said. "I can't leave her in something like this."

"We're gonna go," Is said. "I'm sure this shit will blow over. There'll be an explanation for what we saw. Nothing to worry about, but we're going to leave. Morgan, lead the way."

The group slowly got to their feet. Is, Jack, and Tiffany followed Morgan while Sam, Todd, and Amber stayed together. When they got to the end of the driveway, the friends had an awkward goodbye, no one knowing if they were overreacting or if they would ever see each other again.

Morgan led her group to the south, walking along the sidewalk while Sam, Amber, and Todd cut through some yards to the east. It didn't take long before Morgan couldn't see the other kids anymore. She didn't have high hopes that they would ever see them again.

Morgan jogged at a brisk pace with the others behind her as she tried to figure out a way to explain her role in all of this. She knew that sooner or later she would have to tell them or they would find out. And if they found out, she knew that the friendships she had with them would be destroyed forever. More than once she thought about stopping and coming clean but something prevented her. Morgan knew she couldn't risk it.

The group entered into a parking lot for the large Mall of Genesis. Morgan knew that the entrance to the pipe had been cut into the substructure of the mall during a renovation project that was still ongoing. She had been amazed at how fast Ghost Town Labs could get things built, but figured that when you had an almost unlimited budget that you didn't have to answer for and one person calling the shots there wasn't much that you couldn't get done.

Morgan led her friends into the mall. The Mall of Genesis was full of people, almost to the point where it was hard to move around. The mall always had events and programs going on so it was almost always full. The people in the mall seemed to be on edge today, like there was something strange happening. Morgan couldn't help but notice that there was an abundance of police around.

As Morgan led the others through the opulent mall, they could overhear people talking about the events that happened earlier in the day, a robbery in one of the stores. There seemed to be a lot of talk about it but no one could quite put everything together. People were also very upset with no cellphone or internet service. As the group passed a large cellphone and network store they could hear many angry people yelling at befuddled clerks who had no answers for them.

A voice caught Morgan's ear and she turned to look into the sporting goods store they were walking past. In the store she saw a sight that almost made her stop, the two police from the gas station, Jake Arnold and Ryan Minot, were interviewing Erin Minot, a clerk in the store. When the eyes met, all of them were nervous, none more so than Morgan for she knew that after today they would report that they saw her in the mall, not at the school where she was supposed to be, and that her being in the mall and not found in the city after the events had been hashed out would be an indication that she deserted Ghost Town Labs.

The group entered a door which led down to the control centers of the mall. As they followed Morgan, the desire to come clean with all of these people, her new friends, became stronger and stronger. They twisted and turned through steel and pipe, finally arriving at a door with the Ghost Town Labs symbol on it. Morgan opened the door, ushering the others through.

Inside was a small room with some computer equipment and a pipe that was about six feet tall. There was no lighting in the pipe but there were flashlights next to the computers. Morgan tossed each person a flashlight and was about to enter the pipe when she stopped and turned around.

"I have to confess something to you guys," Morgan said.

"Can't it wait?" Jack asked. "Let's get out of here first."

"It can't wait," Morgan said. "Have you ever been a part of something bad because you loved someone? Have you ever stood aside and allowed others to get hurt because you loved someone?"

"What are you talking about?" Is asked. "We've all messed up before Morgan."

"My father has a madness about him," Morgan said. "He's going to kill a lot of people. I knew about this and have done nothing to stop it."

"What do you mean?" Is asked.

"Does this have anything to do with what we saw?" Tiffany asked.

"It has everything to do with what's going on right now," Morgan said. "My father runs Ghost Town Labs. Ghost Town Labs is using the city of Genesis to test a weapon my father developed. Those women that we saw turn into ghosts…that's the weapon. We have devices running in this city that will turn anyone who dies into a ghost."

"What?" Is asked. "How is that possible?"

"There's no way it's possible," Jack said. "No way."

"He killed everyone in the town of Whiterock," Morgan said. "Everyone. Now we are taking the technology here…here in Genesis…to test it and to show the world what we can do. I tried to stop him, but I didn't try very hard. This is revenge for what happened to my mother and sister. He has told other countries about this, asking them to watch and bid for the technology, but he's not going to sell it, he just wants them to fear what he can do. Those women that had blocked the road and shot the others, those are his women. They are…"

"And what was your role in all of this?" Is interrupted. "What were you to do?"

"I was to pose as a high school student and gather information about the movement of the ghosts and the reactions of the people. I was to monitor and study, that's it," Morgan said.

"Yeah, right," Is said. "You want us to enter that so you can kill us, right?"

"No!" Morgan said, horrified.

"Hang on a minute," Tiffany said. "You really expect us to believe that you have a device that can turn a dead person into a ghost? No way."

"It's true," Morgan said. "But I don't want to be a part of that anymore. I can take you to safety. I know where we can be safe but you have to come with me."

"I'm sorry, Morgan," Is said. "Either you're a monster, a liar, or delusional. It's one of the three. I don't know which but I can't follow you."

"Me neither," Tiffany said.

"Sorry," Jack said.

"She's telling the truth," a woman said, from behind them.

The group turned to see they were being held at gunpoint by two tall, athletic women wearing black spandex singlets, boots, knee and elbow pads, black fingerless gloves, and holding Beretta FS92 9mm handguns. The women had the blue Ghost Town Labs logo on their clothing.

"Good work Morgan," the blonde woman said. "Your father ordered the taking of more test subjects. He will be most pleased with your work."

"You were telling the truth?" Is asked. "I was so wrong about you Morgan. I hope you die a horrible death and rot in hell."

"No, please," Morgan pleaded on the verge of tears. "Not like this. We were supposed to be friends. Not like this."

Before anyone could say anything, Jack, Tiffany then Is fell to the ground. Morgan turned to see a third Ghost Town Labs woman holding a stunner in her hand. The other two worked quickly to get the three bodies onto gurneys before hooking them to a mind control machine.

Morgan saw an open duffel bag on the floor that contained more guns in it. She pulled out a black Beretta 12-gauge shotgun. She noticed that all three of the women had put their weapons down and were working with the mind control machines. Morgan knew she had one chance and had to work quickly.

"There could be more people coming here," Morgan said. "Two of you go check the entrance I came through."

Without questioning the order, two women turned to leave through the door. Once Morgan was between the women leaving and the weapons, she quickly shot the woman standing by herself before turning the gun and shooting both stunned women who were trying to figure out what was going on. Morgan quickly pulled all the bodies out of the room and closed the door, locking it before she went to the mind control machine.

Morgan started to program the machine as fast as she could. She badly wanted to put something in all their of their minds so that they would love her, treat her as their best friend, and make Jack want to be her boyfriend and husband, but she decided against it. She would let the relationships develop on their own. Morgan erased the past few minutes from their minds, erased her confession and the killings. Once the program was set, Morgan got into position, where she was before all this had happened.

One by one, the others got up from the table and stood where they had been when they first entered the room. Morgan had programmed them so they would think it seamless, that the last few minutes had never even taken place. Her speaking was the trigger to wake them up.

"I have a confession to make," Morgan said.

In that instant, their minds went back to normal, except for blocking the past few events out.

"What?" Is asked.

"I'm scared," Morgan said. "I've never had friends before and I don't want to lose you guys."

"You won't lose us," Is said. "We are a team now."

Morgan hugged Is before she led them into the tunnel and into the unknown.

The Mall Part I

As the clerks approached the metal slotted gate separating them from the walkers who were finishing their laps around the mall, the male clerk, a tall and lanky young man with shaggy brown hair and tufts of stubble on his chin, breathed a heavy sigh.

"I hate Mondays," the man said, sounding more dejected than a team that had lost a championship. "Hate them with a passion."

"I'm excited about it," the female clerk said in her thick British accent.

The man looked at his companion and shook his head in disgust. The woman could see in his eyes that he was already dead—a zombie of the world. She could see him as a young man in his mid-twenties that had already seen the best days of his life. He would finish his life by working in this store, drinking beer, and remembering the parties he experienced in high school and college.

"What's your name again?" the man asked.

"Erin Minot," Erin said, showing him her tag.

"I'm Derek Frost," Derek said. "Let me tell you about working here, Erin. The people who come in are rude and demanding. The bosses have unrealistic expectations. We are doing nothing but selling workout clothing and exercise equipment to braindead teens and fat forty year olds who have no intention of using it."

"How long have you been working here Derek?" Erin asked.

"I started my freshman year of college," Derek said. "That was eight years ago. I was part time through college while I got a business major, then I started full time in sales. Two years ago I made assistant manager and got all the glory that comes with it."

Erin stared at Derek. His voice was dripping with sarcasm as he spoke about his life. Derek carried himself like a man defeated. At first glance, Erin was intrigued by his soft face and wild hair, but as he spoke, his true personality came out and she was turned off by the complaining.

Erin studied Derek as he fumbled with his keys to open the gate. They both wore the same outfit—black dress shoes, khaki pants...hers tight and his baggy, with a black polo shirt monogramed with the store name on the left breast, right below where they were required to pin their black nametags.

Erin had her shirt tucked in, with a posh black belt. Derek's shirt was half tucked and half untucked. His brown belt clashed with his shoes, and where Erin's outfit was clean and pressed, his was wrinkled with small stains on the pants. Erin realized that Derek took no pride in his appearance.

Derek opened the gate as he let out a heavy sigh. He looked out at the older people who were finishing up their walks. He knew that none of them would enter the store, but soon there would be all sorts of people bothering him with their little problems.

"It would be so nice if we could just have one day where no one entered the store," Derek said. "Just once, have a day where we could just sit in the break room and not have to do anything...is that too much to ask?"

Erin tried to hide her distain for Derek. She laughed inside, thinking how quickly he was going to die in the events today, how easily he would go, not putting up a fight. As she thought about what would happen she realized that Derek was waiting for her to answer.

"It'd be nice," Erin said. "I'm just happy to have a job here."

"Wow," Derek said, as he walked back to a register and grabbed his large energy drink, taking two massive swallows from it. "Give it a few weeks and that will change. Where is everyone else? We're supposed to have a floor meeting. Damn them, why can't people be on time? I'm trying to do my job here but everyone else is messing it up."

"They are coming," Erin said, pointing.

Derek turned to see the other clerks. Walking in front was Dale Cot—a short, pudgy man with black hair and a full black beard. Although Dale's stomach hung over his belt he looked strong as a bull. He had a powerful walk and his image was enhanced with the tattoos that were covering his arms. Dale wore the same store outfit that Derek and Erin were wearing.

A step behind Dale was Cindy Gray, a stringy woman with dyed black hair that framed out a narrow, sharp face as the straight hair fell to tickle her shoulders. Cindy had a swagger in her walk—a confidence that came from her beauty and experience. In her early thirties, Cindy had a smile on her face and was excited to face the day as the only one with a different outfit than the other clerks—athletic shoes, dark fuchsia tights with black accents, a black workout tank top monogramed with the company logo, and fingerless workout gloves.

"Cindy," Derek said, scoffing, "I see you've decided that you're going to be doing equipment demos today. Did you ask me if that was your position today?"

"No," Cindy said, flatly. "I'm dressed like this because I have to hightail it to the gym when I'm done here. I've got two aerobics classes to lead followed by three personal training sessions. I'm only on until two today. If you want to do the demos, be my guest, but I'd like to point out that I am in the required work uniform, according to the handbook. I know you like it if we all..."

"Whatever," Derek said, interrupting with an exasperated gasp. "Fine, you do the demos. I've been getting my ass chewed lately. Our morning numbers are not where they should be. When someone comes in here to buy a pair of shorts, we need to upsell them—two pairs of shorts, socks, shirts, and our new lines of spandex. We should not be having single item sales. Step it up, people! If we want to last around here, we need to get our act together. It will be just us until more workers arrive at noon. Erin, you will start out in the women's section. Keep an eye on the kids' section across the aisle. Here's a hint, a girl comes in for new spandex and bras for volleyball, sell her a swimsuit for practice or training or whatever."

"That doesn't make sense," Erin said. "Why would she..."

"Don't argue," Derek interrupted. "Just sell. Dale, you've got the men's section. Cindy has the equipment, and Cindy, keep an eye on the new girl, would you? I'll be floating around but mainly at the register. Any questions? No? Good. Get to work."

The others quickly dispersed as Erin smiled and made her way toward the women's clothing. Her entire life she'd been in high pressure, covert operations. She knew what stress was and couldn't contain her laughter as she looked at how stressed Derek was over a simple store. Erin looked over the store as she walked the aisles. It had a lot of clothing, some workout equipment, and game balls. It wasn't very big, a partial selection of a much larger store on the other side of town.

Erin looked over the area she was supposed to work—swimwear and women's clothing. Erin liked the selection of the store, and even liked the work outfit that she got to wear. She knew she couldn't get too comfortable in this role and that very soon she would be fighting for her life with all the ghosts that would be infesting the area. She couldn't wait to see everything in action, couldn't wait to see the ghosts descending on these people. All the people she'd helped were by the orders of Doctor Tesla. Erin was still unsure if her husband Ryan was really on board with Ghost Town Labs, but she had been keeping an eye on him.

"What do you think of the dictator?" Cindy's soft voice spoke behind Erin.

"The dictator?" Erin asked.

"Because he's such a dick," Cindy said, as she started to do some stretching. "You'll get used to him. You're British, aren't you?"

"Yes," Erin said. "Just moved here."

"Welcome," Cindy said. "You'll like it here. This store is pretty laid back. Don't worry about what he was saying about sales. Managers are all the same...more, more, more. According to the managers, every store is on the verge of bankruptcy because they aren't doing enough business. Even the health clubs I work at are the same. We always need more people coming and to do more upselling."

"Why do you work here if you are a personal trainer?" Erin asked.

"Money," Cindy said. "Divorce lawyers are spendy."

"Sorry," Erin said. "What happened?"

"Things were good," Cindy said, "but he was determined to be a power stockbroker, like a hedge fund manager or something. He was spending all his time working and there was no time for us. Then I found out he was having a fling with a woman that worked in his building. He claimed it was just sex, nothing more and that I wasn't there and she was. I tried to work through it with him, showing up at his office when he wanted something and stuff like that, but then there was another girl he was spending money on and I said it stops or I go. He quit for about two weeks before he was back with them. We didn't have much money to start with, and it turned pretty ugly. Looking back, I would have been so much better off to just walk away but I had to get revenge on him, I had to win. I won, that's for sure. I made sure to get the BMW and a couple other things he wanted, but the money I had to spend. Live and learn I guess."

"Sorry," Erin said. "Sounds horrible."

"It is what it is," Cindy said. "So, you married? Kids? Why are you here stateside?"

"Ryan, my husband, is a constable," Erin said, remembering the cover story she'd rehearsed. "We've always wanted to experience America and figured it was now or never. He applied all over the country, we wanted to be in Washington D.C. or New York but this was the only town that would hire him. Once he got hired here, I applied everywhere. I have sales experience but this is the only place that would hire me."

"Ever since Derek moved up there's been a revolving door here," Cindy said.

"Revolving door?" Erin asked.

"People don't last very long here," Cindy said. "Derek doesn't work well with others. Ever since my divorce he's been asking me out—never going to happen, but I don't tell him that. Looks like you got some customers. Remember, 'up sell!'"

Erin looked as Cindy walked away to see two teenaged girls looking over the clothing selection. Both girls were tall and muscular, tanned one with darker hair, the other blonde. They were in identical outfits, sneakers, knee-high tube socks, black kneepads, black volleyball shorts, and cutoff blue t-shirts with a logo on the front for the Genesis Academy High School. The girls looked at Erin as she walked up to them. Both the girls towered over the smaller Erin.

"Good morning," Erin said, in a bright and cheerful voice, laying her accent on as thick as she could. "Welcome to the Genesis Sports Den. My name's Erin, May I assist you in locating something?"

"You can," the blonde said. "I'm Kay and this is Dee."

"Kay and Dee?" Erin asked.

"We're both Nancy," Dee said. "She's Nancy Kay and I'm Nancy Dee. We go by our middle names, it's how people keep us apart. We need swimsuits."

"We have swimsuits," Erin said. "Follow me please."

Erin took them to the swimwear area and paused as they looked over the massive selection.

"What kind of suit are you looking for?" Erin asked.

"Practice," Kay said. "We need something for swimming laps. They have to be black—school rules."

"We have these right here," Erin said, pointing to the rack of black, wide strapped, athletic suits. "Are you allowed to have designs on them?"

"We can," Dee said, "as long as the main color is black."

"I think these are really cute," Erin said, holding up a pair of black suits that had neon green, yellow, and pink splashes on the front. "They are on sale too."

"We'll try them on," Kay said. "Size sixteen for both of us."

Erin looked over the rack and found two in size sixteen. Erin motioned the girls to follow her to the dressing room and opened the rooms for them. Erin stood outside the rooms, listening to the girls talk about some boys that had been talking with them. Erin was stunned at the language the teen girls were using and what they were talking about doing with the boys.

The girls came out of the dressing room, confusing Erin in the fact that they had taken everything else off, the socks and kneepads, and were wearing only the suits and their shoes. The girls looked good in the suits and they fit the girls well. The girls nodded, approving of each other.

"We'll take these," Kay said.

"You need anything else?" Erin asked. "We have a sale on some of our ladies spandex, socks, and underwear. I can help you with any of that."

"We do need some jackets," Dee said. "Black jackets."

"Follow me," Erin said. "We just got some new ones in, a little early to have them out but the manager wanted people to start seeing them before fall."

Erin led the girls to the jacket section and allowed them to look over the black leather duster jackets that they had on display. The girls each grabbed a black duster that was about a size too large for them. They looked in the mirrors at their appearance and both agreed that the jackets were the right ones.

"This is what we'll take," Kay said. "The suits and jackets."

To Erin's horror, Kay and Dee quickly ripped the price tag and bar code off both of the suits and both the jackets, handing them to Erin. Erin didn't know how to react—unsure why the girls didn't take the clothing off to pay for them.

"Be a doll and ring this stuff up," Kay said. "All on one ticket. We'll grab our stuff and meet you at the register."

The girls walked toward the changing rooms as Erin watched them. She made her way to the register, not seeing Derek anywhere near the checkout desk. Erin keyed in her operating code before scanning the tags and waited for the girls to get back.

Erin looked up to see Kay and Dee walking up to her, still just in the jackets and suits, not carrying the clothes that they were wearing when they walked in. Kay had a twenty dollar bill in her hand while Dee had a credit card.

"The total is $299.73," Erin said.

"Before you run the card," Kay asked, "can you be a sweetheart and break this for me? I need a ten and ten ones."

"Sure," Erin said, as she opened the register drawer and counted out the money.

Erin didn't close the drawer as she ran the credit card through the reader. It took a moment before the machine beeped—an error had occurred, the machine wasn't hooked to the internet.

"This is strange," Erin said. "It appears that the reader is down. The internet must be having problems."

"That is a big problem," Kay said. "We need these now. We have to get to practice. Run it again."

Erin scowled at the girl but ran the card again, getting the same result. The look on the girl's faces told Erin that they weren't going to leave without the items and they'd already ripped the tags off so they had to pay for them. As Erin waited on the machine she looked at the credit card Dee had handed her. The name on the card was Andy Huss. Neither girl had given a last name but Erin wasn't sure how she was supposed to handle this.

"I'm sorry," Erin said, trying to sound sympathetic, "but our servers are down. I can't run the card. Do you have another way of paying?"

"Run the damn card," Dee said. "It works. I would also like to take a couple hundred dollars in change from the card. You can do that, can't you?"

"I can't," Erin said. "The machine is down."

"I don't want excuses," Kay said. "I want solutions. Figure it out."

"The internet is down," Erin protested.

"Earn your seven-fifty an hour and figure it out," Dee said, "or maybe, we will come to a different arrangement."

"Arrangement?" Erin asked.

"The anti-theft devices were in the tags," Dee said. "We've been scouting stores that do that. Here's the deal, we walk out of here with the suits and jackets, but before that, you give us the money in the register...all of it."

Erin stared blankly at the girls. They were both teenagers—juniors in high school, maybe seniors. They looked to be fit, healthy, and of good nature. She couldn't believe what she had just heard. It took a few moments to comprehend everything.

"Are you trying to rob the store?" Erin asked.

"Yes," Dee said.

"How stupid are you two?" Erin asked.

"What?" Dee said.

"Let's think about this," Erin said. "Okay, a pair of sixty-dollar swimsuits and eighty-dollar jackets—maybe five or six hundred dollars in cash—you're willing to go to jail for a long time over that? What can you do with that little bit of money? This makes no sense at all."

"Just hand over the money you stupid bitch," Kay said. "We have our plan and you lecturing us isn't part of it."

"I can't just hand over the money," Erin said. "I'll get fired."

"Not our problem," Dee said.

"You think you'll get away with this?" Erin asked. "You're on camera. They will send this picture to every school in Genesis. You'll be found and booted off the volleyball and swimming teams."

"Who said we were on the volleyball team?" Kay asked. "Or swimming?"

"Who said we were from Genesis?" Dee asked. "You see, Erin, we are from a different state. What are the police going to do, pull over every car with two non-descript teenaged girls in it? We have this all planned out. Now give us the money and no one gets hurt."

"Gets hurt?" Erin said, surprised. "What, you got a gun or knife hidden somewhere? Mall security will stop you before you are out of the store."

"Not likely," Kay said. "You've been pushing the silent alarm with your foot, haven't you?"

Erin's eyes got big but she didn't say anything.

"Standard procedure," Dee said. "You are wondering why the security hasn't arrived yet. They are busy. We have some friends on the other side of the mall occupying security. Look, we don't like paying for things. We needed suits and jackets and were going to use this stolen credit card before we cleaned out the register but you're making it difficult."

43

"How's she making it difficult?" Derek said, coming around a corner. "What's going on here?"

"They are trying to rob the store," Erin said. "They ripped the tags off their clothes before paying and they've been demanding money. I've tripped the alarm but no one is coming."

"All the internet and phones are down," Derek said, more upset about the network than the robbery. "Give them the money."

"What?" Erin said, shocked.

"The store is insured," Derek said. "The owners are more afraid of someone getting hurt in a standoff and suing them than they are with a few hundred dollars walking out the door. Give them all the money and let them go. Put it in a shoe box then in a black bag."

Erin complied with Derek, taking all the money and placing it in a black shoebox. She handed the box to the girls who smiled as they took it.

"Anything else you want?" Derek asked. "If you want clothing or anything, go right ahead."

"This is all we need," Dee said. "Thank you."

Kay and Dee rushed out of the store. Erin quickly walked to the dressing room to see that they had left all the clothes they had been wearing when they came in. Erin quickly looked through the clothing but didn't find any identification or anything of value.

When Erin went back to the register, she realized that Derek was already gone. She looked around but didn't see him. Erin looked down at the button on the ground that she was pressing to call security but to her amazement, the button wasn't hooked up, the wire to it had been cut. Erin looked up confused, only to see Cindy and Dale walking toward her.

"Did you see that?" Erin asked.

"I did," Cindy said.

"Is that true?" Erin asked. "The store says *just let the money walk out?*"

"No," Cindy said. "Something strange is going on here. That isn't the first time it happened."

"Odd," Erin said. "And the credit card reader is down."

"My phone is out," Cindy said. "Talk, text, and data. Everything is out."

Just then a woman ran into the store. She was in her mid-thirties and looked to be flustered. She rushed up to Dale.

"Dale," the woman said. "There's been an attack at the Colfax Gallery. I'm so sorry. A bunch of people there are dead."

Dale looked like he could faint. Erin and the other woman helped Dale to the ground as he put his head between her knees.

"I'm so sorry Dale," the woman said. "I couldn't find anything else out. I don't know what's going on or if she was there."

"Who?" Erin asked.

"Dale's sister works at a store in the Colfax Gallery," the woman said.

"I've got to go," Dale said. "Phones are down but I have to find her. Erin, cover for me, I'm going to find my sister."

Before Erin or Cindy could protest, Dale and the woman stood up and rushed out the door, leaving a confused Erin standing in the store.

The Mall Part II

Erin watched as more and more people began talking about the strange events that were going on somewhere within the city. No one seemed to know exactly what was going on but there was no shortage of rumors about the events of the morning. Erin kept slipping out of sight so she could type on her phone—a phone powered by Ghost Town Labs' towers, the only towers in town still working. Erin reported the different events she'd heard about.

Erin was walking near the door of the store, noticing the people within the mall were getting more agitated. The air was ripe with tension and Erin knew that only a small spark would set off a bigger event. Erin was amazed that no one had spoken about ghosts yet, even though Erin knew that by now, the ghosts must have been released and ravaging the area. Somewhere within the city, the ghosts had to be there.

"Hey there pretty lady," a male voice rang out from behind Erin.

"Hey," Erin said, not needing to turn around to know that it was Ryan.

Erin turned to see Ryan and Jake, in full police uniforms, standing behind her. Erin and Ryan shared a quick kiss.

"What brings you two here?" Erin asked.

"We're just making rounds," Ryan said. "All the civilian communication networks are down and we were told to make a pass through the mall to make sure no one was getting out of hand. Have you seen anything strange?"

"I did," Erin said. "Two girls robbed the store and I think the shift manager was in on it."

"They robbed a store in the mall?" Ryan said. "Not very smart."

"They got away with it," Erin said. "Unless the Genesis Police Department wants to investigate the incident."

"We've got enough incidents the way it is," Ryan said. "We had a woman pretty upset at a gas station because they couldn't take her card. All the networks are down."

"I know," Erin said. "We've had some upset people here too."

"Never guess who we saw at the gas station," Jake said. "Morgan. She was with a group of kids."

"Damn teenagers," Ryan said, with a sly smile, "always cutting class and sneaking around."

"Speak of the devil," Erin said, as she looked out into the breezeway of the mall.

Ryan and Jake looked out to see Morgan Tesla, out of her school uniform, rushing through the mall with three other students. Morgan noticed Erin and the police but she didn't make any form of contact with them.

"Strange," Jake said. "What are they doing here?"

"Teenagers at the mall," Erin said.

"They didn't look to be shopping or wasting time," Ryan said. "Let's follow them. Bye honey."

Ryan and Erin had a quick kiss before he and Jake rushed out of the store. Erin watched them as they walked away before turning to go back to work. When she turned, Erin saw Cindy sitting on an exercise machine with a smile on her face.

"He's pretty cute," Cindy said. "Who was the girl you saw?"

"What do you mean?" Erin asked.

"The girl you were just talking about," Cindy said. "The one they went to follow."

"Just a neighbor girl we know," Erin quickly lied.

Cindy was about to speak when a young, fit, blonde woman rushed into the store. The lady looked to be in her early twenties with short hair in a tight braid. She was wearing black tights, an athletic tank top, sneakers and a wide black sweatband. She walked right to Cindy.

"Cindy," the woman said. "I can't believe that you're still at work with all that's going on."

"What's going on?" Cindy asked, standing up. "Donna, this is Erin Minot, Erin this is my friend and another instructor at the fitness center, Donna Sharp."

"It happened at the Colfax Gallery," Donna said. "Rumors are that someone, like a terrorist or something, placed a casket on the sidewalk and when someone opened it, a shooter jumped out and started killing people."

"WHAT?" Cindy yelled.

"That's what I heard," Donna said. "I had a pair of girls at the center and was doing a private aerobics workout with them, senior captains getting ready for volleyball and their mothers came in and got them—said they wanted them at home until they caught the shooter."

"That's horrible," Cindy said. "How can the world allow something like this to happen? I mean, surely someone must have known that this person was going to snap. Where are people when events like this happen?"

"Bad things happen," Erin said. "They just do. No reason or excuse or logic for them."

47

"That's too existential for me," Donna said. "Someone wants to make a statement...and they are doing a good job of it."

"What should we do?" Cindy asked. "What does the radio or the news say?"

"Everything is out," Donna said.

"Everything?"

"Everything," Donna replied. "There are no phones, no internet, on the cellphone or cable. Televisions are out, radios are out...nothing is working."

"This is messed up," Cindy said. "You always fear something like this is going to happen but you never think it will happen to you. I wonder if the mall will be shutting down. Not like we can stay open anyway—without credit card machines there's no way we can process most of the sales."

"What does Derek say?" Donna asked.

"I haven't seen him," Cindy said. "Not since we got robbed this morning. Don't ask, it's a messed up story. I'll find Derek and see what he thinks."

Cindy took off leaving Erin and Donna alone in the store. Erin looked over Donna, a fit young girl who looked to have a lot going for her. She wore no rings, and had no ring tan lines on her bronzed body. Erin was loving the amount of information that she was getting off this encounter. She knew that every piece that she got would help the cause for her and Ghost Town Labs.

"So you're the new worker here?" Donna asked. "Cindy mentioned that an English girl was starting. Where you from?"

"London," Erin said.

"I'm a farm girl, originally," Donna said. "Grew up on the other side of the state, right near the boards of North and South Dakota."

"Near Whiterock?" Erin asked.

"How the hell does a London girl know about Whiterock?" Donna asked, stunned. "I was just a town over from them in Fairmount. Lived about fifteen miles away."

"When my husband Ryan was applying for constable jobs," Erin replied quickly. "There was an opening in Whiterock. He never heard from them though. Once our main choices turned him down we started applying everywhere."

"Ah," Donna said. "How you like it here so far?"

"There are strange things that take getting used to," Erin said. "But we enjoy it. We are doing well here."

Erin noticed that Cindy was coming out of the back room with a confused look on her face. She took a quick lap around the store and came back to the girls. Cindy looked utterly confused by what she had seen.

"He's not in the store," Cindy said. "I checked everywhere."

"Could he have stepped out to go to the bathroom?" Donna asked.

"No," Cindy said. "He hates public restrooms and only uses the small employee one we have in back, but I looked in there."

"Does he have somewhere he likes to hide?" Erin asked.

"No," Cindy said. "He loves sitting at the desk looking important but he's not there either. Those police didn't know anything of any use, I wonder what we're supposed to do."

"I guess we just run the store," Erin said.

"How?" Cindy asked. "With no credit card machine we really can't do anything. I've noticed that the people in the mall are getting upset over something. Look at them out there, everyone looks nervous and is moving faster than normal. What in the world is going on? Did those moms say anything else?"

"No," Donna said. "There was a shooting at the gallery and they wanted their daughters at home. Nothing more was said. We cut our session early and they are paying almost two hundred dollars for each session, nonrefundable of course."

"Then I guess we wait here," Erin said. "Maybe the mall will close down soon and we can go home."

"I don't think I can do that," Cindy said.

"Why?" Erin asked.

"My apartment is on the edge of the Colfax gallery," Cindy said. "If there's been a shooting there or if someone is still on the loose I might not be able to get back there...how could we lose all news sources? That makes no sense."

"A lot of this is strange," Donna said. "I'm staying here with you two though. I don't want to be alone right now."

"That's fine," Cindy said. "Erin, want to make a hot lap around this area and see if Derek is out there somewhere? There's a girl at the coffee cart he likes to flirt with...she flirts back because he tips her so well. Her name is Mary. Ask if she's seen him this morning."

"I can do that," Erin said.

Erin left the two women and headed into the mall. She wanted to reach for her phone and start typing but she began to notice how on edge all the people seemed to be. It was like

49

they could feel the madness of Doctor Tesla descending on them but no one could yet form the words as to what they were feeling.

Everywhere Erin looked it seemed people were starting to act rude and impolite. There was no decorum as she was walking. A man bumped into her and cussed at her as he kept moving. A woman dropped her coffee and started throwing a temper tantrum. A pair of teenaged boys were making harassing comments toward an attractive young woman.

Erin knew what was causing this. She figured that by this point there would be so many ghosts in the city that everyone would be affected by them. Erin reached into her pocket and double checked to make sure that she had the device that would protect her. The black cylinder shaped rod, no bigger than a bottle of lipstick with the red button on top. Erin took comfort in knowing that it was there.

Erin got to the coffee cart but there was no one named Mary there. She looked around the tables but didn't see anyone she knew—just more people acting strangely. Erin wondered at how many of these people would be dead by the end of the day. She had no reservations about what was going to take place, she just knew she wanted to be a part of it.

To Erin, this was nothing more than cutting edge science and the future of warfare. Ever since she was a little girl she wanted to be involved in fighting, conflict and war. She wanted to be on the winning side, and in her mind, from all the studying on war and conflict that she had done, the winning side was always the side that had the best technology.

Erin knew that what Doctor Victor Tesla had done was to take the next step in warfare and create new rules for engagement. Once the world saw the power that Ghost Town Labs possessed there would be no one to stand in their way. Erin hoped she would be the one to lead the clean-up crews once all of this had finished. She imagined that she would be the one to disperse the ghosts as the city of Genesis was rebuilt.

The people in the mall didn't seem to even care about Erin as she continued to walk. She bought herself a bottle of cola and continued walking, not seeing Derek or anyone else. She wondered what the girls that robbed the store were up to, where Morgan had gone and if Ryan and Jake had caught her. Erin circled around and headed back to the store, not knowing at all what happened to Derek, and really not caring.

When Erin was almost to the store, she ducked into the women's restroom, entered a stall, pulled out her phone and quickly jotted down some notes. She didn't want to be seen in the open with a working phone so she hid in the bathroom until she was done with her notes.

Erin checked her phone, looking at the reports that others had posted. She saw everyone was doing well but was confused by Morgan's final post. The final post said that she was at one of the student's houses and they were thinking about staying there. Morgan also said that there were six students with her but Erin only saw three others when she was in the mall. Erin sent Morgan a private message, asking what was going on and offering to provide help if Morgan needed it.

Erin left the bathroom after waiting a minute to see if Morgan would reply to the message but there was nothing. Erin scanned the hallways of the mall but still saw no sign of Derek. When she entered the store, Cindy and Donna were at small display case of hunting knives, both women holding a large knife in their hands.

"What's going on here?" Erin asked as she stayed a few paces back.

"There have been more people talking about this shooter," Cindy said. "It sounds like there's more than one killer on the loose. Man, I wish it was my week to be at the main store. They have every gun you can imagine and a couple of the guys that work there go to shooting competitions. They are world class shots. I'd like to have them defending me. All we have here are knives and pellet guns."

"A pellet gun will only piss someone off," Donna said. "I think you guys should close the store down. You close and lock the gate, we move to the back room, no one can see us or get to us. We wait there until we hear something."

"But I could get fired for locking the door without permission," Cindy said. "I can't lose this job—not now Donna."

"They aren't going to fire you when you think your life is in danger," Donna said. "You could also say that people were getting upset about not being able to use a credit card, so by closing the doors you were not pissing them off when they came to buy something."

"The corporate suits would never buy that," Cindy said. "They don't care if we are in danger or not. They want their money and their sales. Erin, what do you think we should do?"

"I think we should keep the doors open," Erin said. "Until we know more about what's going on. For safety, we should position ourselves so that we cannot be seen by someone walking by. If a shooter comes here, I doubt they would come into a store that looks empty first. We might be able to get out of the building before he found us."

"That's a horrible thought," Cindy said, "but I like it. I agree. Follow me."

Cindy took the others to the women's swimwear aisle. Toward the back of the aisle was a grouping of chairs. They each took a chair and positioned it so they could see if someone walked in but no one from the hallway could see the girls. As they sat there in silence, Erin wondered how long it would be before someone started talking about what was really going on. It didn't take long for that question to be answered. A group of people began running through the hallway of the mall, all screaming the same thing: "GHOSTS!"

The Mall Part III

It started simple at first, welling into a wave of violence and madness. The first store to be hit was an electronics store that was just across the breezeway from the sporting goods store where Erin, Cindy, and Donna were hiding. They couldn't tell for sure who started it, but the looting started when someone tried to walk out with electronics.

Once the clerks tried to stop the men who were stealing, the men threw punches and all hell broke loose. There was pandemonium throughout the mall. Everyone started to rush into stores and tried to steal things. As the melee broke out, Cindy rushed to the door and began to close it. As she was closing it, a man and woman slid underneath in an attempt to loot the store.

The man was tall but thin, in his early twenties, looking fit and athletic. He wore khaki shorts, a t-shirt with a local baseball team logo and a baseball hat to match. The man was shaved bald but had a goatee. The woman was short but thick, athletic, wearing a baseball t-shirt identical to the man's with black shorts.

The pair went right for a rack of clothing and began grabbing items as Cindy finished closing the door and snapped a padlock shut. Erin rushed over to the pair, trying to charge the man as Cindy and Donna grabbed the woman. The man pushed Erin back, almost knocking her over—but Erin, who'd been through multiple mind-control trainings, was ready for him.

She spun around quickly, using the spin to build momentum as she drove the point of her shoe into the back of the man's right knee. The man screamed in pain as he dropped down to one knee. With absolute precision, Erin moved to the front of the man and put all of her weight and force into a straight right punch to the man's nose.

Blood splattered like a geyser from the man's nose as Cindy and Donna held the woman down—all of them stunned at what they were seeing. The man fell to the ground as blood filled his eyes, blinding him. The man was trying to hold his knee, screaming in agony. Erin calmly grabbed a rope off the wall, a rope that was for towing water skiers, and she quickly tied both the man and woman up. Erin, Cindy, and Donna stood back to look over their work.

"Why did you tie them up?" Cindy asked. "Why don't we just throw them out the door?"

"Look at it out there," Erin said.

The trio looked out the door and saw that it was a total riot in the mall. People were looting and destroying anything they could. There was glass being broken out of store windows and doors, people fighting—it was complete disorder. Cindy quickly lowered more metal grated gates that covered the window areas, sealing the store off from the mall.

"You open that door," Erin said, as Cindy walked back to them. "And there'll be no way that we can stop them from coming in."

"You're right," Cindy said. "What are we supposed to do now?"

"Let us go," the tied up woman said. "Release us before you get into trouble."

"This is a citizen's arrest," Cindy said. "We're holding you until the police can get here and process you for trying to steal from the store."

"Where did you learn to fight like that?" Donna asked, looking at Erin.

"Since my husband was an officer of the law," Erin said, quickly coming up with a plausible lie, "he needed to know how to defend himself. He was in a fighting league. Quite good at it too. I would always watch. I was fit and healthy and there were some women in the league but they wanted more. They asked me, so I trained and had a couple fights."

"How many have you won?" Donna asked.

"That was my first win," Erin said, with a smile. "Although the moves I used here wouldn't have been very sportsman-like in organized combat."

"That's all well and good," Cindy said, "but what are we going to do about what's going on out there?"

"I say we leave everything locked," Donna said, "and move into the employee room. Bar the door and wait."

"I agree," Cindy said.

"Wait for what?" Erin asked.

Erin was about to ask her question again but noticed Cindy and Donna both standing with their jaws hanging open, eyes wide as dinner plates, trembling. The color had been drained from their skin and they were in utter shock. Erin didn't need to turn around to know what she was going to see.

As Erin slowly turned, she saw a ghost in the mall. It was a man, in his mid-forties, who was wandering aimlessly throughout the concourse. The man was in jeans and a t-shirt, looked to be fit, except that he was transparent. The man had no idea why people were recoiling at the sight of him.

Erin grabbed the other two and hid behind a clothing rack, watching the man as he milled about in front of the store, trying to get someone to talk to him. The man couldn't speak and he didn't know why. Erin couldn't tell how he died, there was nothing to indicate what had happened. She knew that there was a separator running in the substructure of the mall so that if anyone died in the mall they would be turned.

As the man was looking around, a young girl, not more than twelve years old approached him. She was a ghost too, her red pigtails completely transparent. The girl seemed to have a smile on her face, seemed to know what her condition was. Erin guessed that the man was a spirit and the girl was a shadow. Erin was excited to see what would happen, see how the ghosts would perform.

To Erin's surprise, when the girl got almost to the man, he turned on her, taking her and making himself stronger. The confusion had been an act. The man started going after people in the breezeway. He was killing—and more people were turning into ghosts. When there was no one left in immediate sight, the man noticed the couple that was still tied up in the store.

The man rushed in, passing right through the grates. He quickly took both people and their spirits that returned with them. He was very powerful now, surely an apparition, Erin thought. The man had killed everyone in his field of vision in the breezeway and taken their spirits that had returned.

Erin slowly lowered her hand into her pocket and fingered the device she carried with her. She placed her hand on the button, wondering what the other's would say when the ghost just magically disappeared. As Erin was getting ready to depress the button, there was a bang behind her and a whooshing sound flew above her head.

Erin was watching the ghost and saw him vanish, dispersed in front of her eyes as a trail of fire, like a shooting star, hung in the air. Erin turned around to see Cindy holding a smoking flare gun. Cindy was trembling, not knowing what to do, tears running down her cheeks.

Cindy quickly reloaded the gun and looked around. Erin was impressed. She didn't know that a flare gun would work, but it made sense since the ghosts had no tolerance to flame and fire. Erin wanted to send out a memo to all the Ghost Town Lab employees right away, but she knew she would have to deal with the women in the store first.

Donna was in the process of loading a flare gun for herself as she tossed Erin a loaded flare. They grabbed all the flare ammunition off the shelves and moved into the employee room, locking and barricading the door behind them. Both Cindy and Donna were nervous wrecks. Erin was calm, but was trying to appear nervous to match the others.

"What the hell was that?" Cindy asked.

"It looked like a ghost," Donna said.

"I know what it looked like," Cindy said. "I want to know what it really was."

"How did you know that a flare gun would work?" Erin asked.

"I didn't," Cindy said. "I just grabbed the first thing I thought would come in handy. I figured that we were going to die just like the others so trying something was better than just sitting there."

"Good idea," Donna said. "Is everyone okay?"

"I am," Cindy said.

"Me too," Erin replied. "But what are we supposed to do now? All those people out there looked to have been turned into ghosts. There were so many bodies on the floor."

"I don't know," Cindy said. "This must have something to do with the shooter at the Colfax Gallery. I don't know. I think that we are safest here. We know how to kill them, we have food and water plus a radio with an emergency band. We could hold here for a while."

"It looks calm out there now," Donna said. "We should sneak out and grab as much from the cooler of drinks and the racks of jerky and candy as we can. Erin, you should change out of those clothes, there's blood on them."

"Good idea," Cindy said. "Take whatever you want to wear." Cindy grabbed a duffel bag from the floor. "I've got drinks—Donna, you grab food."

They nodded as they slowly crept out of the room—guns drawn, ready to fire at anything that moved. Erin rushed to the women's section and grabbed a blue and gray spandex racer-backed tank top and matching running shorts—an outfit that she had been eyeing since entering the store that morning—and some new underwear to go along with it. As Erin moved toward the fitting rooms she looked out to the hallways but saw no one out there, just bodies still on the floor.

Erin entered the fitting room and noted that no one had bothered to move the clothing the two girls had left. She still couldn't figure out what that had been about, or if Derek was really in on the scam with them or if he just left to go somewhere and never made it back. Either way, Erin figured she would never really know what had happened to them. She quickly changed and moved back to the room with the others.

Both Cindy and Donna were back in the room. Cindy locked the door once Erin entered. Donna was trying the radio, but all bands were static, including the weather and emergency frequencies. The three women sat back in chairs in the small employee area. The room was painted white, with a utilitarian table and chairs in the middle, a sink, refrigerator, and microwave against one wall, television against the other. There were two doors, one leading to the store, the other to an office.

"There's nothing on the radio," Donna said. "I don't understand this."

"Something big is going on," Cindy said. "I don't care what they say, for something this big to happen the government has to be involved."

"You always think the government is involved," Donna said. "There's always a conspiracy. The government has better things to do than mess around like this. There's enough world events going on to keep them busy."

"Who else could do something like this Donna?" Cindy asked. "Think about the level of training this requires—the resources! Who other than a government would have that ability?"

"What did we see out there?" Donna asked. "That was a ghost. A ghost...no one has the ability to create ghosts. Why would they? Something is messed up, but blaming the government isn't going to get us any closer to figuring out what the hell just happened out there. Erin, what do you think?"

"I have no idea," Erin said, trying to sound upset and nervous. "At least we know that we can get rid of those things. Maybe we should search out the mall and see if there is anyone else or someone who knows what's going on."

"These things are single shot," Cindy said. "And take a few moments to reload. If we happened to run into a group of those things then we would be sitting ducks. There would be nothing that we could do."

Erin nodded. She so badly wanted to explore the mall, see what kind of damage had been done, what the people were like, find survivors and hear the stories that they would have to tell. Erin wanted more than anything to be the person with the best information from this event.

Erin knew that once they went outside they would be in no real danger. All she had to do was push the button on the device she had in her pocket and all the ghosts around them would be gone. But there was no way that she could explain that to the others—no way she could let them know she was involved with the ghost they'd just seen.

"She may be right, though," Donna said, to Erin's surprise and enjoyment. "If there are people around we might owe it to them to show them how to survive. We could find a group of people, get them up here, and go out and get more. There are plenty of flare guns and flares here. If the three of us are together, knowing that if we encounter a grouping...Cindy, you take the first shot, then me, then Erin, the other's reloading, we might stand a chance. If we could find more people, and more who will come with us, then we could have five or six, all armed. We would have a fighting chance."

Cindy looked at Donna, then Erin. Erin couldn't read her expression, didn't know if Cindy was in the process of agreeing with them or not. Cindy seemed stronger than Erin first thought when she'd met her. Erin wondered if there was a ghost nearby, affecting their emotions, but she'd felt firsthand what those things could do and she was positive that they were alone.

"If we go out there," Cindy said, speaking in a slow, controlled tone, "there is a good chance we could never come back. Are both of you willing to take that risk?"

"Think about it for a moment, Cindy," Donna said. "If there are ghosts out there...ghosts like the one we saw, then it will only be a matter of time before we are found here. There isn't anything that could prevent that. We have enough food and water to last maybe a week, and that's not living very well. We hole up in here and we are guaranteeing our deaths. I know that you've always been a fighter, you've never given up. Why would you give up now and resign yourself to die in this room?"

Cindy stared at her friend. Erin smiled inwardly, knowing that Donna had just said the right thing to get Cindy on board with moving out.

"So we get fifty people here," Cindy said. "Then what? We would only have food and drinks for a couple days."

"We would get all of them and make a break for it," Donna said. "There has to be some way we could get out of here. The more people we have the better chance we have of surviving."

"Erin," Cindy asked, "what do you think?"

"I think we should go," Erin said. "We have the weapons, and sitting here will get us nowhere. Think about it, there may be rescue trucks outside the mall right now but we'd never know about them because we're sitting in here. There may be people we can help, there may be lives we can save. I say, if we have the ability to help, we have the responsibility to help."

"Okay," Cindy said. "But we are going to follow one rule...if it gets too hot out there, we come back here...agreed?"

Both Erin and Donna nodded their heads in agreement. Cindy grabbed a smaller backpack and filled it to the top with all the flare ammunition she could get. Each lady grabbed an extra gun and the group took the barricade off the door.

Cindy was first out, her gun leading the way as she poked her head out of the break room door. The store was devoid of people, save the two bodies on the floor. They looked past the sales floor, there was nothing in the breezeway, no movement, no noises, and no people. Cindy made it fully out of the door with Donna and Erin following quickly behind her.

When they reached the locked gate, Cindy pulled her keys out and tried to open the gate as quietly as possible. She only opened it high enough for the women to slip underneath it, then closed it when they were on the outside. Cindy kept the padlock with her so that no one could lock them out while they were searching the mall.

As the women looked down the breezeways of the mall, there was an eerie silence. In the halls that were filled just minutes before, was nothing. No people nor the sounds of people. As the women slowly crept along, stepping around the dead bodies that were on the floor, they all kept their guns at the ready, up in the air, fingers on the triggers.

The group made it to a central area where more hallways met up with the one they were in. They could see down the central corridor of the mall but it looked the same as the hallway they had just come through—dead bodies everywhere, but no people. What scared Erin the most was that there weren't even the sounds of people anywhere. Erin reached for her device as she walked along, keeping it ready in her hand even as she held the flare gun.

"Let's go this way," Cindy said, pointing toward a bank of windows about a hundred yards away from them. "Those windows overlook the parking lot and have a pretty good view beyond that. Maybe we could see something…or someone to help us."

The women crept along, looking over all corners of the building to make sure they weren't surprised by some ghosts. As they went along, Erin noticed that there were people in another store. The store was a hobby and game shop, and they had the gate closed and the lights out, but Erin could see movement there.

"Hey guys," Erin said, in a hushed voice. "There are people behind that gate, in the game store."

Cindy and Donna looked, pausing as they both aimed their guns in that direction.

"You sure they are real?" Cindy asked. "How are we to know? How can we see them in the dark like that? I say we press on."

"We walked out here to help people," Donna protested, "not leave them to die."

"You want to just walk up there and knock?" Cindy asked.

"They can see us," Erin said. "Look, they are coming to the window."

Erin could see three people near the window looking out toward her. It looked like three tall, lanky men. From the way they were dressed, Erin figured that they were all employees of the store. They were motioning to the girls but Erin couldn't figure out what they were trying to say.

Erin, Cindy, and Donna started to move closer to the guys. As she stepped closer, Erin could feel something in her stomach—a pang that she hadn't felt in a long time—the unmistakable gut feeling of the attraction to a man. The last time she'd felt it was when she met Ryan. Just looking at the three men in the window she was more and more attracted to them. Erin smiled inside, knowing in that instant that all three of the men were ghosts.

Erin wasn't sure how to play the situation. She wanted to just depress the button and disperse these ghosts but that might raise questions with the other girls. She could wait to see how it played out but that would lead to unnecessary risks. Erin was hoping the ghosts would make the first move, allowing her time to observe how they act and the other women would react.

As the women were within a couple feet of the gate, one of the men stepped right through the gate. Cindy jumped with fear while Donna raised her gun and fired. The ghost dispersed without a problem. The other two ghosts stayed behind the gate, with no way for the women to get a clean shot at them. The two ghosts started to back away as Donna reloaded her gun.

"What's the matter?" Donna shouted as she closed her gun and cocked it, making it ready to fire. "Can't stand a little heat? Come out here and I'll kick your ass myself! Just come over here and everything will be made right."

"What did you do to our friend?" one of the men shouted. "How were you able to do that?"

"Seems that your kind doesn't take to well to flare guns," Donna shouted. "Makes it easier for us to get rid of you demons."

"You simple fool," the man shouted. "You think that you can defeat us? You have no idea what's happened to your town. We can feel it. There are thousands of us here already and soon there will be thousands more. No one in this town will be safe from the destruction that we will cause."

"You sound pretty tough," Donna said, with a smile, "while you're standing behind a gate. All I ask is that you come over here and we can settle this like adults. There's no reason to shout taunts back and forth to each other."

"If you only knew," the man said.

"How many of you are in the mall?" Donna asked. "How many of you are here?"

"More than you have ammunition for," the other man said.

The women looked around the hallway but they didn't see anyone else in the area. There were no ghosts, but no sounds either. A thought was starting to worry Erin; all the dead bodies in the breezeways but yet they hadn't seen very many ghosts. The man and girl outside the store and these three. There was a chance that they could have taken the other ghosts before the others got too strong, but then they would be very powerful, apparition level at least. Erin couldn't tell how strong they were but she kept her finger on the button of her device.

"What do you want?" Cindy called out to the men. "Why are you here?"

"We want death," the man said, in a cold voice. "That's all we want. We can do all the things we never could as humans without cause or concern. All we want to see is death and destruction."

"Either come out or shut up," Donna said. "We don't have time to talk to you all damn day."

"Strong words," the man said as they started to step forward.

The two men stepped out of the gate and Cindy fired first, hitting one of them and dispersing him. Donna fired the next and the man was gone. Both women started to reload when they noticed that hundreds of ghosts were coming toward them from all directions. The women froze, not knowing what to do, they were totally surrounded.

Erin wasted no time in pushing the button on top of the device. In an instant, all the ghosts were gone—dispersed. Cindy and Donna looked around confused. In one moment they were certainly dead, in the next, they were safe.

"What just happened here?" Cindy asked.

"I have no damn idea," Donna said. "Erin?"

"No clue," Erin said, looking around. "Maybe something within the mall took care of them. Or maybe they are playing with us. Let's get to the window."

The group rushed to the window, hoping to see something that would help them. When they got to the floor to ceiling windows and looked out over the majestic city—they were all stunned. There were hundreds of people, people who'd been in the mall but must have rushed out, and were now in the parking lot. From the second story window they had a bird's eye view of the horror.

The people were being held in a tight circle as a few ghosts picked the people off one by one in a gruesome show of power.

The Mall Part IV

Erin, Cindy, and Donna sat cowering in the break room of the athletic store. For the past hour, no one had said a word. Donna sat on the floor, with her back to the wall, holding Cindy's head in her lap. Cindy wept, curled into a ball ever since they rushed back to their hideout. Cindy had locked the gate, taking all of her abilities to continue to function until she was able to collapse on the floor. Donna tried to comfort her friend but nothing worked. They just sat in the room, listening to Cindy cry.

Erin had paced, like a caged cat, back and forth, the entire time fingering her device. She was hoping it would last until she was able to get back to the Ghost Town Labs' compound. Erin knew she was between the main office complex where Ghost Town Labs had their main station and the mobile unit that Doctor Tesla had taken her in the night before.

The clocked ticked away, letting Erin know that every second that passed there were more ghosts running around outside. Erin didn't know if there were more ghosts in the mall or if a ghost would enter trying to find more people. One thing Ghost Town Labs didn't know was if a ghost was able to detect humans and how sensitive that sense was.

Erin looked to Donna and made a motion indicating that she was going to the bathroom. Donna nodded as Erin entered the bathroom. Once the door was locked Erin pulled out her phone and began looking through the data. There was an abundance of information on the ghosts and how they were progressing. They estimated that at one o'clock in the afternoon about thirty percent of the one-million, two-hundred-thousand people in Genesis had been turned into ghosts.

More detailed reports had come in. Ryan had reported that they didn't find Morgan but they did find three dead Ghost Town Labs women. They reported that the mind control device had been used but the programming the last users entered had been erased so they didn't know what the mind control was used for—but they reported that three people had gone through the programming.

Reports were that the Colfax Gallery was deserted already, and the ghosts that had been changed there had left. The report continued that the downtown area was now crawling with ghosts and there was a lot of action there. It continued that people were trying different things to stop the ghosts and someone had discovered that fire worked. Erin quickly posted that flare guns work incredibly well before she called to Doctor Tesla's mobile command post.

"Hello?" a woman's voice answered.

"I need to speak to Dr. Tesla," Erin said. "This is Erin Minot."

"Just a moment," the voice said.

Erin had to wait over a minute before her call was taken off hold.

"Hello, this is Tesla," Victor said.

"Doctor Tesla," Erin said, quietly, "this is Erin. I had submitted reports and am wondering what my next moves should be."

"What is your status?" Dr. Tesla asked.

"We are trapped in the mall," Erin said. "We have locked ourselves in the store break room. One of the women with me has discovered that flare guns will take out the ghosts, even big ones."

"Good, good," Victor said. "We need to get more people downtown. There's a massing of ghosts that are ravaging the area. How many are with you?"

"Two women," Erin said.

"Good, good," Victor said. "There's a mind control device in the mall, near the entrance to the tunnel. Get the women down there and run the basic warrior program on both of them. Don't worry about getting them uniforms right away, just get to the downtown area and keep gathering data."

"Orders received and understood," Erin said. "I'm on my way, Doctor Tesla."

Erin hung up her phone, wondering how she was going to get Cindy and Donna to move. Donna was still rational but Erin thought Cindy has lost it. She'd done nothing but cry since they got back. As Erin walked back to the room she knew that she would have to handle the situation with finesse.

"We need to do something guys," Erin said, softly. "We can't just wait here to die."

"What are we supposed to do?" Cindy shouted. "Can you tell me that there is something that will bring all the dead back? Is there a way to forget what we saw out that window? These things are just playing with us and we will all die soon."

"I don't want to die," Erin said. "And you don't either. We have to get out of the mall. We have to get out of town."

"And go where?" Cindy yelled. "What, start a new life in a new town? There are ghosts out there. I always knew that one day we would be wiped from the face of the earth like a dog shaking off its fleas. This is it, the human race is going extinct. We are in the final days of earth."

"That's not true," Erin said. "We can't be certain what will happen but I, for one, have no desire to stay here and die cowering, hidden in a place that has no meaning to me."

"What are we to do?" Donna said.

"I have to find my husband," Erin said. "He's a cop. He'll know what to do."

"That's a good plan," Cindy said. "Except there's GHOSTS out there and we have no phones. How do you propose that we find him?"

"If things have gotten really bad," Erin said, "they would pull him in to man the dispatch center. He focused on police logistics when we were in London. I'm betting that he's at the main police center in the downtown area."

"Do you really think we could get there?" Donna asked.

"We could," Erin said. "I have a Hummer. My husband wanted to make sure I was in a car that I am safe in. We could go to the parking ramp and get out of here. The Hummer can make it through anything."

"She might have a point," Donna said. "What do you think Cindy, we really should do something. I don't want to die here."

"I don't want to die either," Cindy said. "But what about those things out there? What if we turn into one of them?"

"Then we will die trying," Donna said. "Not die cowering in the break room. Come on, Cindy, I know that you are a fighter. You have always fought. You never give up and I'm not going to let you now. If there's a chance, a chance of any kind, we have to take it. I'm going with Erin so that means that your options are to sit here and cry by yourself or to fight alongside of us...so which is it going to be?"

Cindy looked up at her friend, then to Erin as she tried to dry her eyes. There was an unfathomable amount of stress in her eyes. Erin didn't know how much Cindy would be able to take, but she knew that all she needed to do was get the women in the basement of the mall and then everything would be different. The warrior program would make the women mentally tough as well as skilled. The normal warriors spend many hours in the gym, crafting the strongest bodies possible, something these women wouldn't get until after the Genesis Event, but they would be fine for the day.

"I will go," Cindy said, standing up. "You're right. I've had so many fights in my life that I'm not going to let this stop me. Lead the way, Erin, lead the way."

Erin smiled at the women before she motioned for them to leave the break room. Erin led the way as Cindy followed and Donna pulled up the rear, each woman holding their gun at the ready. They reached the gate, not seeing movement anywhere in the mall. Cindy unlocked the door and they opened it wide, walking into the breezeway.

The breezeway of the mall was still deserted, bodies still on the ground. Nothing had moved and the girls couldn't see any movement as they snuck along.

"There is one good thing here," Cindy said.

"What's that?" Donna asked.

"The bodies are still here," Cindy said. "Don't have to worry about zombies running around."

"That's a positive," Donna said, laughing.

The women continued through the hall to an elevator. Erin pushed the button to call the elevator, keeping a sharp eye in all directions to make sure they wouldn't be surprised by something or someone. The elevator doors started to open and all the women raised their guns, ready for something to spring out at them but there was nothing there.

They got it and Erin pushed the button for the basement, leading to the underground parking ramp. When the elevator stopped and the doors opened, the girls slowly made their way out, keeping their guns at the ready, sweeping from side to side making sure they wouldn't get attacked. Donna noticed the first ghost and took the shot, dispersing the ghost when the flare hit.

Erin noticed that there were more ghosts hiding behind the rows and rows of cars— ready to attack, but holding off after they saw the first ghost get dispersed. Erin could hardly believe what she was seeing. She didn't know if she was reading into something that wasn't there, but it appeared the ghosts were afraid of getting dispersed.

The implications of that thought were staggering. It meant that the ghosts had full awareness of what they were and that they could end up facing the eternal judgment of what lies beyond their plane of existence. Erin didn't know if anyone else had observed the phenomenon, but she knew it would have to be reported.

As they were walking, Erin noticed the door that led to the tunnel. She could see the Hummer sitting in the lot, the only big vehicle in the parking garage of sedans and compacts. It had been a nightmare to park but she had instructions to keep it near the tunnel door in case people needed to enter. Her Hummer was outfitted with a system to protect the passengers from ghosts. As long as they were inside and the car was running they would be safe.

"There's so many of them out there," Donna said, looking at the ghosts that were hiding between the cars. "How are we supposed to get out of here?"

"Service tunnels," Erin said, as she opened the door to the tunnel area. "There may be a way out through here."

Cindy and Donna quickly followed Erin through the door. When the door closed, Erin heard the clicking sound of the electrified field that protected the tunnel entrance. She knew that they were perfectly safe in the room, no ghost could enter.

As they walked into the room they walked over the three bodies of the Ghost Town Labs' women who had been shot. Erin was confused as to how the women died, no one should have been shooting in this room. She wondered why Ryan and Jake didn't report what had went on down there. As they walked into the room with the mind control device, Erin wondered how she was going to get the women into the mind control system.

Erin knew she would only have one shot at this. She knew that only three warrior women were guarding the entrance, so there would be no one else in the room. Erin took a step behind the women as they were looking at the tunnel. It was an abyss of blackness extending into the unknown. They couldn't see anything within the tunnel. Donna aimed her gun and shot a flare into the tunnel.

"That goes on for a ways," Donna said. "But I wonder where it leads to?"

"Should we walk down it?" Cindy asked.

Neither of the women noticed that Erin had picked up a heavy flashlight that was sitting near the controls of the mind control system. With a fluid motion, Erin hit Donna in the head, followed by Cindy. Cindy fell to the ground unconscious but Donna wasn't knocked out.

"What the hell?" Donna stammered before Erin hit her again.

Donna fell in a pile out cold. Erin quickly pushed the mind control system toward the women on the floor. Erin hooked the needle to the back of their necks, put the clip on their right index finger, the headphones on their ears, and placed the goggles over their eyes. She turned on the computer and ran a warrior training program. As the program was running, Erin quickly programmed another program that would cause Cindy and Donna to follow orders from Erin without question.

When both the programs had run, Erin turned the mind control off and helped the women take the equipment off.

"What are our orders?" Cindy asked, standing and saluting.

"I'm going to call Victor again," Erin said. "Something doesn't seem right about what happened here. There's Electro-Plasma Distorters hidden somewhere in here. Find them and post up while I call."

Erin pulled her phone and dialed as Cindy and Donna went to a cabinet, discovering a collection of E.P.D. guns. They both pulled out a black gun that looked like a standard AR15 assault rifle but took an E.P.D. round. They moved near the door and stood like stone statues, ready to spring into action at a moment's notice.

"Hello?" a female voice said, through Erin's phone.

"This is Erin Minot," Erin said. "I need to speak to Doctor Tesla."

"One moment please," the woman said.

Erin waited, thinking about what could have happened here. She couldn't understand how the warriors could be killed and was starting to worry about what happened to Ryan and Jake. It seemed like a lifetime for Victor to get to the phone.

"Hello?" Doctor's Tesla's dark voice came onto the phone.

"Doctor," Erin said, quickly, "this is Erin. We have a problem here at the mall. I got both women with me through the program but there are three dead warriors here. They've been shot. I saw Morgan in the mall. Ryan and Jake were going to follow her but I've not heard from any of them. What do you recommend?"

"I spoke with Ryan and Jake," Victor said, easing Erin's nerves. "Things happened and we need to adjust. The reason I wanted you with the other ladies was to stake a building downtown but now I think due to the deaths, you should stay there to guard the tunnel."

"What happened here?" Erin asked.

"That's classified right now," Doctor Tesla said. "There are reasons and you'll know in the course of time but for now there are other problems. We are having difficulties controlling some of the ghosts. I've been losing warrior women all over the city. The ghosts are more powerful than we could have ever imagined. Erin, we may need that tunnel very soon. Estimates say that we will need to implement containment procedures very soon. Guard the tunnel at all costs."

"The parking ramp that leads to the tunnel is infested with ghosts," Erin said. "There must have been hundreds of ghosts around the cars. If a team tried to get to the tunnel they would be slaughtered."

"I knew we should have made a secret entrance to that room," Doctor Tesla sighed. "You have no other choice but to clean out the parking area. I want every ghost in that area dispersed."

"Orders received and understood," Erin said.

"And Erin," Doctor Tesla said, "there's one more thing…if anyone I haven't told you about tries to enter from the tunnel, kill them on the spot. I want no one coming into the city. I will tell you if I authorize someone to enter."

"Understood," Erin said, as she heard the doctor end the call. "We have to clean the ramp out. We must make sure there are no ghosts left in the area. Also, if someone tries to enter Genesis from the tunnel we are to kill them unless Doctor Tesla informs us that they are coming."

"Then let's get moving," Cindy said, tossing Erin her gun and grabbing another from the cabinet.

Cindy took a number of loaded magazines for the guns and handed them to the other women. They took black vests from the cabinet that resembled bulletproof vests but were simply an electric field generator to protect them from the ghosts.

Erin opened the door and entered the parking garage with the other two close behind her. They could see the ghosts behind the cars and wasted no time in rushing toward the ghosts, firing their guns as quickly as they could to disperse the ghosts. Once the ghosts realized they stood no chance against the powerful guns, they started to merge together and move toward the women.

Erin motioned for the others to fall back and place their backs against the wall so they didn't have to worry about sneak attacks. Erin couldn't believe how many ghosts were coming. They each burned through the clips they had and the spare ones they brought, but they still hadn't taken out even half the ghosts. Most ghosts needed two or three shots before they would disperse.

The women spent their extra clips and still had ghosts moving in on them. Erin pulled out her device and waited for more of the ghosts to get near them. She studied the ghosts as they moved in. They all looked like the standard shoppers who'd been at the mall. She couldn't believe there were so many of them—that they'd all been turned so easily.

Once enough of the ghosts were close enough, Erin depressed the button on the device and many of the ghosts dispersed at once but there was still many ghosts behind the cars. Erin couldn't figure out what to do. She knew with the amount of ammunition they burned through to get to this point that they would have to use everything they had to finish the rest of the ghosts off.

The group moved back into the room and sealed the door shut. Cindy rushed to the back door that led into the mall and sealed it, closing the women in completely. Erin looked over their ammunition supply and she knew that they were trapped. They had to defend the tunnel but they wouldn't be able to clear the parking ramp. She sent a report on the situation to Doctor Tesla and waited for a reply.

"What is our next move?" Cindy asked.

"We guard the tunnel," Erin said. "It is our responsibility to make sure no ghosts go through the tunnel and no one enters the area without our knowledge. We have protection here."

Erin and the other women took their vests off and took positions in the room. Erin was checking her phone every few moments to see if there would be new orders. As the time ticked away Erin wondered what was happening in the main part of the city. When her phone beeped that it had received a message Erin nearly jumped out of her skin.

Erin's eyes scanned the message as quickly as she could. There was a number of reports that confirmed what she had noticed—the ghosts seemed to be afraid when they saw one of their own getting killed. The reports said that the ghosts seemed to have reached a peak. Indications from satellite imaging showed that there hadn't been a massive attack and turning event for almost an hour. What worried them the most was that they had lost intelligence on Hannah. They could not locate her and didn't know where she had gone.

Erin saw the note for her from Doctor Tesla—they were to defend the tunnel at all costs. He had ordered more warriors to enter the area and they would be arriving near nightfall, entering through the tunnel. Erin and her partners were to wait there and keep the room secure.

"I guess we have it easy for a while," Erin said. "We are to wait here and keep the tunnel entrance for Ghost Town Labs."

"That should be easy enough," Cindy said, looking over their weapons supply. "The ghosts can't enter this room and we have enough ammo and protection to at least get to the Hummer and get out of here."

"Reinforcements are coming," Erin said. "We will greet them when they come through the tunnel. They think that the ghosts have reached a plateau. They aren't turning the living as fast as we thought they would."

"Do you believe everything in those reports?" Cindy asked.

"Yes," Erin replied. "Why?"

"If the ghosts have plateaued and everything is under control," Cindy asked, "why are they sending reinforcements?"

The Bank Part I

Mackenzie Hanson smiled through gritted teeth as she handed a stack of crisp, new twenty dollar bills to a forty year old man that had pathetically tried to get her phone number. Mackenzie, extremely trigger-happy once she'd joined Ghost Town Labs, thought how fun it would be to pull out her Beretta FS92 9mm handgun that she had concealed on herself and waste this loser.

Mackenzie could feel the weight of the gun pulling against the top of her skirt, the gun clipped to the back of her tight, gray, short business skirt and covered by the matching gray jacket that was over Mackenzie's black tank top. With her long legs in dark pantyhose and her black pumps, Mackenzie could see why men would be hitting on her today, but she didn't think it would be that bad in a professional setting like a bank.

Mackenzie watched the businessman leave the bank with his money in hand. She'd given him a number, the local call in number to receive the weather report, and hoped that he'd call it before he was killed in today's slaughter. She knew that people like him wouldn't last very long once the ghosts started to take the city.

Mackenzie was stationed at the Genesis First Bank and Trust, situated right on the edge of the Colfax Gallery. The lobby of the bank was opulent, black marble so polished you could see your reflection anywhere on the floor, white pillars lining the lobby, partially hiding the doors to the offices and more artwork and relief busts than there was room for. The bank had a majestic feel, like you were walking into a palace, but the main offices for the bank were upstairs and they'd wanted to impress people when they stepped through the laser-etched glass double doors.

Mackenzie had caught herself more than once staring at the marble fountain that stood in the middle of the lobby floor. The fountain contained a ten-foot-diameter pool that contained four granite men, all looking like Greek gods, looking out. Water was springing from each of the men's mouths while a waterfall of water cascaded down from the second floor.

A noise at Mackenzie's station caught her attention; the vibration of her cellphone. She wasn't supposed to have her phone on during working hours—bank rules—but she really didn't think they would have time to fire her today before the destruction began. Mackenzie looked at the number, seeing that it was from the F.B.I. main office. She'd never given any communication back to the feds after she and Hannah returned into the woods at Whiterock— never let them know what happened to her.

Mackenzie smiled as she ignored the call, letting the feds hang, not letting them know what had happened to her. Mackenzie was sure that by now, they must know she was alive and had been working for Ghost Town Labs the entire time, but she reveled in the fact that she was able to feed them so much misinformation about Ghost Town Labs. Hannah had been very easy to lie to, being a naïve girl and Hannah had reported everything Mackenzie said as the total truth.

Mackenzie hoped that from her vantage point she would be able to see the casket but it was on the other side of the gallery. Mackenzie knew that when the lid was opened all hell would break loose and they would hear the screams right away. Mackenzie was excited for the event, she knew that everyone that did well would get a promotion within the Ghost Town Labs Company and she couldn't wait to be even closer to Doctor Tesla, helping him as he showed the world what true power was.

Mackenzie looked as her next customer was walking toward her; an early twenties woman, an attractive black woman, who looked to still be wearing her pajamas but her hair and makeup had been done nice. Mackenzie smiled at the woman who smiled back.

"Welcome to Genesis First Bank and Trust," Mackenzie said. "How may I assist you today?"

"I need to cash a check," the woman said handing Mackenzie a check and her driver's license. "Big bills please."

"Thank you," Mackenzie said, as she took the items.

Mackenzie looked at the check, it was for $2,000, from a personal account. The name on the check and the name on the license matched, so Mackenzie started to process the transaction. She ran the woman's name to verify that she had enough in her account to allow the check to be cashed in her name, but the computer wouldn't work—there was no internet. Mackenzie knew what was going on, but she had to act surprised so no one would get suspicious.

"This is strange," Mackenzie said. "The computer isn't working. It's like the internet is no longer running. I'm not sure what I'm supposed to do here."

"Could you just give me the money please?" the woman asked. "I really need to get moving. I have to get somewhere and I need the money."

"Just a moment," Mackenzie said. "I have to get a manager."

Mackenzie started to walk to the manager's office but saw she was already on her way over. A tall woman, in her early forties, short brunette hair with frosted spikes atop a narrow, pointed face, with squinted hazel eyes. The woman was dressed to enhance her attractive, shapely body with black, form-fitting slacks, a gray, sleeveless blouse with a swooping neckline, a clustering of gold necklaces around her neck, a black belt, black pumps, golden bracelets and both hands full of gold and diamond rings.

The manager had a powerful, confident walk with a face that looked like it could melt the coldest of hearts. Her long, pronounced eyelashes fluttered as she blinked quickly, an almost seductive gesture that, even though she was also a woman, put the waiting customer at ease.

"Is there a problem here?" she asked as she reached the counter.

"There is," Mackenzie said. "This customer wants to cash a check but the internet is down. I can't access accounts."

"I'm Ashley Wilson," Ashley said, extending her hand.

"Charmed," the woman said. "Please, I'm in a terrible rush, can you help?"

"Let me see what I can do," Ashley said, as she typed at the computer. "The internet is down—typical...I can see from the in-house computer you have the funds. I authorize the transaction Mackenzie, you can cash her check."

"Thank you," the woman said, as Mackenzie counted out the hundred dollar bills.

Mackenzie counted the money again, and a third time as she handed it to the woman while Ashley watched. The woman smiled, took the money, and walked out. Mackenzie looked to Ashley as the woman moved out of their sight.

"She's good for the money," Ashley said. "Her father is very successful. He started building houses, working carpentry after high school and worked his way up. He now has one of the most successful home building companies in town. They run a number of crews and she works for them. Uses the money to get things done quickly, permit wise I mean."

Mackenzie mouthed a silent 'oh' as she thought about the implications. She knew that the world was a cutthroat place and people in power would use that power to get whatever they wanted. She felt no different working for Ghost Town Labs, but at least they were honest about what they were doing.

"I didn't know it was Halloween already," Ashley said, softly, while looking at the door.

Mackenzie turned to look and saw two very athletic teen girls walking in the door. They looked to all the world like normal girls, except the fact that they were only wearing black with neon yellow, pink, and green splashes, one-piece athletic swimsuits with a black duster jacket over the top. Both girls had running shoes with no socks showing. As far as Mackenzie and Ashley could tell, that was all the girls were wearing.

The girls were set in a conversation amongst themselves as they walked through the lobby of the bank. They were not paying attention to anything around them. The girls didn't even seem to notice anyone until they were almost at the teller windows. The girls looked up, realizing that most of the people in the bank were staring at them. They smiled, looking for a window to approach. The girls looked right at Mackenzie and started walking toward her.

"Ashley," a male teller called out beside them, "I need a secure form authorization. Could you grab one for me and fill out your part?"

"Sure thing Andy," Ashley said, walking back to her office as the girls approached Mackenzie.

71

"Good morning and welcome to Genesis First Bank and Trust," Mackenzie said, with a smile. "How may I assist you this morning?"

"We need a withdrawal," the blonde girl said.

"I can help you with that," Mackenzie said. "What's your account number and how much do you need?"

"Account number 8-6-7-5-3-0-9," the brunette said. "We need twenty-thousand dollars."

Mackenzie's eyes got huge. She couldn't believe what she'd just heard. She wondered how these two teenagers could have that much money in an account. As she started typing the account number in, she realized that she'd heard that number before. Mackenzie looked up and saw the girls were both making eyes with Andy, something was going on between them. Mackenzie finished typing the number but the computer couldn't find an account linked to it.

"I'm sorry," Mackenzie said. "There's no account with that number. Are you sure it's right?"

"We are," the blonde said. "We need to get that money. We have a big shopping trip today. Please, check it again."

"The computer can't find it," Mackenzie said. "And if it's not an in-house account, we can't find it anyway, the internet is down."

"You'd better call then," the blonde said. "I'm getting tired of waiting."

"Of course," Mackenzie said, as she lifted the phone up. "What the name on the account?"

"I'm Nancy Kay," the blonde said. "And she's Nancy Dee. We go by Kay and Dee."

"Okay," Mackenzie said, as she started to dial. Mackenzie looked at the phone and depressed the receiver button a number of times, "I'm sorry Kay but the phones are down too. I can't get you the money right now."

"That doesn't work for me," Kay said. "But how about this..."

Both Kay and Dee slightly opened their duster jackets to reveal that they had shotguns concealed within. Mackenzie's eyes got big and she swallowed in a dry throat. She found it funny, the terror that was about to befall this town yet here she was, getting robbed by a pair of teenagers. Mackenzie thought about pulling her pistol but decided against it. She gently pushed the call button at her foot to alert security that she was being robbed.

"Are you trying to rob the bank?" Mackenzie asked.

"Boy," Kay said, sarcastically, "you're a bright one. Hand over the money bitch, or we start wasting people. You'll be first."

Mackenzie tried pushing the button again but no one was coming. She looked over to Andy Huss who'd been listening to the whole thing. Andy was in his late twenties, and seemed to be a bit of a whiner. He wore a navy, off-the-rack suit, that didn't fit him very well. His rusty hair and beard needed a trim while his hazel eyes seemed to be very shifty. He took a step closer to Mackenzie.

"Mackenzie," Andy said, softly, "give them all the money in your drawer, but not the bottom four bills off each slide—they are marked."

Andy handed the girls a bag of money from his till.

"What?" Mackenzie asked.

"The bank is insured," Andy said. "The suits in the office are more worried about someone getting hurt in a standoff and suing then they are with a few thousand dollars walking out of the building. Just give them the money and everything will be fine, I promise."

Mackenzie continued to stare at Andy. She couldn't believe what she was hearing.

"Trust me," Andy said. "It will be fine."

"Maybe you understand this," Kay said, as she took her jacket off, showing off her tone, muscular arms and broad, defined shoulder and neck muscles. "Give me the money or I come over this counter and beat you within an inch of your life before my friend shoots you."

"Just give them the money and get them out of here," Andy said, in a whiney tone. "Don't be a hero Mackenzie. You won't be in trouble and you won't get fired."

"Okay," Mackenzie said, as she opened the cash drawer and pulled out a bag, "fine, here's the stupid money. I hope you two are caught and locked away for a long time because of this."

Mackenzie finished loading the bag with money as Kay put her jacket back on. Mackenzie handed Dee the money and the girls quickly took off with over twenty-thousand dollars between the two bags. Mackenzie dropped to her knees to inspect the call switch that she had pressed with her foot and to her surprise, the wire running to it was cut.

Mackenzie stood back up to see that Ashley was standing near her, holding some papers, but Andy was nowhere to be seen.

"Where'd Andy go?" Ashley asked. "I have the papers he asked for."

"I'm not sure," Mackenzie said. "We were just robbed."

"WHAT?" Ashley shouted as she dropped the papers. "What happened? Why didn't security stop it?"

"I don't know," Mackenzie said. "I was at my window when those two girls asked for money. They had shotguns underneath their jackets. I pushed the call button a number of times but no one came. They were at my window but Andy handed them the money from his window and told me to give them mine. He said the bank was insured for things like that. I gave them the money and they left. I was just checking the call button but the wire has been cut and now Andy isn't here."

"Son of a bitch," Ashley said, shaking her head. "Andy's been here for a long time but I've noticed some strange behavior in him lately. I didn't know what it was and tried to talk to him about it but he always blocked me out...I shouldn't judge too quickly though. We were just robbed. Maybe he had to go to the bathroom or something. I can't say anything until we know for sure what is going on."

"All I know is that everything is out," Mackenzie said.

"Everything?" Ashley asked.

"Everything," Mackenzie repeated. "Phones, internet, cell service—the works."

"That's a problem," Ashley said. "This place gets very busy in about an hour. If the service isn't up by then I don't know what we'll do. Mackenzie, go through the building and look for Andy. He drives a red Honda car that's usually in the back row. See if it's there. If you find him, have him come to me to give a statement. I'll try to get police here and tell the people upstairs what happened. We've got a record here, this building has never been robbed in the five years that we've been here. People have tried, but this is the first time they made it out the door with the money."

"I'll find Andy," Mackenzie said, as she took off from her window.

Mackenzie was glad to be away from the window. She knew that very soon the casket would be opening and she was hoping to get front row tickets to the show. There was a window on the second floor of the bank that Mackenzie rushed to. It looked over the employee parking lot, but to the other side of the window was the Colfax Gallery where she would have a perfect view of the casket.

As Mackenzie reached the window she looked out over the lot. She knew the red Honda that Ashley had mentioned since she had parked beside it that morning. Mackenzie looked out, her black Hummer was in the lot with the space next to it full—the Honda was there. Mackenzie wondered if there was something more to the robbery than she had seen but she didn't worry too long. Mackenzie filed a report on her phone and looked toward the casket.

The black, shiny casket trimmed with polished bronze sat on a wheeled gurney that had had its wheels locked and a piece of black cloth draped around it. The gallery was packed with people, many not even bothering to take a second, or even first look at the casket set in the

74

middle of the stone brick area. Mackenzie looked at her watch, knowing that very soon, all these people would be running for their lives.

Mackenzie notice a boy, not more than ten years old, down on the galley floor that seemed to be awe struck with the casket. His mother was in an animated conversation with another lady and neither were paying attention to the boy. The boy kept pulling at his mother's hand to move closer to the casket but finally the mother had had enough and simply let go of the boy's hand. The little blonde boy moved closer and closer to the casket, staring at it with sad, curious eyes.

Mackenzie could hardly believe it, the boy was going to open the lid. Mackenzie would get a firsthand account of the event as it happened. She would get to see Hannah exit the casket and take her first victims. As the boy had his hand on lid, ready to open it, his mother rushed to him and pulled him back. Mackenzie winced, not getting to see the first event.

"Find him?" Ashley asked, coming up behind Mackenzie.

"No," Mackenzie said, turning. "His car is here though."

Ashley walked up to Mackenzie, trapping her between the window and her powerful, commanding presences. Mackenzie, even though she had a gun clipped to her back, felt twinges of fear. Ashley was a dominate woman, someone not to be taken lightly, with an air of mystique about her, something that commanded those around her.

"And you have no idea what was going on?" Ashley asked.

"Nothing," Mackenzie said, looking Ashley straight in the eyes. "I swear to you that I am just trying to earn a living here. I wasn't in on it."

"You lying to me?" Ashley asked flatly.

"I'm not," Mackenzie said. "I didn't have anything to do with it."

"I believe you," Ashley said. "I can tell when a person is lying or not. It's a gift. I knew that Andy had been lying about something recently. I wasn't sure what but his girlfriend had broken up with him and he was having a rough patch with some friends. I know that he'd been going to parties near the college—and once you're out of college it's a horrible thing to do. I knew something wasn't right."

"How will we catch them?" Mackenzie asked.

"That's a good question," Ashley said. "I have some ideas. Andy will be easy enough to trace. We have all the information we need on him. This is just so frustrating though."

"What's that?" Mackenzie asked.

"Getting robbed," Ashley said, as she moved a step to the side and looked out the window. "I've been working with Genesis First Bank and Trust since I was in high school. I started as a cleaning lady after hours. Once I turned eighteen, I started working the tills. I got a business degree and masters—fought and clawed my way up to this position. When I got it everyone thought it was because I was dating the son of one of the board members. That may have helped but it wasn't the reason. I was the best person for this position and I've been proving that since I got here. It's hard being a woman in a man's line of work."

"You still dating him?" Mackenzie asked.

"No," Ashley said. "I knew that the position was coming up and there was some intense competition. I went out with him for about a year. Judge me if you want, but I was the best person for the job. I shouldn't have had to do that to get the spot...hang on, what's that out there?"

"The casket?" Mackenzie asked.

"Yeah," Ashley said. "Such a strange place to leave a casket. I wonder if one of the businesses out there is trying some tacky promotional gambit with it. There are a couple store managers out there that would be short sighted enough to try something like that."

Mackenzie was about to answer when the lid of the casket slowly started to rise. Mackenzie felt her heart instantly start to race as she noticed her palms were sweaty. The anticipation of this moment had been building inside her and she couldn't believe that she was going to witness one of the darkest moments of mankind. Mackenzie and Ashley watched as Hannah, dressed to the nines in her red party dress, stepped out of the casket. Hannah looked around the gallery with a predatory smile as people began to notice her. Hannah licked her lips as she took her first victim.

The Bank Part II

It started so simply, an attractive blonde woman, dressed in a sparkly red party dress, stepped out of a casket in a packed gallery. As she exited the casket, few people noticed—jaded people who'd lived lives of simple complexity, lives that were just moments from being destroyed. Hannah Jones, the woman stepping out of the casket, felt nothing for these people, all she wanted was to destroy, the only emotion that she could feel was death and destruction. Hannah was the Genesis Ghost, the ghost who would trigger the darkest chapter in mankind.

Hannah looked around the gallery area at all the people. She wanted her first victim to be perfect. As she scanned the area she noticed a couple, a man and woman who looked to be in their early twenties that were having a fight. The man and woman were yelling at each other, the woman in tears, the man clearly upset. Hannah looked at the man, a buff, strong bald-headed man in tight jeans and an even tighter gray t-shirt. The woman looked soft and dull, brunette hair in a ponytail, too much makeup for a day of shopping, in a red skirt and white tank top.

Hannah sauntered over to the couple arguing. Their voices getting louder, arguing over money, spending habits and the girl bringing up how little the guy isn't at home anymore. Hannah got closer and closer, most people trying their best to ignore the couple, the only other person paying attention to them, a police officer standing twenty feet to the man's left near a tree. Hannah got so close that the couple couldn't ignore her any longer.

"Can I help you?" the man snapped. "You want something?"

"Don't snap at her," the woman said, between her tears. "You shouldn't get involved."

"Oh let me help you," Hannah said, glowing with excitement. "I've never been in a fight with my boyfriend. I've never had a boyfriend come to think of it. See, I was dedicated to work, dedicated to my life. I never took time for myself. I was so focused that I let my life pass me by. That all changes now. That changes today. I can help you. No matter what problems you are having, I can help you."

"Oh gee thanks," the man mocked. "Please help us random strange lady. Get moving, freak."

"Danny!" the woman shouted. "I'm so sorry ma'am, he's usually not like this. It has been rough at work for him."

"That's okay," Hannah said. "You look pretty strong, like you can protect yourself. You've been in fights before but this is one you can't win. I have a secret, something that will make everything better."

"Get to the point freak," the man said.

"With pleasure," Hannah said.

Hannah took a step back before rushing toward the man and passing right through him. The man's body fell to the ground yet his spirit stood where his body did, looking down at himself. Hannah wasted no time in taking what was left of the spirit. The woman took a moment to register what had just happened. It was so quick that she wasn't even sure if she really saw what she thought she saw.

Hannah turned to the woman, waiting for her to scream but the woman was so confused she didn't know what to do. The police officer was making his way over to them, concerned that the man was on the ground. The officer was taking his gun out of his holster as Hannah rushed him, taking him to the ground and taking his soul the second it returned.

The woman began screaming hysterically. Everyone in the gallery started looking at her and saw the bodies on the ground. People started moving away but they couldn't get away fast enough, Hannah started turning on everyone, killing as fast as she could. There were bodies everywhere, spirits wandering around, some taking others, some taking humans, all keeping their distance from Hannah.

Mackenzie and Ashley watched in sheer terror; Ashley sweating and trembling, Mackenzie stunned silent, having seen things like this happen in training but never in real life. The people that were being killed were real, out in the open, and there was no way to reverse what had just happened.

As they were watching, Ashley grabbed Mackenzie's hand and squeezed tight. She was white as a ghost, sweat pouring from her forehead. Mackenzie couldn't take her eyes off the destruction. She knew that she would be getting a promotion with the data that she was gathering. Mackenzie couldn't wait to report what she'd seen. The women could hear the screams coming from the gallery.

Ashley turned her head backwards, looking back into the bank. There was a panic going on in the lobby. People were rushing, running, and screaming. Mackenzie looked to see a woman dive into the fountain in an attempt to hide. It took Mackenzie a split second to realize what was going on—ghosts had already entered the bank.

Mackenzie felt herself being pulled away from the lobby. Ashley had Mackenzie's hand held tight and was moving up a flight of stairs. Mackenzie was amazed at how powerful Ashley was, almost dragging Mackenzie with her. The pair got to the top of the stairs and Ashley started to race down a hall. Mackenzie needed everything she had to keep up.

They moved down hallways, up another flight of stairs, this one a back set that Ashley had to use a key card to access. At the top of the stairs was a hallway with a vault door in the middle. Ashley used two metal keys, a key card, and a hand print to open the door. Once everything was verified, a wheel on the door started to spin and the door opened.

Ashley pushed Mackenzie in the vault first before she rushed in and pulled the door shut behind her. Mackenzie looked around the room. It was warm, a pleasant temperature with a slight breeze smelling of vanilla and rain air fresheners. The walls that could be seen were painted a dark blue, matching the plush, soft blue carpet. On one wall, from the floor to the fifteen-foot ceiling, were safety deposit boxes. The opposite wall had larger boxes, the doors two feet by two feet. The wall opposite them was adorned with art and the wall the door was on had a mural of the Genesis Skyline at dusk, brilliantly painted to make the wall almost seem alive.

In the middle of the room was a pair of black leather sofas, four black leather easy chairs, and a row of waiting chairs that surrounded a dark mahogany coffee table. Past that was a larger conference table surrounded by black leather office chairs. The entire area was like a fancy office. Mackenzie scanned the room quickly, noticing that there were two other doors on the far side of the room, almost concealed within the wall.

Ashley double checked the door to make sure it was locked before motioning Mackenzie to come to one of the doors on the other side. She opened the door revealing a small room that was actually a large refrigerator that was stocked full with bottles of sparkling water, soda, and some snack food. Ashley took a bottle of water and motioned to Mackenzie to take something. Mackenzie grabbed a cola before they closed the door and moved to the plush leather chairs.

Ashley took a drink from her water, trying to process everything that she'd seen. She pulled out her cellphone and tried to access news. There was nothing there, the net was still down. Ashley tried to access the net through the bank system but that route was down too.

"What is this room?" Mackenzie asked. "I thought the safety deposit boxes were on the first floor."

"This is for some of our bigger clients," Ashley said. "If you look at blueprints of this building, this area is offices. There's billions of dollars in this vault; gold and silver bullion, jewelry, collectables and the like. These boxes hold documents that are very important to families, there are wills in here that direct billion dollar estates. This room is where they can meet in total secrecy. There's no way to listen inside this room from the outside. No long range device can penetrate the metal in the walls, there's electricity running through them, scrambles any listening device. We have bug detectors in here as well. This room can be rented out for meetings."

"Does it get used a lot?" Mackenzie asked.

"All the time," Ashley replied. "Politian's meeting with businesses, company owners meeting for takeover talks, hell, we even have school boards that meets here to discuss school business away from prying eyes."

"How much?"

"One-thousand an hour," Ashley said. "Back door entrance, we can have anything they need here, catering, booze...women, no questions asked."

"How is the air supplied?" Mackenzie asked.

"There is a recirculating system with a purifier," Ashley said. "Totally contained—no chance of someone listening through it. We can stay here and never be found. Only I and two others have all the keys to enter. I entered by myself which means that all the boxes in the room are locked. You have to have two handprints to unlock the magnetic locks that hold the faces on the boxes. One person can access the room, two are needed to access the content."

"How much food?" Mackenzie asked.

"There was a meeting that was going to take place this evening," Ashley said. "I had brought some of the needed items. There is enough water and soda to last the pair of us for months--food, we could get by for a couple weeks before it got tight."

"You think we should stay here?" Mackenzie asked. "I mean, what if there are more survivors in the bank? Shouldn't we go out there and get them?"

"It's a nice thought," Ashley said. "But I don't think so. If what I saw out there was real, what I think I saw, I plan on staying here until...I don't know, but I'm not heading out there."

"Even if it means people die because we don't help them?" Mackenzie asked.

"Let me ask you a question," Ashley asked. "What do you think we saw out there?"

"Someone was killing people," Mackenzie said. "I don't know how, but people were dying. It's an attack of some kind."

"There were ghosts out there," Ashley said. "Somehow, that lady in the red dress was turning people into ghosts."

"You seem very calm about this," Mackenzie said.

"I was military," Ashley said. "Guards from eighteen until thirty. Saw some action overseas. They trained us to keep calm in intense situations. Inside, I'm a wreck, thinking that I'm seeing things, wondering if I'm crazy. Outside however, I'm very calm and together, giving orders, keeping people safe like I did back then. You are very calm about it as well, why?"

"I lived in a haunted house growing up," Mackenzie said, repeating the lie she'd come up with in case anyone ever asked. "My best friend for five years was a little ghost boy who'd been killed by his father. Everyone thought he was an imaginary friend but he was there. I've seen other ghosts, this is no different."

"Interesting," Ashley said. "Remember when I said I could tell if a person was lying or not?"

Mackenzie nodded her head while swallowing in a dry throat.

"You're lying to me right now," Ashley said. "Your eyes betray you. I also know that you're not telling me the whole truth about working here. I was told that you were starting today, by some higher-ups in the board, board members who met with strange people in this very room not days before I was told you would be starting...you know what's going on out there, don't you?"

"No I don't Ashley," Mackenzie said, searching for what to say, amazed at how well Ashley had pinned her in her words. "I've never seen anything like that before."

"They say that compulsive liars will repeat a lie so much in their minds that it becomes the truth," Ashley said. "They believe the lie so fully that even a lie detector test will show they're telling the truth. There's a fine line between truth and falsehood. There's no truth in your words Mackenzie, none at all. Please tell me what is going on."

Mackenzie stared at Ashley. She couldn't believe how perceptive that Ashley was, how she picked up on the subtleties of what was going on. After what Mackenzie saw out there she was content to stay in this vault. If Ashley was telling the truth, and the interior of these walls were metal with electricity running through them, then they could stay here and be safe, having seen enough for a good report.

Mackenzie knew that to stay here though, she would have to convince Ashley of her innocence. Mackenzie didn't know what to do, but she knew it had to be bold. Mackenzie quickly stood, moved to Ashley, and pressed her lips against Ashley's. Mackenzie kissed Ashley for a moment, Ashley not pushing her away but not inviting her to go further. Mackenzie kept the kiss going for a few moments before pulling away and looking into Ashley's eyes.

"I've been wanting to do that for some time," Mackenzie said. "I've wanted to be close to you since I first saw you a year ago. I was here, cashing a check and saw you walk behind the counter. I found out what I could and did what I could to get hired here. It took a year but I did it. I'm not letting you go Ashley."

Mackenzie thought she may have found a route in with Ashley. Mackenzie had read a report of personnel of the bank, knew everything about them. Mackenzie knew that Ashley favored women, not exclusively, but that she'd recently ended a long-term relationship with a woman, and that the reason it ended was Ashley was playing around with some younger women on the side.

"You're not gay," Ashley said, smiling at Mackenzie. "Hell, you're not even bi. Maybe you practiced with your girlfriends when you were a teenager; that's the furthest you've ever gone. The fact you tried that tells me you know my background and you know what I like...you've studied me, you were looking at that casket when I found you on the second level. You are involved with this. How?"

"Who the hell *are* you?" Mackenzie asked. "How the hell can you tell all that from what just happened here?"

"I told you," Ashley said. "I can read truth in words and I've developed a high ability of logic and reasoning. I needed it to get where I am in the bank. Now, you're going to tell me, right now, who you are."

Mackenzie slowly started to reach for the gun that she had clipped to her skirt. She thought that maybe the quickest way would be to shoot Ashley now but Mackenzie's arm stopped when a thought crossed her mind, 'what if Ashley turns here? My protective device is in my purse at my station. Are the separators powerful enough to create a ghost in this room?'

The thought was powerful enough that Mackenzie decided against shooting Ashley but Ashley still had her eyes glued to Mackenzie. This was the first time since she'd started working for Ghost Town Labs that Mackenzie didn't know what to do. Ashley pushed Mackenzie away and stood up.

"I've got some supplies in the other room," Ashley said, walking toward the door. "Change of clothes and whatnot. I'll be out in a moment."

Ashley disappeared through the door. Mackenzie took her phone out and started checking reports. There was utter chaos in the gallery, the bank was surely overtaken. Mackenzie noticed reports from Erin about two teenaged girls who robbed her sporting goods store, stealing money and outfits matching what the girls wore in the bank, giving Erin the same names they gave Mackenzie.

As Mackenzie looked over the reports that were pouring in she wondered if she should head to the second floor of the bank. There was a mezzanine area that looked over the lobby. She could get a good view of the first floor and the horror that was taking place down there. Mackenzie cursed, realizing that she left the magazines loaded with EPD rounds for her gun in her bag that was at her station at the teller windows.

Mackenzie continued to look over the reports that were coming in. The Ghost Town Labs' women were in position around the town, blocking every exit. They'd only had problems in one location with the local police. For the most part, Ghost Town Labs had the metropolis of Genesis under control.

There were reports coming in from Maria, who was near the gallery, but was now called away because how hot the area was getting. Maria had a ground floor view of the casket being opened. Mackenzie thought back to the event, to the opening, but couldn't remember seeing Maria anywhere.

Mackenzie looked around the room. She wondered how many backdoor, crooked deals were made in this room, how many drug deals had been made. She knew the price of business but had never seen it up close and personal. Her role in Ghost Town Labs had been research into the reactions of normal people upon seeing the ghosts. She'd been placed into the FBI, partnered with Hannah for years before Whiterock.

When she was in the FBI, Mackenzie studied everything about the organization. She was tracking how information flowed, who gave reports to who, and who made the final orders. She saw many backdoor deals, many events go unnoticed because there wasn't profit involved or because someone had received a payoff. Ghost Town Labs used all the information to manipulate the feds so all eyes were focused today on Fargo North Dakota, not Genesis

Minnesota. Mackenzie felt a degree of pride, knowing that her dealings were the ones that led them to the deceptions they gave the feds.

Mackenzie looked back to the door that Ashley had passed through, wondering what was taking her so long, wondering why she had a change of clothes in this room. Mackenzie was still trying to figure out how Ashley saw through her. Nothing that Mackenzie tired had worked. Mackenzie knew that she would have to come clean with Ashley but the truth seemed stranger than fiction in this deal.

As Mackenzie debated what to say, she heard the door open. Mackenzie didn't turn around right away—she wanted to let some tension build. Mackenzie was still trying to figure out what to say when she turned around to look at Ashley. When Mackenzie saw Ashley her jaw dropped and her eyes went big, stunned at what she was seeing.

Ashley was in solid black from head to toe; tights, long sleeved form-fitting top, knee high boots, gloves, bulletproof vest, a bandana tied over her hair and black tinted goggles. Ashley was ready for combat, ready for a shootout. The outfit wasn't the most disturbing thing about Ashley. The most disturbing thing was that Ashley was holding a black 12-gauge shotgun, a short barrel shotgun with the stock removed and replaced with a pistol grip that was being held up and pointed directly at Mackenzie's head.

"Okay bitch," Ashley said, as she walked up to Mackenzie and pressed the barrel of the gun into Mackenzie's head. "Let's try this one more time. Tell me who you are, what you know about what's going on out there, and why you are working here."

The Bank Part III

Mackenzie was frozen. She never pegged Ashley for a violent type of person, she couldn't believe Ashley was holding a gun to her head. Mackenzie thought about trying for the pistol on her back but knew that Ashley would fire if she tried for it. Mackenzie was certain that if she confessed, Ashley would pull the trigger anyway. She only saw only way out of this; fight.

Mackenzie dropped and spun, kicking Ashley in the back of the left knee as she moved out of the way of the gun. Ashley let out a yelp of pain as she tried to keep her balance and bring the gun back onto Mackenzie. Mackenzie quickly got behind Ashley, trapping her right arm while placing her foot on the back of Ashley's knee, forcing Ashley onto her knees.

Mackenzie tried to grab the gun from her back but Ashley tried to swing around, causing Mackenzie to have to hold on to not lose her advantage. The pair struggled in the hold—Ashley to get out, Mackenzie to keep her in the hold. Ashley began to power out of the hold, using her upper body to knock Mackenzie off balance. In the blink of an eye, Ashley was out and swinging the gun, using the barrel to smack Mackenzie on the side of the head, landing the blow with a sickening thud.

Mackenzie stumbled back while reaching for her gun. Ashley rushed and grabbed Mackenzie's jacket, pulling it up over her head so Mackenzie couldn't use her arms. Ashley saw the gun on her back, threw some punches to Mackenzie's head and stomach, and as Mackenzie fell to the ground, Ashley took the pistol away from Mackenzie.

Ashley ripped the jacket off Mackenzie, using it to choke Mackenzie. Ashley on top, Mackenzie was face down, turning blue as she gasped for air, wondering if Ashley was going to kill her here and now or if she would be allowed to live. Ashley didn't let up until Mackenzie gave up the struggle and blacked out.

Mackenzie awoke in a comfortable chair but in extreme pain. Her head was throbbing, her stomach experiencing sharp pains, with aches all over. Mackenzie tried to rub her eyes before she opened them but something prevented her from moving her arms, there was metal around her wrists. Handcuffs.

Mackenzie opened her eyes to see that she was in a chair that was chained to the wall and the handcuffs were attached to the chains. Mackenzie scanned the room and finally located Ashley, laying on one of the sofas, bulletproof vest on the floor next to her, Ashley looking through Mackenzie's phone. Mackenzie tried to get out but she knew that she was locked up tight.

"You shouldn't be looking through that," Mackenzie said. "There are things in there you shouldn't see."

"Very interesting," Ashley said, standing and walking over to Mackenzie. Ashley cuffed Mackenzie across the face. "That's a start. How in the world could you get involved with something like this? You think it's funny to destroy the world?"

"This is evolution of the species," Mackenzie said. "It would have happened whether I was involved or not. I tend to be on the winning side of things...you didn't send any information out of here, did you?"

"I've forwarded every report that you sent and received to a friend," Mackenzie said. "A friend that lives in a different town. She will expose everything if we don't make it out of here alive."

"What do you mean," Mackenzie said. "Make it out of here alive? What are you talking about?"

"You are going to guide me out of this town," Ashley said. "All my friends and family are out of town this week, I don't need to get anyone. It will be just you and me. You will lead me out of here and to safety."

"I don't know how to get out of the town," Mackenzie said. "All the routes are sealed and guarded. They will never let you pass."

"Now that's something I know is a lie," Ashley said. "There's an exit strategy. I've seen references in the reports to a tunnel and that your team controls the airport. You have something that can get you out."

"Even if it were possible," Mackenzie said, "why would I help you? Why would you trust me? I could turn on you, give you to the ghosts, before you were able to shoot me."

"You won't," Ashley said. "I can kill you right now and if I could beat you before, I can do it again."

"You're not as tough as you think," Mackenzie said. "But I won't argue the point."

Mackenzie's mind raced. She knew that she had a device that could protect them from a ghost attack in her bag, could maybe get Ashley to the tunnel. Mackenzie knew they would be safe in her modified Hummer and they could move around the town, getting reports, but she really wanted to stay in the vault, stay where they would be safe. Mackenzie thought that Ashley might make a good addition to Ghost Town Labs, she could be put in the mind control and they would have a new powerhouse to work with.

"Okay," Mackenzie said. "I will lead you out. What's with the doofy outfit? Where did you get it and why do you have it in here?"

"The gun and vest I keep it here in case the bank goes into lockdown," Ashley said. "If there's a shootout or something. I need something to wear underneath it, and considering what the situation would be like, the base layers work. I also keep these clothes here in case I need to work the system when people are in here. There are a few outfits back there, this one is mine but some of the other women here wear other things. We don't do anything with them, we're just eye candy."

"You got something I can wear?" Mackenzie asked. "I don't want to be running around out there in a skirt and heels."

"I'll grab you something," Ashley said, as she walked to the door.

Mackenzie watched as Ashley entered the room. She was still locked up, unable to move, and couldn't see where her pistol was. Mackenzie knew that she was in a tough spot, but if they could get to the Hummer, then to the mall, she could put Ashley in the mind control and have a new helper for the rest of the day. Ashley wouldn't know the difference and would go along.

Ashley returned from the room, tossing Mackenzie some new clothes before unlocking the cuffs. Ashley held her at gun point while Mackenzie changed into the black tights and matching tank top. Mackenzie didn't leave the room or even bother to turn away as she put on the new clothing. She wanted to try to show Ashley that she wasn't afraid of her. Ashley just watched with a smile.

"Suppose you liked that," Mackenzie said, trying to sound tough. "Want to see it again?"

"Not really," Ashley said. "I've seen better...much better. Try these for shoes."

Ashley tossed Mackenzie a pair of black sneakers. Mackenzie put them on, looking them over. The shoes were a men's, about a size too big, but better than the heels she'd been wearing. Ashley picked up a bulletproof vest and tossed it to Mackenzie. Mackenzie looked at the vest as Ashley started to put hers on.

"Don't bother," Mackenzie said, tossing the vest on the ground.

"Why?" Ashley asked.

"There won't be anyone to shoot us," Mackenzie said. "The Ghost Town Warriors shoot two in the heart one in the head so unless there's helmets here to go with them, there's no reason. No one else will be shooting at us. The weight of the vests will only slow us down, we need to be able to move as quickly as possible."

"Fine," Ashley said, as she took the vest off and left it on the floor. "We need to move."

"I'm only going to tell you this one time," Mackenzie said, "I'm not slowing down for you. You slow down, you will be left behind. There is a warzone outside, not like anything you've ever seen before. The ghosts, once they developed for a few minutes, become cunning, blood-thirsty killers that will do anything to capture and kill."

"I understand," Ashley said. "I'm not afraid. What's your plan?"

"There's a tunnel that was built into the substructure of the mall," Mackenzie said. "It's the only unguarded path out."

"Try again honey," Ashley said. "I saw some of the reports on your little phone there and that path is blocked. How else can we get out?"

"That path is blocked?" Mackenzie asked, surprised. "I guess the other option would be to go to the airport. We have control of the grounds there so I could get you out on a chopper."

"Just know one thing," Ashley said. "I've already forwarded the reports to my friend and she will send them to the news, to the government if I don't make it out alive. Everything that Ghost Town Labs had done will be known, you won't get away with this."

"We had no intention of getting away with this," Mackenzie said. "Hell, Doctor Tesla has a press conference planned for tonight. He's going to show the world what he can do and there will be fear. Once the fear truly sets in...money. Every terrorist group and country in the world will be bidding on this technology."

"You people are monsters," Ashley said. "Let's get moving."

"We need to get to my station in the bank," Mackenzie said, as she followed Ashley to the door. "I have bullets in my purse that can disperse these things. I'll need my gun back."

"When we have the new bullets," Ashley said.

Ashley went through the keys to open the door. There was a rush of wind as the door cracked open. Ashley stuck her head out the door, slowly looking around. There was nothing in the hallway outside the vault. Ashley opened the door further, motioning for Mackenzie to lead the way.

Mackenzie crept outside the door, realizing how dangerous and dumb this was, not having any attack against the ghosts, not even her lip-stick sized device that could protect them. Mackenzie had the device in her bag, wishing it was in her hand, as she moved along the hall, keeping her back toward the wall.

At a meeting of hallways, Mackenzie paused and listened. She strained to hear anything but there were no sounds in the bank. There was an eerie quiet that caused Mackenzie's pulse to race. The air was ripe with tension. Something told Mackenzie that there was trouble ahead as she peeked around the corner, looking for anything out of place.

There was a bank man standing in the hallway so Mackenzie slowly moved toward a flight of stairs going down, away from the man. As the women were halfway between the hallway they came from and the stairs, a grouping of ghosts, ten in all, rushed up from the stairs heading right toward the man. He screamed, getting ready to run but frozen in terror, could only watch as the ghosts got closer. When they were close enough, Mackenzie saw the ghost take the man, then disappear.

Ashley opened her eyes, expecting to be dead, but they were again standing alone in the hallway. Mackenzie wiped sweat from her brow, looking around the hall. There was a tense moment before either woman was ready to move again.

"We have to keep moving if we want to stay alive," Mackenzie said.

"What happened to them," Ashley said, "are all the ghost attacks similar to that?"

"No," Mackenzie said, flatly. "I don't know what happened. I've never seen them disappear like that. Something isn't right. We have to get the bullets as quickly as we can. We must move silently, and draw no attention to ourselves."

Ashley nodded as they moved along. They moved down the stairs, walking as softly as they could, moving swiftly with their backs against the wall. They arrived at the mezzanine area without any incidents but as they looked down from the second floor, they saw the lobby was full of ghosts. There were people everywhere, all transparent, fighting amongst each other, each ghosts trying to take others to become stronger.

The women watched in horror as the ghosts attacked. One ghost, a thirty-year-old man in jeans and a black t-shirt, with short black hair and matching goatee, big arms, and very strong, was dominating the other ghosts. He was in the process of taking two other ghosts at once. After the man had taken them, he looked into one of the offices that was partially hidden by a marble pillar. The woman watched as the man walked into the office and found a human, a bank worker, hiding. The man took the bank man and then the spirit that returned.

The man walked back into the open lobby and started taking ghosts as fast as he could. Of the sixty or so ghosts that were in the lobby, there was only one left when the man got done—another man, late teens, shaggy red hair, and baggy clothing. The younger man squared off with the older man. They didn't say anything, didn't wait—just started fighting. They were very evenly matched, fighting all over the lobby, destroying anything that hadn't already been destroyed. It took almost two minutes, but the older man took the younger.

He laughed as he looked over the damage he'd caused to the bank. Nothing was moving but the water that was spilling over the now broken fountain. Lights had been broken out, plants and art were on the ground. The man started to walk toward the door when it swung open and someone swaggered in.

It took Mackenzie's eyes a moment to adjust to the light that poured in to see who'd entered the bank, but when she could see the outline, she knew who it was—The Genesis Ghost: Hannah. Hannah, still in her party dress, looked over the lobby and at the man. She started walking toward him.

"That's her," Ashley whispered. "The woman from the casket."

"Quiet," Mackenzie hushed her. "I need to see what happens here."

The man started running toward Hannah but when he reached her she simply swatted him away like a person would to a pesky fly. The man sailed across the room, landing in a pile of rubble. The man stood and ran with all his force at Hannah but when he reached her, in the blink of an eye he was on the ground with Hannah on top of him.

"What are you?" the man stuttered with fear in his eyes.

"I am the first," Hannah said. "I am the Genesis Ghost. I am the one who caused all of this. The world, humanity, will crumble at my hands. I can't do it alone though. I need powerful ghosts to help me. What is your name?"

"David," David replied.

"Congratulations, David," Hannah said, as she let him up. "You are now a member of my coven. Together we will destroy the world. Get any funny ideas, remember that I can destroy you in an instant."

"I understand," David said, as he stood fully to his feet.

Hannah motioned and David followed her out of the bank. The lobby was deserted except the bodies that were strewn around the floor. Mackenzie and Ashley quickly rushed to the stairs and down. At the bottom of the stairs they paused before rushing to the teller windows. Mackenzie grabbed her bag, pulling out clips loaded with EPD rounds.

Ashley handed Mackenzie her gun, pulling out the magazine before handing it to her. Mackenzie loaded the new mag and chambered a shell. She pulled another pistol, an identical Beretta FS92, loaded it with an EPD magazine, and handed it to Ashley.

"This is loaded with an Electro Plasma Distorter round," Mackenzie said. "It will disperse the ghosts. Some only need one hit, others need many rounds. Don't hesitate if you're unsure if the mark is human or ghost. One shot won't kill a human."

"I understand," Ashley said, looking the gun over.

"We have to get to my Hummer," Mackenzie said. "That will be the best vehicle to take out of here. Once outside, we have to move quickly. Don't hesitate, okay?"

"Got it," Ashley said. "Lead the way."

Mackenzie crept along toward the back of the bank. They moved along a deserted hallway to the back door. Mackenzie peeked through the window on the door, looking in all directions to see if there was anything in the way. The area looked clear, so Mackenzie opened the door and moved out.

Once both women were outside, they saw the ghosts. Mackenzie took the first shot, dispersing a female with one round. The other ghosts paused, but soon, as Mackenzie and Ashley moved further away from the bank, the ghosts started moving toward them.

"How many more clips do you have?" Ashley asked.

"Four more on me," Mackenzie said. "A lot more in the Hummer. We have to get there. We'll shoot a couple more then run for the truck."

As Mackenzie finished speaking she took a number of shots. Ashley started firing, aiming at the ghosts heads. The women moved toward the Hummer as they were shooting. More ghosts started to move in the direction of the women but they held back as they realized that ghosts were dispersing. Mackenzie looked toward the truck and saw a clear path, motioned for Ashley to rush to the truck. As the pair were closing in, David appeared next to the driver's door of the Hummer.

"It's blocked," Mackenzie said, as she put a new clip in her gun. "I don't think we have the firepower here to repel him."

"What do we do then?" Ashley asked.

While Mackenzie tried to think, Ashley turned her gun and took two shots at the man. The shots knocked him to his knees but he quickly stood again. Ashley turned her gun back to the ghosts that were closing in on them. Mackenzie realized that they were running out of ammo. Mackenzie motioned Ashley to stop shooting. She looked around and saw the path back to the bank was open.

"We should go back to the bank," Mackenzie said. "There's no way we can match this guy with our firepower. There's simply too many of them here."

"What will we do in there?" Ashley asked. "Let's push on."

"We can go back to the vault," Mackenzie said. "They can't enter the electric field. I can send a message that I need extraction. A team of warriors will be here to take us out. That's the only way we are going to survive this."

"Okay," Ashley said. "Let's move."

The women pulled up their guns and prepared to shoot as they rushed toward the back door of the bank. They had to use almost all the ammo they had left in the magazines to clear the way to the door. Mackenzie reached the door first, opened it, ushering Ashley through. Mackenzie cleared the door and closed it, starting to run, following Ashley, not looking back at the door to see if the ghosts were following.

The pair raced through hallways, up flights of stairs, and around corners. Mackenzie thought that they had gotten away, thought that they were safe when they came around the corner to the hallway containing the door to the vault. Both women skidded to a stop when they saw someone standing in front of the door, someone in a sparkly red party dress. Hannah turned and smiled at the pair.

"Mackenzie," Hannah said, as she took a step toward the pair of women. "I've been meaning to ask you, my dearest friend, look at me now—take a look at what I've done, do you still consider me, how did your report to Doctor Tesla put it...*a naïve, weak little girl who'd been sheltered for too long*?"

"Hannah," Mackenzie said, putting her hands up, "that was before, in the past. Let's not do anything rash."

"Why would I do anything rash?" Hannah asked with a sinister grin. "David, would I do something rash?"

Mackenzie and Ashley turned to see David was blocking their exit from the hallway.

"I made you what you are," Mackenzie yelled. "Doctor Tesla told me to kill you when we left New Church—leave you for dead in the woods. I saved you because I felt sorry for your pathetic ass. If it wasn't for me, your corpse would be rotting in the woods and you'd be gone, not on this plane of existence."

"I'm touched," Hannah said. "You have no idea how touching your words are to me. You really think that I care what happened? You think there's anything that's going to save you from what I'm about to do?"

Mackenzie looked everywhere in the hallway for something that they could use as a weapon against the two very powerful ghosts. There was nothing that presented itself. Mackenzie could only watch as David stood his ground and Hannah started stalking toward Mackenzie and Ashley. Mackenzie and Ashley were pressed up against a wall as Hannah rushed toward them with death in her eyes.

The Bank Part IV

Mackenzie couldn't believe the turn of events, couldn't believe what was about to happen. Hannah had rushed Mackenzie and Ashley in the hallway and instead of killing them, she'd captured them, dragging both into the vault, and cuffing them up. Once they were inside the vault, Hannah forced Ashley to turn on the electric field so that no other ghosts could enter the room.

Hannah paced in the room, smiling, laughing, and speaking to herself. Mackenzie was trying to use logic and reason to figure out what Hannah's plan was going to be, but she couldn't come up with any reasons as to why Hannah kept them alive.

"Hannah," Mackenzie said. "You were my friend, no matter what that report said. I had to talk you down to Victor, that's what he wanted and we all had to give Victor what he wanted."

"I'm not going to kill you, Mackenzie," Hannah said. "You know, when we were first partnered together in the FBI, I was jealous of you. Really, I'm serious. You'd lived such an amazing life and everything I'd done was just plain and boring. I wanted your life but now look at us. I'm not far away from controlling the world. Everything will be mine, everyone will bow to me and you're nothing but bait for my plans."

"Bait?" Mackenzie asked.

"I'm going to send a message with your phone," Hannah said. "I'm going to tell Victor that you are trapped, in danger, and in need of help. He'll not let you die. Victor will send his lovely warrior women. I'll allow them into the bank, let them get to at least the second floor, that's when we'll have ourselves a jolly good time. I have selected eleven ghosts, other than myself and David, to be my first coven. I will allow them to become powerful before we leave Genesis and show the world what we can do."

"Leave Genesis?" Mackenzie said. "You must not know the full extent of what's happened. You cannot leave this town. Doctor Tesla has made sure…"

"That I cannot be away from a separator," Hannah interrupted. "Whoops, I guess I wasn't supposed to know about them, but I do. I know everything. Once I have my coven set up we will find one of the separators and take it, allowing us to go anywhere that we please. My coven will destroy you, Victor, Ghost Town Labs, and anything that gets in our world. Now silence."

Mackenzie complied with Hannah's command. She remained silent while Hannah entered a report on Mackenzie's phone. Mackenzie was hoping there would be something she could do to prevent damage to the company. Hannah smiled before throwing the phone against the wall, shattering the screen, and spilling the internal components on the ground.

Mackenzie winced as the final pieces of her phone landed on the ground. That phone was her lifeblood for this event. She now had no way to contact anyone within the city of

Genesis to receive reports; no way to warn Doctor Tesla about the trap his women would be stepping into. Mackenzie wondered what Hannah would do with them, how this would be handled. Hannah was again pacing, trying to figure something out.

"Once they arrive it will be a massacre out there," Hannah said. "I can't miss this. They should be arriving in about ten minutes."

Hannah rushed to Ashley and undid her bindings. Hannah drug Ashley to the door and threw the keys at her.

"Open the door," Hannah barked. "You two will stay in here. I'm setting David to post outside this door. You try to leave and he will kill you. I have to watch my coven in action. I have to see what they can do. Don't leave. I will be back for you shortly."

Ashley opened the door and Hannah rushed out. In the blink of an eye, David was standing in front of the door. Ashley quickly closed and locked the door before he could enter, making sure that the electricity was running through the door so there would be no way for the ghosts to enter.

The only sound in the room was the hum of electricity that was running through the walls. Mackenzie and Ashley were both stunned silent from what they'd seen. Ashley quickly removed Mackenzie's cuffs and allowed Mackenzie to get out of the chair.

"Please tell me," Mackenzie said, "that this is a really crooked bank and there's a hidden entrance into this room."

"There's not a hidden entrance," Ashley said. "That would violate the agreement that we have with many of our people. Trust in the bank is the most important thing for us. If our clients don't trust us, there's no working relationship."

"So we sit here until we die or she comes back for us and kills us?"

"As I said," Ashley said, moving to the wall with larger safety deposit boxes. "We have some big meetings here. Sometimes people meet in this room and they cannot be seen together. Strange events go on here. There's no hidden entrance, but there is a hidden exit."

Ashley opened one smaller safety deposit box but many of them on the same panel swung open revealing an opening about four feet high and three feet wide. Mackenzie looked into the opening but all she could see was black.

"We do have an escape route though," Ashley said, with a smile.

"Where does that lead?"

"We can go a number of places," Ashley said. "The best would be the service elevator. That could take us to the parking lot without having to go through the bank. The elevator doors are closer to your truck than the main door is. We could try that again."

"Good idea," Mackenzie said. "The ghosts should have moved out of the area. They think we're trapped here so no one will be concerned with us...although I would like to see this coven in action, see what happens to the women."

"What women are you talking about?" Ashley asked.

"They work for Ghost Town Labs," Mackenzie said. "They have been trained to be cold-blooded killers. They may look like women, but trust me, they can kill in the blink of an eye. I've seen them kill men—men much bigger than they are, with their hands. They know death and have no fear at all. If you see one, run—if you're lucky, they won't waste their time chasing you."

"They are the ones who've been through mind control?" Ashley asked. "In the black fighter gear?"

"Yes," Mackenzie replied. "You read about them on my phone?"

"I saw some reports," Ashley said. "Okay, this tunnel will lead to a hallway. From there we can get to the service elevator. That hallway won't be on the route the women will take to get to the vault, so we shouldn't run into any of your friends."

"We can hope," Mackenzie said.

"Let's just get moving," Ashley said.

Ashley flicked a switch in the dark tunnel and a cool blue rope light illuminated the tunnel. The rope lights were secured to the top of the tunnel, bathing the light in blue. As the women moved into the tunnel, they were forced to move on their hands and knees. Mackenzie wondered why they didn't build it tall enough to walk upright, but only twenty feet in, the tunnel made two turns and they were able to stand, the tunnel taking the dimensions of a normal hallway.

Mackenzie raced to keep up with Ashley, amazed at how fast the older woman could run. They raced along, passing different exits—some tall, some small, until they reached a door that was only about three feet tall and two feet wide. The doorway looked like a little tunnel of its own, sticking out three feet from the interior wall. Mackenzie couldn't figure out what the tunnel was.

Ashley found the latch that opened the tunnel, swinging a side panel out. Before they exited the escape route, Ashley turned the blue lights off. The women entered an office room, their entrance into the room through a two-drawer file cabinet against a wall. There were other, identical cabinets in the room, no way to tell the regular from the hidden tunnel. Mackenzie tried to open some of the other file cabinets but they were all locked.

"Perfectly hidden in plain sight," Ashley said. "Like most of the evils in this world."

"There is no evil in the world," Mackenzie said. "Only things that people turn into evil."

"I'll remember that the next time we're hunted by ghosts," Ashley said, as she moved to the main door of the opulent office. "Follow me."

Ashley looked out the door, inspecting the hallway. She couldn't see anything moving, couldn't hear anyone. Ashley looked back into the room, looking at Mackenzie, motioning that they should move. The women were starting to leave when Mackenzie grabbed Ashley's arm. A noise had caused her to pause—a voice.

"What?" Ashley whispered.

"I heard someone," Mackenzie said. "I know it."

"Help us," a voice meekly said, from somewhere in the room. "Please, Ashley, help us."

"Come out," Ashley commanded. "It will be safe with us."

Mackenzie kept her finger on her device, hoping that she wouldn't have to use it. She didn't think that they were about to encounter ghosts, figuring the ghosts would have attacked, not pleaded for help but she wasn't about to take any chances.

Mackenzie was stunned when a tile on the suspended ceiling above the wooden desk was moved and three people came out. All younger, in their twenties, a handsome man in a gray suit, and two attractive women, one in a black skirt and red blouse, the other in a black business dress. All three looked to be scared to death.

"What the hell is going on?" one of the women asked. "How can this be happening?"

"I don't fully know," Ashley said. "We have a plan to get out of here. You three can stick with us as long as you don't slow us down."

"You were in the vault, Ashley," the man said. "You changed. Why were you there?"

"It seemed the safest place to hide, Darrel," Ashley said. "I wasn't sure what else to do. Why did you hide in the ceiling above your desk and why were these two here with you?"

"They'd brought reports," Darrel said. "We didn't know what else to do either. What's your plan? How do you think that you can get out of here?"

"We just do," Mackenzie snapped. "You want to get out, stick with us...otherwise go back to hiding in the ceiling."

"And you are?" one of the women asked.

"My name's Mackenzie," Mackenzie said. "I work for the company that did this. I was put here in the bank to gather information and data on people's reactions to the ghosts. My Hummer is outfitted with an electric field, which is one thing the ghosts cannot pass through— they will be dispersed if they get hit with electricity. Fire is another thing that can destroy them. I have guns in the truck that can stop them, but only enough for us to get away."

"Then why the hell should we go with you?" the other woman asked. "You're part of the monsters that brought this destruction here."

"We follow her," Ashley said, "because I already kicked her ass and will do it again if she doesn't help me. Now we have four on one, she doesn't stand a chance. She will get us out of here if she wants to live and not become one of those demons herself."

"Why don't we go back to the vault?" the woman asked. "We could stay there until this is over."

"There is a plan in place," Mackenzie said. "Most of the people in Ghost Town Labs don't know that this is even going to happen. Doctor Tesla, the person who created these things and runs Ghost Town Labs, has a backup plan in case the ghosts get out of control. The rivers around Genesis will turn to fire and the city will be consumed."

"Consumed?" Darrel asked.

"There's enough explosives planted around the city to level it in one giant ball of fire," Mackenzie said. "There will be nothing left and it will destroy all the ghosts."

"Bullshit," the man shouted. "He'd never get away with it."

"Terrorists will be blamed," Mackenzie said. "They'll probably be dumb enough to take the credit for it in the first place."

"When is this supposed to happen?" Ashley asked. "And why is this the first time I'm hearing about it?"

"I didn't tell you," Mackenzie said, "because you didn't need to know. As for when it's going to happen, well, that's a harder question to answer. The reason it was set up was to prevent the ghosts from leaving Genesis if they get too powerful. There is a device called a separator, which separates the soul from the body—one of them needs to be running to keep the ghost...here. In theory, the ghosts could become powerful enough that they don't need a separator running, in theory. If that becomes the case we burn them all. That wouldn't happen until tonight but I plan on being a long way from here."

"Okay," Ashley said. "Back to the main plan. We get to your Hummer and go to the airport. You'd better be able to get us on a plane out of here."

"Don't worry," Mackenzie said. "You get us on the service elevator and I will take it from there."

Ashley nodded as she looked out the door. The hallway was empty but she knew that could change in the blink of an eye. Ashley led the group out of the office and down the hallway. They couldn't hear anything in the building, everything was silent. At every doorway, Ashley was waiting for ghosts to jump out but they never did.

After a couple twists and turns, they were at the door for the service elevator. Ashley pushed the button and waited. Mackenzie had everyone get behind her, with her finger on the button of her device in case ghosts came out of the elevator when it arrived.

The car arrived and the doors opened. The car was clean. The group entered and Ashley pushed the button for the service entrance. The elevator car started to move. Mackenzie hoped that no other floors would light up, indicating they would be picking someone up.

As the car descended slowly, Mackenzie tried to come up with a plan. When it was just Ashley, a woman stronger than she was, Mackenzie knew that she was going to have to jump her from behind, one strong blow to the head and Ashley would be ready for the mind control machine. The problem now was the other three. The two women Mackenzie knew she could take out. Darrel on the other hand looked to be fit and strong, and easily a hundred pounds heavier than Mackenzie.

Mackenzie knew she would only get one sneak attack—either Darrel or Ashley, and then it would be a straight fight with the other, which she would lose against either of the two. She could try to divide the group up, but that had problems as well. Mackenzie knew that Darrel was no good in the mind control machine. His mind was not emotional enough to accept the suggestions and the training. The only option would be to shoot Darrel and hope the others would follow her as opposed to dying.

The elevator car came to the bottom and the doors opened, doors on both sides of the car so they could go back into the bank or to the parking lot. The elevator was on a loading dock, with a large garage door going into the back of the bank next to it. The group moved along the wall, looking out to see if there were any ghosts hiding around the cars.

Mackenzie could see her Hummer and thought she had a clear shot at it. As she was about to signal the group to run to the cars, four Ghost Town Labs Hummers raced into the lot, sliding to a stop. Warrior Women jumped out with their guns drawn. The women started to run toward the bank.

"DON'T ENTER THE BANK!" Mackenzie screamed as she jumped off the loading dock and ran toward them. "Don't enter the bank, it's a setup."

The women stopped and looked at Mackenzie. The leader of the team, a massive six-foot-three-inch tall black woman who was ripped with muscle ordered her team to stop but to remain on high alert as she approached Mackenzie.

"Mackenzie," the woman said, recognizing Mackenzie. "What's going on here?"

"My phone was taken by Hannah," Mackenzie said. "She's more powerful than you could imagine. She sent a communication to get you here so that her coven of ghosts can grow more powerful. They set a trap in the bank."

"Then we spring the trap," the woman said. "Strike team, EMP bomb first floor, detonation in thirty seconds."

"What's going on?" Ashley asked approaching the team of women.

"An electromagnetic pulse bomb," Mackenzie said. "That should destroy the ghosts in the building. That might kill Hannah too."

"She's too powerful," the leader said. "I have orders from Doctor Tesla himself."

A blonde warrior was moving toward the bank with a suitcase-sized box when the door opened and three ghosts rushed out. The woman dropped the box and pulled up her gun. She shot one of the ghosts while other warriors got the other two. The woman picked the box up again and was almost to the door when another ghost rushed out. The male ghost got hit with three bullets, but it wasn't enough to stop him before he got the warrior.

More ghosts started pouring out of the building, coming from all the doors and windows. The warriors took defensive positions, firing their guns while the leader was barking orders to set off the bomb. Two different women tried to make it to the bomb but they were both killed, their spirits returning only to be taken by the ghosts.

As more ghosts arrived, the leader tossed Mackenzie a gun while members of the team pulled another EMP bomb from one of the Hummers. The woman holding the bomb realized that more ghosts were coming right for her so she detonated the bomb where she stood. Mackenzie felt the blast rush past her—the electricity in the air. Many of the ghosts that were attacking them vanished, leaving an eerie mist handing in the air.

Although a number of the ghosts had been dispersed, more kept coming from the bank. An endless stream of them. More were coming from the area around the bank. The leader of the women was on her phone giving orders, saying they were overrun and in trouble. Mackenzie was watching as more bombs were being removed from the Hummers.

Another EMP ripped through the area, destroying a number of the ghosts as EPD bullets were flying everywhere. Mackenzie tried to see what happened to the others that were with her. She looked around for Ashley and the bank workers, but she didn't see them right away. She only noticed them when Ashley stuck her head out of the window of one of the warrior's Hummers. They were safely hidden.

As more ghosts started coming to the parking lot, Mackenzie wondered how the supply of bullets for the women were holding out. She didn't know if this group had seen action somewhere else or if they were freshly supplied. The women didn't seem to be concerned and were performing perfectly.

Mackenzie noticed someone coming out of the bank slowly. It was Hannah and David. Hannah was grinning from ear to ear as she watched what was happening. A warrior was about to detonate another EMP but Hannah instructed David to stop her. David wasted no time in killing the warrior then killing what returned of her.

Hannah and David started to take more and more of the people and ghosts. Mackenzie realized that it was going to be tough to stop them. The bullets were having no effects on the two powerful ghosts. Mackenzie noticed that more ghosts were coming from the bank. They all looked somewhat similar; black gothic clothing, long hair, the men with long beards, and there were eleven of them—Hannah's first coven.

Mackenzie fired shots at some of the people in the coven but the bullets had no effect. Mackenzie started to make her way toward a Hummer, hoping to get an EMP but as she got closer she realized that the warriors were losing. Hannah took the leader of the group before the real terror began.

The members of the coven took the last of the warrior women and the hundreds of ghosts that were in the parking lot. When they stopped, only Mackenzie remained. Mackenzie looked around, seeing the dead bodies of Ashley, Darrel, and the other two women. She couldn't believe it. There were no ghosts other than the coven. Hannah sauntered up to Mackenzie.

"Believe," Hannah said. "I am the Genesis Ghost. No one will have more power than I. I will control them all. Doctor Tesla will die at my hands."

"You don't make threats to..." Mackenzie was cut off as Hannah destroyed her. Mackenzie felt strange, warm, like submerging herself in a warm bath. Her mind had been full of thoughts and knowledge before, but it was empty now, and try as she might, nothing would come back to her. Mackenzie looked down to see her body on the ground. She couldn't figure out how she could be looking at her body.

"Hannah?" Mackenzie asked. "What's going on?"

"I'm killing you," Hannah replied.

Before the words could register, Hannah devoured Mackenzie's spirit, leaving only a dead body on the ground. A gentle breeze passed through the bank parking lot as Hannah looked over her work. Only her coven remained. She motioned them and they followed her. Hannah smiled, knowing that the day was only just getting started.

Maria wiped the sweat from her brow, leaving a trail of dirt on her forehead. She looked at her progress, weeding the flowerbeds that were spread around the Colfax Gallery in Genesis, and realized that she barely had a good start on the process. Her two partners, Terry Dins and Tanya Henns, seemed to know exactly how to make this job stretch out for the entire day. Maria thought the three of them should have been able to do this weeding job in a couple hours, but with the instructions they gave her, it was a day process.

Maria looked around for the pair but she couldn't see them. Not because of all the people that were crowding around the gallery, but because they weren't at the flowerbeds they were supposed to be cleaning. Maria swept the area with her gaze and noticed them easily because of their outfits. The mid-twenty-year-olds were on a bench, kissing.

The trio wore very similar outfits; blue jeans, tan work boots, yellow and silver high-visibility vests with white garments underneath. Terry wore a plain t-shirt, Maria and Tanya wore ribbed cotton tank tops. The vests were what caught Maria's eyes. The sunlight hitting the vest grabbed attention, no matter where the person was standing.

Maria didn't like either of them. They were both lazy and didn't care about their job. Maria lived a hard life growing up—she had to work, struggle and fight just to survive. She thought Maria and Tanya didn't even know the meaning of the word *work*. Maria was glad they would both be dead soon, easily falling to the ghosts.

As Maria got back to her work she looked across the gallery to see the casket. The bronze-trimmed black casket sat on a cart with black cloth around it. It amazed her that so few people were even paying attention to it. The darkest chapter in mankind was about to start in this very gallery, the madness of Doctor Tesla was about to change the history of the world, yet all the people walking about were too busy to look up from their phones to realize the world was about to change. Most people didn't even realize the casket was there.

Maria thought back to Doctor Tesla and the way they met. It seemed like such a long time ago although it had really only been a few years. He'd seen her in competitive combat and wanted her to help with the training of some warriors. Maria jumped at the offer, having been fighting for food and a place to stay, stealing both when she didn't win. It was all she knew and this was the only way she saw to get out of her situation.

Maria and Doctor Tesla didn't fall in love right away, that took a few months, but since their first night together, they were inseparable. Maria laughed at the two kids who were supposed to be working with her; so young, so naïve. They thought they knew how the world worked, they thought they were going to get married in the fall and live happily ever after, they thought they were going to have a boring day at work.

Maria stood from the flowerbed, filled with yellows and pinks, reds and blues, and aroma assaulting her nostrils and decided it was time for a break. She walked over to the plain white city pickup, a regular old beat up truck that had seen better days. In the back, amongst the gardener's tools and cleaning supplies was a five gallon water jug that was filled to the brim with ice cold water. Maria took her gas station coffee cup off the dash of the truck, tossed the remaining cold, bland coffee on the ground and filled the cup with water.

Maria drank slowly, savoring the water. She knew that very soon the casket would be opened and all hell would break lose in the gallery. Maria was amazed when she got the assignment for the day. She figured she would be off in the town somewhere, maybe mowing lawn or cleaning drainage pipes, but they put her in the heart of the action.

Maria had never been much of a people watcher in the past, but as she leaned against the truck she couldn't help but notice the people in the gallery—all ages and races, young and old alike. Maria noticed a young man and woman coming out of one of the shops, starting to argue. She noticed a mother and her young boy, in a conversation with another woman. There were professionally dressed people, others who looked like they'd just gotten out of bed and others who looked like they were ready for a party or the beach.

Two women caught Maria's eyes. They were tall, athletic girls who looked to be near the end of high school, wearing identical black swimsuits with duster jackets over the top. The girls were carrying bags that had the markings of the Genesis First Bank and Trust, the bank where Maria knew Mackenzie was working. The women were walking fast, looking over their shoulders, eyes shifting like they were looking for someone. The women stopped when they realized that Maria was staring at them.

The two girls paused, confused for a moment. Maria couldn't figure out why they were looking at her so strangely. Maria looked down, making sure that her clothing was on right and nothing was open. Her hair was in a ponytail and in its proper place. It was then that Maria noticed there was a man also looking at her, a man who was standing to her left.

The man was a tall and lanky young man with shaggy brown hair and tufts of stubble on his chin. He wore khaki pants with a black polo shirt, a red monogram sewn into the left breast, indicating that he worked at a sporting goods store. The man and the girls were all looking over Maria, wondering what to do. The blonde girl started walking forward.

"Morning," the blonde said. "Beautiful day out, isn't it?"

"Depends," Maria said.

"Depends on what?" the blonde asked.

"If you dislike sunny days," Maria said, pouring her Russian accent on heavier than normal, "then a day like this is miserable. If you like, how do you say it...overcast, dreary, rainy days then today is a horrible day."

Maria smiled. The blonde was thrown for a loop, not knowing how to respond to Maria's cynical comment. Maria loved messing with people she viewed as weaker and beneath her.

"I, for one, love days like this," the blonde said. "I love being at the beach, the rays of the sun massaging my skin, the warmth of the day soaking in, the feel of my bikini on my body, the surf, the waves, days like this are what make life worth living."

"There's no beach and surf here," Maria said, looking around. "And that's a workout suit, not a bikini."

"Technicalities," the blonde said. "I have a slight issue. Thing of it is...I'm Kay by the way. Nancy Kay. That is my friend Nancy Dee. People call me Kay and her Dee so we don't get mixed up. See, we have our friend over there, Derek Frost, and we have another friend coming, Andy, and we are working on a project. It's a really cool project but I can't tell you too much about it. For this project to work we need to get into the storm drains...specifically, the storm drain that your truck is parked over right now...would you be a sweetheart and please move your truck so we can enter it?"

Maria studied the girls. There was something about them that didn't seem true, something about them said they were not what they seemed. Maria looked over the bags they were holding and began to think the bags were full of money. With the way they were acting, looking back toward the bank, looking at the cops who were paying attention to the fighting couple, Maria wondered if these girls just robbed the bank.

Her answer came when Andy, a short man in a gray suit, arrived. Maria first noticed he had a nametag from the bank on his jacket. He seemed bewildered that the storm drain wasn't open and that his friends were still in sight.

"Come on people," Andy said, walking up to the group. "Why haven't we advanced to phase three yet?"

"The cover to the drain is blocked," Kay said. "I asked this friend very nicely to move her truck so we can have access but she hasn't answered me yet."

"Ask her?" Andy said, angrily. "Look lady, we pay your salary. You want to keep your city job? Move the damn truck right now or I call city hall and you can walk home."

Maria looked over Andy. He was short and skinny with a dull disposition about him. Maria moved herself off the truck and straightened up, allowing them to see how tall she really was. With her tank top and vest, her muscular arms were in full view for all of them to see. Growing up, Maria had taken her share of beatings from people bigger than her and had learned a thing or two about fighting. She wasn't going to let some twerp order her around. Maria walked right into Andy's face.

"Please explain to me," Maria said, in her dark voice, "how you are going to make that telephone call to city hall when both your hands are broken."

Andy swallowed as he started taking small steps back. Kay and Dee moved forward, not setting the bags down, but getting ready for action. Maria knew she could easily handle any one of these people on their own, but together, if all four of them were ganged up on her; that would be a different story. Maria had a Beretta FS92 concealed in her boot, with extra clips, both regular and EPD in the other boot, but she didn't want to start shooting just yet.

"Please," Kay said, reaching out and touching Maria's arm. "Don't listen to him. He's in a bad mood. Just move the truck so we can access the drain."

Maria didn't answer them. She noticed that a young boy was about to open the casket that was about one hundred yards away from them. Maria desperately wanted to see this, see the casket opening, but then, she thought that if the drain was opened it might provide a good escape route if the action on the surface got too hot.

"I'll gladly move it," Maria said, with a smile. "No problems at all."

Maria moved to the cab of the truck while the others looked around confused at what had just happened. Maria quickly pulled the truck forward, exposing a manhole cover in the ground. Andy and Derek quickly moved in and removed the cover. Right as the group was about to enter the hole, a scream rang out over the gallery. Maria, exiting the truck, looked to see a man on the ground, his wife hysterical next to his body, his spirit standing over him, and Hannah licking her lips as she took his spirit.

In the first moments of the destruction, no one knew, no one could comprehend, what was going on. The sight was so foreign that people could not process what they were seeing; ghosts. It was as difficult to process as a UFO landing or a dimension opening up; no one knew what to do, they could only stand, watch, and take it all in. Maria noticed that her two coworkers, Terry and Tanya, were already laying on the ground as cold dead corpses. The pair, so in love and full of promise, didn't last thirty seconds in the destruction. There were ghosts starting to form, starting to take other people, Hannah having her hands full with all the destruction, like a kid in a candy store, as more and more screams started to ring out.

Maria noticed that Kay and Dee were starting to move toward the manhole. Andy was the first to go in, while Derek was frozen. Kay grabbed him by the arm and pulled him toward the opening. Kay was the last one standing on the ground, the others had disappeared into the hole. Kay grabbed Maria's arm.

"Come with us," Kay said. "You will die up here."

Maria thought for a moment but realized that Kay was right. No matter how badly she wanted to stay and observe, there was nothing for her to do here. The people she'd been placed with were dead and she knew nothing of how the city workers conducted business. Maria nodded to Kay and went into the hole. Kay followed and covered the manhole, bathing the hole in darkness save for the small shafts of light coming from some little holes.

Maria climbed down the cold metal ladder, the sounds of water dripping around her, until she reached the ground. There was no light in the tunnel, no way to see where things went. Maria moved away from the ladder, giving Kay room to reach the ground floor.

Maria heard Kay's feet hit the ground before Kay grabbed Maria's hand. Kay pulled Maria to the left, into the darkness. Maria wondered how Kay was walking with no lights but Kay kept moving at a quick pace.

"We had this planned out," Kay said. "I've walked this path a number of times, I know how many paces we need to go to reach the door."

As Kay finished speaking she stopped, Maria bumping into her. Kay was opening a door. Light spilled into the hallway as Kay quickly rushed Maria into the room and closed the door behind them.

Maria's eyes adjusted to their new surroundings. They were in a dimly lit room, filled with metal counters and computer screens, buttons and controls everywhere. There was information running across the screens and lights flashing on the panels. Andy, Derek, and Dee were sitting on utilitarian chairs that were spread out throughout the small room.

"Why did you bring her?" Derek asked. "I'm not splitting the loot with anyone else."

"Look at her," Kay said. "If she didn't move the truck we would have died up there with the others. She tough and we can use her in a fight."

"What the hell is going on up there?" Andy screamed. "Did you see those ghosts up there? We're done for. Give me the gun, I'm going to kill myself right now!"

"Sit down, Andy," Kay said. "You're not going to do anything."

"Yes, I am," Andy said. "Kill me now. I don't want to live with what I saw up there."

Andy walked to Kay and tried to reach inside her duster jacket. Kay tried to move out of the way but Andy positioned her against a wall so she couldn't back away. Andy tried again to reach in the jacket but Kay quickly took him to the ground, so swiftly that Maria wondered what type of fight training this girl had. Kay kept Andy on the ground for a moment before letting him up.

"Next time," Kay said. "I'm breaking something. Keep your shit together Andy."

"But there were ghosts up there," Derek yelled. "What is going on?"

"I don't know," Kay said. "We should be safe here. No one knows that we're going to be here."

"Except the city workers that were going to meet us to guide us through here," Andy said. "I saw them up top—Terry and Tanya, they were both dead."

"What's going on here?" Maria asked. "What are you people doing?"

"It was planned to be the perfect robbery," Dee said, standing. "We already hit a store and a bank. We were going to hit three more places before using this tunnel to get out of the city. Kay and I aren't from Genesis, the guys are. They were going to help us. By nightfall, we were going to be out of state, and a hell of a lot richer."

"What's with the outfits?" Maria asked. "Dusters and swimsuits?"

"Confusion," Kay said. "I mean, come on, if the police heard a report about robbers in these outfits, what do you think they are going to think? Plus, any guy that sees us is going to be more interested in our bodies than our faces, makes it hard to give the police a facial description. We have more outfits to change into throughout the day. Next up was superheroes, then movie characters, and finishing out in black."

"Who gives a shit about the plan?" Derek yelled. "Andy is right, we should all just kill ourselves. Who knows what is going to be out there to get us. We don't have guides to get through these tunnels."

"What is this room?" Maria asked. "How did you find it so easily?"

"This room is a control room for the city water and sewer," Kay said. "It's remote operated but this room is here in case the remote system goes down. It's the manual control. Dee and I have been planning this operation for almost a year, lining up the routes, getting people on our side, figuring out which stores to rob, and making sure no one is paying attention to us."

"How old are you two?" Maria asked.

"Seventeen," Dee said. "You know how expensive college is these days? It's the only way we could pay for it without going into a lifetime of debt."

"We found people who wanted a new life," Kay said. "Offered them a cut to get help. It was a good plan."

Maria nodded. She had so many questions for these two, but the more pressing point was what to do now. Maria figured it best to head back to the command center where Doctor Tesla was at, report on her findings at the release site, and see what Victor wanted her to do next.

"Hang on one second," Kay said. "What is your name?"

"Maria," Maria said.

"Well, Maria," Kay continued, "something doesn't make sense here. If you're a city worker, why did you need to ask what this room was? Shouldn't you have known about it?"

"I only do above ground maintenance," Maria replied. "Plus, I just started working for the city. I'm a grunt laborer, you really think I should know anything that's going on?"

"Okay," Kay said, nodding. "We need a plan. These tunnels will take us to a point in the city near a park that has a boat docked and ready for us to use to escape but we weren't going to take the tunnels there and I don't think we should go above ground. The only problem is that there is a labyrinth of tunnels down here. We need to find a map of some kind to figure out the path."

"Is that the best option?" Dee asked. "Maybe we should stay here for now and see what happens."

"With the ghosts up there?" Andy snapped.

"What's your idea?" Dee shot back. "Sit here and wait to die?"

"We have to move forward," Kay said. "Whatever's going on up there will go on up there whether we sit here or move. If this is where the shit is happening, I say we get the hell away as quickly as we can. Start searching these computers and see if we can find a map."

Kay, Dee, and Maria started working on the computers, quickly going through screen after screen to try and find something that would be useful to them. Maria found cameras to the surface, but everything was out of focus, looking at water outlets and drainage pipes. The computers were on an internal hardwired system, something that wasn't affected by the damage that Ghost Town Labs had caused.

Maria quickly realized she could access everything in the city systems with these computers. She quickly switched the monitor to the security cameras at the main police station. In grainy, black and white images, were amazing people running in all directions, total pandemonium. She could see that everyone was trying to use their cellphones or desk phones, but nothing was working. People were starting to rush into the station, yelling and screaming, trying to get someone to help them.

"Found it," Kay said. "I've got a map that can lead us to the park where our boat is."

"Do you think we can follow it?" Dee asked.

"There are markings down here as to what street the tunnel is running along," Kay said. "All we need to do is follow them. I know the path to get us there."

"Is that what we want to do?" Derek asked. "What if we see more of those ghosts in the tunnels?"

"I'd rather meet one trying to escape," Kay said, "than meet one waiting to die."

"I agree," Dee said. "Maria, what's your vote?"

Maria thought about the information she could gather with these computers while she weighed that against the information she would experience in the tunnels with these people. Maria knew that she had to keep moving.

"I'll go with you," Maria said.

"That's three votes," Kay said. "We go. Boys, if you want to come with, fine. If you want to stay, fine. But know one thing, the money goes with us."

Kay and Dee started to walk out of the room. Maria quickly followed. It took the men a moment to think the situation over, then they rushed to catch up to the women, trekking down the darkened drainage tunnels, hoping the boat would be there when they arrived.

City Workers Part II

The group twisted and turned in the tunnels as they raced along, following Kay as she navigated the dark tunnels. Maria could hear the water on the cement floors of the tunnel as they ran along. She was amazed that the city had such nice tunnels underneath the city streets. Maria tried to see what streets they were near as the names were written on the top of the tunnel, a sign at each junction, but the light was too dim and Maria wasn't close enough to Kay to see the signs with her flashlight.

Kay motioned the group to stop. She was looking at a junction of tunnels, a place where three tunnels met, there were five other directions to travel, not including the tunnel they came from. Kay was shining her flashlight on the signs above them, going from one to the next to determine which route to take.

"What's the problem?" Derek asked impatiently. "We need to be moving."

"This place wasn't on the map," Kay said. "We need to enter the 6th street tunnel, this one." Kay shined her light down one of the tunnels, "but on the map we didn't enter it here, we need to be a half-mile down the tunnels before entering. I don't know if this will get us where we need to go."

"Is there another control room around here?" Dee asked. "We can check the computer maps again."

"I don't know their locations," Kay said.

"Oh for God's sake," Andy rolled his eyes. "Never let women give the directions. Come on, Derek, let's go up that ladder and look out. We can gain our bearings above ground."

"I wouldn't do that," Kay said. "We don't know what's up there."

"We'll be back before you know it," Derek said as he started climbing the ladder. "This will be the simplest way to find the right path."

Andy quickly followed Derek up the ladder. Derek needed all his strength to remove the manhole cover that connected the tunnel to the streets above. Once the opening was big enough, Derek slipped out of the tunnel and onto the street. Before he even had a chance to let the others know what the surface looked like, Andy exited the hole.

The women watched from the tunnel as the men looked around. Maria couldn't see Derek or Andy but she could see their shadows moving around above the cover. Maria couldn't hear the surface due to the noise in the tunnels, but she did hear the screams that started as the shadows of the men moved away from the cover. The screams were piercing, bloodcurdling, and horrifying.

It was Derek's body that fell first, his eyes open, looking into the tunnel. Andy was still moving around, trying to avoid something, but he fell too. Kay was the first to start running,

running as fast as she could down the 6th street tunnel. Dee followed and Maria pulled up the rear, hoping no ghosts would enter the tunnel through the open manhole cover.

The women ran, pushing themselves as hard as they could. Maria's feet were starting to hurt, sharp pains in the heels as a dull ache started in her calves. Maria knew it was because the heavy work boots weren't designed for running. Maria didn't know how long she could continue at the pace they were running while she was wearing those shoes.

The women continued the fast pace for over twenty minutes, running through the tunnels, taking turns and making corners where Kay thought they should go. When they had pushed themselves as hard as they could, Kay noticed a control room. She rushed into the room, holding the door open for Dee and Maria. Maria got into the room and collapsed on a dusty, dirty sofa while both Kay and Dee took their jackets off, throwing them over the back of an office chair.

The lights in the room were dim, but enough to see everything. Kay was looking over the room. It took her a moment to find a small dorm–room-sized refrigerator. Kay opened it and took out three bottles of water, handing one to Dee, one to Maria, and keeping the other for herself. The women all took a large drink from their water bottle before Kay and Dee sat down on office chairs.

"I'm sorry about your friends," Maria said, breaking the silence. "That was a tragedy."

"Not really," Kay said.

"What do you mean?" Maria asked.

"We planned to set up the guys to take the fall for all the robberies," Dee said. "In the end, Andy, Derek, Terry, and Tanya would have been arrested for everything. I know they were your co-workers, but we have our lives to live."

"You didn't care about them at all?" Maria asked.

"We did care," Kay said. "They were going to make sure we got away with everything. It took a long time to find Andy and Derek. We have ads on the web in many cities trying to find people who were a match for what we needed. I didn't think that we would find two who were so perfect in the same city. Yeah, we had to do some things with them to get them fully on board, but they gave us access to everything."

"What if they located you after everything was over?" Maria asked.

"Everything we told them was a lie," Dee said. "From our names, our hometowns, our backgrounds...everything. There would be no way that they could ever find us."

"Why did you do it?" Maria asked. "The real reason?"

"We needed money for college," Kay said. "There's so much expense there. We were both working on getting scholarships from sports and grades, but neither of us received anything. This day was going to make sure we would have four years fully paid for at a private school. We are both going for teaching, high school math teachers."

"How were you going to launder the money?" Maria asked. "Weren't you concerned mysteriously getting all this money would raise some red flags?"

"There is a company that helps people with stuff like that," Kay said. "For ten percent of the total laundered amount, they make it look like you worked for them. They produce videos and movies, low budget local stuff. Doesn't make much money but they do this on the side. We would have made enough to cover our schooling while paying them. It was a good plan."

"Not really," Maria said. "You were stealing and doing some very risky things. How did you know the others wouldn't sell you out?"

"We had certain controls over Andy and Derek," Kay said. "While Terry and Tanya were very dumb."

"No arguments here," Maria said. "Back to the issue at hand, where are we?"

"I think we've been running along the streets we need," Kay said. "We should be close to where we need to go. The final scam, we were going to have them hit one more store while we got the boat ready to go. There's a pontoon docked at a park that has enough gas to get into the water before dying. While they were robbing the store we were going to call the police, tell them that the others did everything, and tell them where to find the pontoon. We have two personal water crafts we were going to take off on, that's why we needed the swimsuits, we'll be getting out of here on smaller, stand up jet skis, heading north on the river into the suburbs to our car."

"The only problem," Dee said, slowly, "is that only one person can ride each one. I don't think that we can get you on one of them with us."

"I'll give you a try," Kay said. "You can ride with me. The personal water crafts should have enough power to plane out with both of us on it."

Maria nodded, knowing the plan wouldn't work, knowing the Ghost Town Labs' warrior women would shoot them if they were on the water, that is, if Victor hadn't gone ahead with some of the containment procedures yet. Maria wondered what she could do to help these two. Maria knew that they would be great to have on the team, both powerful and able to handle themselves, if she could only get them into the mind control system. Maria wanted to check her phone but didn't want to show the girls she had a phone that worked. Maria noticed Kay and Dee talking to each other. Dee whispered into Kay's ear and Kay nodded, trying not to look at Maria.

Kay and Dee quickly stood up and rushed over to Maria, pulling her off the sofa and onto the ground. Maria landed on her back, still too tired from the run to mount an effective defense against the strong girls. Kay quickly sat on Maria's upper body, putting all her weight on Maria to make sure she stayed down.

Maria tried to struggle but Kay was very powerful. As Kay struggled with Maria, Dee quickly started patting her down, finding the pistol and extra clips in her boots. Kay patted down Maria's upper body, starting by ripping the high visibility vest off and running her hands underneath the white tank top. When they were satisfied with what they had found, Kay and Dee allowed Maria up, with Dee keeping the pistol aimed at Maria at all times.

"Interesting choice of tools for a city worker," Dee said. "Is this standard issue?"

"You know how dangerous it is out there," Maria said. "A girl needs to protect herself."

"Why do you have this gun?" Dee barked. "Answer now! Were you working with Terry and Tanya to set us up and steal the money? What was your plan?"

"I wasn't working with them," Maria said. "I have my own ends."

As Maria finished speaking she ducked and rushed toward Kay, grabbing the girl and turning, keeping Kay between Maria and Dee with the gun. Maria locked Kay into a hold, applying heavy pressure to hurt the girl. Dee's eyes went big with surprise as she tried to keep Maria sighted into the gun but couldn't, Maria knew her position far too well.

"Put the gun down and slide it over to me," Maria said, as Kay tried to struggle. "I don't want to hurt either of you. I can help you get out of here."

"Do it," Kay screamed as she struggled in pain. "Do what she says before she breaks something. I can't fight her."

Dee dropped the gun and kicked it away from the group. As Maria started to release the hold, Kay kicked her leg back, meeting the heel of her shoe into Maria's shin. Maria gasped more in shock than in pain. Kay spun around, throwing a punch that connected to Maria's head. As Maria staggered a step back, Kay lifted a knee into Maria's stomach causing Maria to double over in pain.

Dee came from behind, wrapping her arms around Maria's waist, lifting, turning, and releasing, dropping Maria hard on the ground. Face down Maria tried to roll to her back, tried to get some kind of defense against the pair of girls but Kay quickly grabbed Maria's arms and locked them into a hold, putting all of her weight on Maria, driving Maria's chest into the cement floor. Dee grabbed the gun from the floor and aimed it at Maria's head.

"Let's try this again," Dee said. "I want to know who you are and why you are carrying this gun. We can do this all day if you want…kicking your ass, beating you to the ground. You may look tough and strong, but there are two of us and only one of you. Tell us what the hell is going on."

Maria was amazed. Growing up, she'd been in so many fights, been involved in both gang fights involving many people on both sides, and in one on one fights, but she couldn't believe how good these two were. They'd gotten the jump on her both times, Maria did not expecting this kind of attack from them and she was upset they'd been able to beat her. Maria realized she had no choice, she had to work with them.

"There's something you need to know," Maria said, calmly, "but first, I have a question. You both seem to be very calm about everything that's happened outside. The ghosts. Why?"

Kay and Dee exchanged a glance, a grimace came across their faces. An entire conversation passed between their eyes in that single glance. Neither of the girls seemed to want to say anything. Kay tightened her grip and put more pressure on Maria.

"We've been through a lot," Kay said. "We've seen a lot. I still don't know what we saw up there. I'm not ready to admit that it was ghosts."

"What have you two ever been through?" Maria snapped, thinking back to her upbringing. "When have you ever experienced any form of real pain? You're both yuppie middle class spoiled brat girls who've had everything handed to them and the second that you're being forced out on your own, instead of working to get there you're just stealing what you can. You're nothing but a pair of worthless crooks."

There was a silence in the room. Kay and Dee were stunned at what Maria had said. Kay tightened her grip on the hold even more, putting more pressure and pain on Maria. Maria struggled slightly, trying to relax the hold but she could feel the pain shooting through her body. Dee bent over and cuffed Maria across the head as hard as she could. Maria saw stars the hit was so hard.

"You have no idea the pressures we are under," Dee said, trying to mask tears. "We're expected to be perfect, get good grades, dominate in sports, and be the perfect girlfriends. Don't even get me started on that, the pressures of modern dating, what we're expected to do, what we have to put up with. In case you hadn't figured it out, Kay and I are in love. This is our ticket out. This money will get us to a California private college and allow us to be happy together. We're from the east coast and both are damn tired of our family and friends out there. We need a new beginning and aren't going to let anything get in our way."

"Why do you have the gun Maria?" Kay asked. "Just tell us everything and it will be okay. We promised to get you out of here and we will do just that."

"I had the gun," Maria said, "because I knew there was going to be an attack today. If you look at the extra magazines that I was carrying, the blue tinted ones contain a special bullet that will get rid of those ghosts...it will disperse them from this existence."

"How did you know about it?" Kay asked. "How did you get those bullets?"

"I work for a company called Ghost Town Labs," Maria said. "We are the ones that caused this. What's happening in Genesis is nothing but a test for us to see what our ghosts can do. Once we have all that data about our project, we'll see which country is the highest bidder and sell it."

"What?" Dee asked.

"That's all there is to it," Maria said. "If you want to get out of here we need to move quickly, although I don't think you'll be able to get out on the river. We have troops stationed that will kill anyone trying to cross and if that doesn't get you, very soon the river could be a raging inferno."

"Why?" Kay asked.

"We know of three ways to stop those things up there," Maria said. "The Electro Plasma Distorters, which the bullets in that gun are made of, fire and electricity. Our leader is going to flood the top of the river with a combustible that will stay afloat and burn or hours, making sure the ghosts cannot cross the river."

"What kind of madness came up with a plan like this?" Kay asked.

"Government madness," Maria said. "The government hired someone to make a weapon and this is what they came up with, a person who couldn't be killed. Imagine the damage that could be done in war with this technology. The government knew how powerful it was, so they tried to kill the person who invented it, but he escaped with the technology in hand. Now, it's up for sale."

"That is horrible," Dee said. "The names you called us for stealing some money when you are going to bring down a plague that could destroy the world. We should kill you now for what you've done."

"You should," Maria said. "But you kill me and you kill yourselves. If I die down here then I will turn into one of those ghosts. There is a machine running that makes all spirits stay here on earth. Once you turn, death and destruction is your only concern. Even if you get past me, there will be no way to exit the city, you'll be trapped and dead before you know it. I can get you out of here...I can give you everything that you want."

"What do we want?" Kay sneered. "How would you know what we want?"

"I can give you a job with Ghost Town Labs," Maria said. "You will be in positions of power within two years, I can guarantee that. You won't have to deal with your parents or old friends again, plus you can live the lifestyle you want without worry or care."

"Interesting," Dee said. "No college needed?"

"None," Maria said. "We have our own training programs and it works so much better if you haven't been corrupted by a university. You two will go far in our programs. If you want to be teachers, we can have you guys training new recruits. You would be perfect for it. We have many different locations all over the world. Enlist with me and you will go far."

Kay and Dee looked at each other for a moment. Neither was sure what to do, but with what they'd seen, what they'd been though, they thought that this would be the best option.

With Maria they could have what they wanted; a life away from the pain of their past. The girls let Maria up and shook her hand.

"It's a deal," Kay said.

"Good," Maria said, taking her gun back. "I think you two will go far, but if you lay a finger on me again, I will destroy you."

"What's the plan then?" Dee asked. "Where are we going to go from here?"

"We need to get you both to the main command center for this operation," Maria said as she pulled out her phone. "All communications are down in Genesis but Ghost Town Labs has its own phones, our own cellphone towers that are still active. I can use the GPS to find the quickest way there."

"Where's the command center at?" Kay asked.

"On a bluff near the river," Maria said. "On the east side overlooking the downtown area."

"We're not far from there," Dee said. "We studied this town well before we hit it. We should have no problems getting there, except these tunnels don't run very far to the east."

"And we have a bigger problem," Maria said. "A very big problem."

"What's that?" Kay asked.

"The ghosts are spreading," Maria said. "We are going to have to travel through a hotbed of ghosts."

City Workers Part III

The midday sun was high in the sky, beating down bright, hot and intense as screams rang out over the city streets. People were running everywhere, a strip mall parking lot full of cars on the north side of the road, some restaurants and gas stations on the south of the four lane road. Ghosts were attacking everything that was moving, allowing no escape for the people on the surface.

The road was blocked with traffic, everyone was trying to leave at the same time but there was nowhere for the cars to go. The air was thick with the sounds of car horns blasting while peopled screamed at each other. There were fistfights and fender benders, all while ghosts ravaged the area.

People were trying to crowd into a large convenience store that had ten fuel pumps in the lot. Some people were trying to loot the store, others were hiding in fear as a woman walked into the store with a pistol drawn. She was cool, calm, and collected as she walked right up to a freckle-faced college girl who was behind the counter, trying to keep order.

"Turn on all the fuel pumps," Maria barked at the girl.

"What?" the girl stuttered.

"Turn the pumps on," Maria yelled, pulling her gun and aiming at the clerk. "Turn them on now."

The girl, scared and confused, complied. Maria and the clerk looked out to see Kay and Dee going pump to pump, taking the hoses off the stands and turning them on, letting gas run on the ground.

"What are you doing?" the clerk asked.

"If I were you, I'd run," Maria said. "Run fast."

Maria took off before the clerk could say anything else. She met with Kay and Dee in the lot as they'd gotten the last of the pumps running. The women ran to a manhole cover, Maria and Kay going down in the hole while Dee lit a Molotov cocktail. Dee used all her power to throw the flaming bottle before she went into the hole, pulling the cover shut.

The bottle hit the ground just short of the gas spilling from the pumps. There were spots of fire on the cement ground as gas trickled down the parking lot. The women in the manhole cover were waiting for the explosion, hoping that it would take, fearing what it would mean if it didn't take. The women didn't have to wait much more than a couple breaths before the ground shook and heat enveloped them.

From the surface, the people who were fighting, struggling to escape from the ghosts, had a new problem to worry about; a raging inferno that rose above the street and buildings, vaporizing everything in its path. The heat was intense, the power of the explosion so powerful that building windows three blocks away were blown out. The block the gas station was on had been leveled completely, the nearby blocks were reduced to rubble.

The people and ghosts who'd been in the vicinity were gone—cars overturned, and an eerie silence covered the area once the violence of the inferno had subsided. The area was empty, one of the biggest hotbeds of ghosts in the town was now silent, deserted, save for the three women who were coming out of a manhole cover. Maria looked over the area, proud of the way they were able to clear the area.

"We should have a few minutes to get through here," Maria said. "We can get to a different underground system that will take us to the compound."

"Won't the blast attract more ghosts?" Kay asked. "What about the people who died here? Won't they be ghosts soon?"

"That's why we need to move fast," Maria said. "Come on."

Kay and Dee buttoned their duster jackets up to protect their bodies from the heat and debris that was still in the area. The trio took off running, trying to be as direct as possible to get to the other tunnels. Maria led the way, the scent of ash assaulting their nostrils, the vapors of the explosion still hanging in the air.

Maria kept her eyes open as she ran, scanning everywhere for more ghosts. The area was deserted as ash fell like snow from the sky. Maria worried there would be more underground fuel tanks that would explode without warning, so she tried to keep a distance from the crater that used to be the gas station. As they ran past, the trio could see the mangled mess of pipes and rubble that used to be a popular gas station.

As the trio reached the edge of the blast zone, Maria could see some movement in the distance, along houses, in the houses, and between the cars on the road. She couldn't see any people out in the open, everyone was hidden from them. Maria held her gun close to her, Kay and Dee had their shotguns at the ready, even though they only had regular bullets for the shotguns.

As the trio moved they started to attract considerable attention from figures that were moving in the hidden areas of the residential area. Maria hoped that they would have enough time to get to the tunnel entrance. She'd found it interesting that no ghosts had entered the tunnels when they were underground before, causing her mind to reel, wondering if there was some unknown reason as to why they didn't go underground.

Maria knew they were just a couple blocks from where the tunnel entrance should be, but she had some reservations regarding problems with the entrance. As they moved along, figures started coming into the light, ghosts that had the trio of women in their sights.

Maria noticed a shambling ghost, an older woman dressed in business garb, her gray suit almost matching the gray in her brown hair. She was confused, stumbling around, asking for help, not understanding why no one was helping, wondering why a number of people, both men and women, were looking at her like she was a snack to eat. Maria pulled up her gun and took a shot—one EPD bullet was all that was needed to disperse the woman.

All the ghosts in the area stopped and stared at Maria. Maria kept her team moving forward, glad she'd seen the report that said they took pause when a ghost near them is dispersed. The ghosts seemed to know what was happening to them.

As the team moved around a corner of a house, ducking through backyards, jumping over gardens and outdoor toys, Maria grimaced, seeing a wreck of vehicles over where she thought the manhole cover was going to be. Two cars and a large SUV were piled in a twisted, mangled pile above the cover. Maria looked around, hoping to see some form of construction equipment or a truck that could push the wreck out of the way but there was nothing available to them.

"The cover is blocked," Maria said. "There's no way we could get through that wreck and there's nothing to move it with."

"What should we do?" Kay asked. "Where's the nearest entrance from here?"

"I don't know," Maria said. "We need to get out of sight so we can figure this out."

"There's movement in that basement," Dee said, pointing to a window.

The others looked, seeing an egressed window on a large white house. All the houses in the area were large, well decorated, with perfectly manicured lawns. They didn't see any movement but Maria was already on her way to the door. Kay and Dee quickly followed.

Maria was running when she reached the door, ghosts started to move into the area. Maria was ready to break the door in but to her amazement, the door was unlocked. Maria entered the house, ushering the others in before taking a few shots, dispersing a number of ghosts, giving the attackers pause as she closed the door.

"They won't enter," Maria said. "Not right away, we've shown them that we can hurt them."

"Will they find their way in here?" Dee asked. "Can they sense us in here?"

"They'd have to see us," Maria said. "When I was in Whiterock I saw these demons set traps, look like humans, and have conversations with people in attempt to trick them. Never let your guard down, not when there's the possibility of ghosts around."

"Who the hell are you!" a male voice rang out.

Maria turned to see a young male, teenager, in black gym shorts, holding a black pistol at them. Maria raised an eyebrow as she looked the boy over. Maria showed him that she also had a gun, causing the young man to start to tremble as he tried to keep a tough face.

"We are running from those things," Maria said. "We are here to help you. We can help you get out of town."

"What's out there?" the boy yelled. "What are those things?"

"They are ghosts," Maria said.

"My mom was one of those things," the boy said. "She was taken by another one. Why did this happen? Is the world going to be full of those things?"

"No," Maria said. "We need to stop them. We found a way to stop them; fire. We blew up a gas station and got rid of many of those demons. With your help we can stop this from happening somewhere else...what's your name? Are you alone here?"

The boy stared at Maria, Kay, and Dee. He didn't know what to make of them. As he was looking, two more people came through a door into the room, another boy dressed the same and a cheerleader type girl in red gym shorts and a t-shirt. There was a slight stand off before the girl stepped forward.

"I'm Amber Dean," Amber said. "This is Todd, and the guy with the gun is my boyfriend Sam. Who are you?"

"I'm Maria," Maria said, trying to think up a lie quickly. "This is Kay and Dee. We are with the government. We know how to defeat these things."

Amber looked them over with skepticism. Kay and Dee had their jackets open, showing their black bathing suits while Maria was still in her city outfit, minus the vest. The three looked strange, not like they were supposed to be with the government.

Maria wanted this standoff over quickly. She didn't care how many people came with them, she would put all of them through the mind control. The boys would have a role to play, something they could be used for, and the girl could become a warrior of some kind. Maria knew that she had to get back to the compound.

"How can we defeat them?" Amber asked.

"Fire works best," Maria said. "I also have bullets that can stop them."

"I saw that," Amber said. "How do they work?"

"It's called an Electro Plasma Distorter round," Maria said. "An EPD round. We knew that Ghost Town Labs was going to be coming here to try something and we got some people on the ground to try and stop it. They moved faster than we did and the government wasn't able to stop it in time. We are trying to make it to a compound where we know that some of the leaders of Ghost Town Labs are at. We will make them pay for what they've done here."

"I just want to go back downstairs," Sam said, the gun's barrel moving around in his trembling hands. "I don't want to see those things anymore."

"If you come with us you will be safe," Maria said. "We have a way to get to the compound...well, we *had* a way. There's a tunnel but those cars out there are on top of the manhole cover. We need to look at some maps to find the nearest entrance."

"We don't have any paper maps here," Sam said.

"And all cellphones are down," Amber chimed in.

"I have a government phone," Maria said, as she slowly took out her phone. "It still has service. It doesn't run on normal cell towers. If you lower your gun I can work on it and we can get out of here."

Maria held her breath waiting. Sam was trembling, on the verge of breaking down crying. Maria didn't know what he would do, she knew that intense situations like this could cause normal people to do things without thinking. Maria was worried that she might have pressed her luck with what she told them, worried that he was going to shoot, but Sam lowered the gun, clicking the safety back on.

"What do we need to do?" Sam asked as the tension was released from the room.

"I need to check my phone," Maria said.

Maria quickly looked over her phone, looking at the tunnel system of the city, trying to find the nearest cover. Maria noticed that other close covers would not take them into the tunnel they needed to enter. She found a tunnel that was only two blocks away that would work, but it involved going through a very hot area. Maria didn't think that any of these three would be able to survive going that far in the open.

"There's a tunnel we can enter," Maria said, "but it's two blocks away, through a hot zone. We will have to go through a number of dangerous areas. Are you three up for it?"

"No," Sam said.

"We can't sit here and wait to die Sam," Amber pleaded. "I want to go. I want to at least fight to try and survive. There's no honor in dying while cowering in fear. That's no how I want to go."

"But those things out there," Sam said. "There's no way we could survive. If we stay here, if we stay hidden, we can last these things out. It's our best shot."

"Todd," Amber asked. "What do you think?"

"I can't leave here," Todd said. "I don't want to turn into one of those things. I agree we should stay here."

"Sam," Amber said, sharply, "we are going. I'm not going to die in this house. We are not going to die today. We have our lives planned out—college, marriage, spending our lives together. I'm going and you are coming with me."

"I can't Amber," Sam said.

"Why not?" Amber demanded.

"I'm scared," Sam said. "Our other friends left and we will never see them again."

"You don't know that," Amber said. "You don't know what will become of Tiffany, Jack, Is, and Morgan. We may see them before the day is over. I know we can make it."

"I'm not leaving," Sam said. "I don't want to leave this place. I want you to stay with me Amber. This is my decision. We will be safe if we stay here. Amber, we will stay here."

"No Sam," Amber said, anger starting to show in her voice. "We cannot wait here to die. I'm not debating this. I'm leaving, you can come with me or this will be goodbye."

Sam's jaw dropped as his eyes widened. He couldn't believe that Amber was making him choose. Sam wondered why she didn't want to stay in the house, stay with him. Sam realized Amber was determined to go and he didn't know why.

"Amber please," Sam said. "Let's go into the other room and talk about this alone. I don't understand why you are so intent to leave here. If you would just trust me we could survive this."

"Why can't you trust my judgment?" Amber asked. "You always do this to me, anytime I have an idea, anytime I want something, you always have to change it, make it yours. This time we are doing things my way."

"That's cute and all," Sam shot back. "You want to be heard but this is not the time. You need to trust me on this. We leave this house and we die."

"We stay and we die," Amber shouted. "You want to die a coward? Die hiding in a basement? I want to fight. I would rather die fighting than die hiding."

"But if we stay here we wouldn't have to die," Sam said. "We could survive."

Maria knew the teenagers wouldn't resolve their spat anytime soon. In the moment, Maria wanted to kill both of them simply for how childish they were being, but she tempered herself and decided to try and gently move things along.

"We have to move," Maria said. "Decide now, are you in or out?"

"I'm going," Amber said. "End of discussion. Sam, I love you, but I'm going. Are you coming with or are you staying?"

"I'm staying," Sam said. "I can't leave. Todd, what are you doing?"

"I'll stay with you Sam," Todd said. "There's no reason to leave. I don't understand what you are trying to do."

"Let's move out," Amber said. "I'll follow you."

Sam and Todd watched as the group moved out of the house and into the yard. They were keeping a tight group as they were moving along. Tears were streaming down Sam's face. All he could think about was all the times he and Amber had together, all the fun and plans they had made. He couldn't understand why she wanted to leave him now, why she would leave with three strange strangers instead of staying with him.

With every breath Sam took he was waiting for a ghost to jump out and take the group. He was positive they wouldn't be able to last out in the open; the plan they had wouldn't work. Every moment the group of women got further away, Sam had a feeling they were going to be destroyed, that the ghosts would get them.

"Why do I think this is the last time I will ever see her?" Sam asked.

Todd didn't reply. Sam turned around to see why his friend didn't answer. The sight was shocking; Todd, transparent, his body on the ground, standing next to a stunning blonde woman. The blonde smiled as she took Todd's ghost. Sam didn't know what to do, he looked out the window but the women were gone. Sam turned around as the blonde rushed him, taking him and the spirit that returned.

City Workers Part IV

Maria, Kay, Dee, and Amber rushed as fast as they could, as close to the houses as they could. The group didn't want to be in the open, didn't want to be easily spotted by the ghosts. Maria stopped the group at the corner of a massive brick house, looking out over the street, seeing the cover to the tunnel they needed to get to and checking the scene over, making sure they could make it.

Maria gave a hand signal, indicating they needed to run as fast as they could. She did a silent finger countdown and the group took off. When they got to the cover, Kay and Dee quickly removed the cover, Maria going in first, followed by Amber, then Kay and Dee, who replaced the cover leaving no indication that someone had breached the tunnels.

As Maria reached the base of the metal ladder, she grimaced; water was over the top of her feet. Maria could hear water running. She noticed the air smelled fresh, not stale, like there was at least two major openings in the tunnel allowing air to move around. As the rest of the group reached the bottom, Maria wondered if the water would stay nice and shallow or if it got deeper in the tunnel.

Maria looked at her phone, using the GPS signal to guide her through the darkened tunnel. It took a moment for her eyes to adjust, hoping she could see enough to go through the tunnel without tripping on anything. The group held hands in a line to prevent getting separated in the darkness.

Maria moved them at a fast pace, only glancing down every few moments to look at her phone, making sure that they were on the right path. The water level varied from pools under their feet to knee deep. Maria, concerned they might fall into deeper water or trip on something, slowed the pace but didn't allow time for rest.

Maria knew that this tunnel ran from the upper bluff to the top of the hills where the compound was situated. She knew that they had to be getting close as the water started getting deeper and was moving quicker.

The group arrived at the exit point that would get them very close to the compound. Silently, Maria climbed the ladder, opened the cover, stuck her head out, and looked around. Maria was amazed at how quiet it was on the hill. She could see the black semi-tractor-trailer combo that served as the base. There was one Ghost Town Labs' Hummer parked outside but nothing else.

Maria motioned for the others to follow her out of the tunnel. Maria looked over the area—it was grass, with small shrubs behind the trailer that led to the bluff cliff to the river. Looking to the west, Maria could see the town, smoke rising from a number of locations, cars and activity everywhere. In the distance, on the other side of the river, Maria could see Ghost Town Labs' vehicles.

As the others made it out of the tunnel, Maria was amazed that there were no ghosts in the immediate vicinity. It was all quiet. Maria wondered how she was going to explain everything to Amber, wondered how she would explain that they weren't with the government but with the enemy that killed all of her friends and family.

The group rushed from the tunnel on the street to the trailer compound. Maria led the way and rushed inside, stunned it was completely empty; no people, no bodies, nothing to indicate what had happened. Maria sat down at a computer in the narrow, dark trailer that was stuffed full of electronic equipment and started to type.

"What is going on?" Amber asked. "We just rushed into the den of the enemy. Shouldn't this place have been crawling with defenses?"

"Something isn't right here," Maria said. "There should have been people here. Doctor Tesla should have been here."

"Is there anything on the computers?" Kay asked.

"This is amazing," Maria said. "The damage these ghosts have caused. We're at twenty percent of the population of Genesis being converted. No one within the city has been able to mount any kind of defense."

"What are you talking about?" Amber asked impatiently. "What is going on?"

Maria stood up and walked up to Amber. Amber tried to take a step back but she was pressed back against a wall of electronics. Maria took a swing, connecting with a heavy blow to the side of the head, knocking Amber to the ground out cold.

Maria moved quickly to find a mind control device, hooking Amber up while Kay and Dee looked on. Maria was glad the pair just observed while she was working, Maria didn't want to answer questions as to what was going on. Once the device was hooked up, Maria moved to the controlling computer and brought up a list of mind control programs.

Maria looked at the programs, what they would do, as she looked over Amber. Maria knew that Amber, although fit, wasn't strong enough to be a warrior. She scrolled the list until she found a loyalty program, a training system that would make Amber believe that she is a secret agent for Ghost Town Labs, make her an expert on espionage, a computer expert, and gave her some combat training so she could survive the rest of the day.

It only took a few moments in the training before Amber removed the goggles, opened her eyes, and stood up. She took the other mind control systems off as she looked around the room, confused. Amber stood at attention before Maria.

"Sorry Maria," Amber said, in a powerful tone. "I don't know what happened. What is our status report?"

"The report," Maria replied, "is that we don't know what's going on. This command center was supposed to be where Doctor Tesla was stationed for the day but he is not here, no indication as to where he went."

"Allow me," Amber said.

Amber moved to a computer and started typing. It only took her a few moments before all the screens in the trailer were showing the same thing, a large office, filled to capacity with computers and electronics, so many warrior women moving about that they could barely walk without tripping on one another. In the middle, watching a monitor, was Doctor Tesla.

"Doctor Tesla moved to the main compound in the downtown area," Amber said. "He left here almost two hours ago when this area became too hot. Everything was left as is because he intends to return here before nightfall."

"We can man this location until he returns," Maria said. "Kay, Dee, come here. I'm going to hook you into a training program. Everything will make sense then."

"Hang on a minute," Kay said. "That is not the same girl you put that stuff on. She's totally different. What the hell is that thing?"

"It's a training system," Maria said.

"I don't know," Dee said. "I'm having second thoughts about this."

"I am too," Kay agreed. "I think that the best thing for us might be to go."

"Where?" Maria asked sarcastically. "I'll tell you this right now, there is no way out of this city; none."

"If we take that truck out front," Kay said. "It's got the Ghost Town Labs symbol on the door. I bet no one would question us, and I'm willing to bet that vehicle has electricity running through the skin, preventing any kind of attack from the ghosts."

"We've already shown we can kick your ass," Dee said. "Don't make us embarrass you again."

"Get on the ground," Amber said, as the chambering of a shotgun shell rang out. "Now."

The group looked to see that Amber was holding a black 12-gauge shotgun, aimed right at Kay's head. Both Kay and Dee put their hands up in the air as tension blanketed the small room. Maria was amazed that Amber was so aggressive, she didn't think the program she ran Amber through would have done that to her. Amber was calm and steady as she held the gun.

"Get on your knees right now!" Amber barked out. "The both of you. Our commander gave you an order and you'd best follow it."

Kay and Dee both fell to their knees. Maria quickly went to work putting the mind control devices on them. Maria knew she was going to run these two through the warrior program, she knew both of them were strong enough to be fighters. As she was about ready to start the program, Kay called out.

"Maria," Kay said, tears in her voice. "Please, I don't know what this thing is. After seeing what it did to Amber I can only imagine how we are going to turn out, but please, please promise me one thing."

"What's that?" Maria asked.

"Don't do anything to tamper with or erase the love I feel for Dee," Kay said. "Please, just let us be together. No matter what we have to do or go through, let us be together."

"I will," Maria said, touched by the sincerity of Kay's words.

Maria quickly ran a warrior training program but programmed a separate system that would keep Kay and Dee's love for each other untouched, unchanged. Maria thought about enhancing it or doing something to make it better, but decided to leave it as it was. Maria noticed Amber watching every move like a hawk, not putting the gun down until the training system was over.

When the system was finished, Kay and Dee took the mind control equipment off and looked around their surroundings. They both looked at their clothing, taking their jackets off and going to a supply closet. In the closet they found the standard black clothing that the warriors wore; boots, knee pads, elbow pads, and fingerless gloves. The pair put all that on, opting to leave the swimming suits on instead of putting on the warrior singlet with the Ghost Town Labs' Logo on the stomach.

Without a word, Kay and Dee hefted up assault rifles and took guard positions by the door as Maria and Amber went to work on the computers. Maria studied the town and all the reports that had come in. As far as she could tell, the warrior women were working perfectly, keeping everything under control. The ghosts were incredible, killing humans and each other without a care or concern.

As Maria was scanning the various cameras that were positioned around the city, something caught her eye. Maria switched all the screens in front of her to one camera in the downtown area, not far from the Colfax Gallery. It was there that she saw Hannah, having a delightful time in toying with a group of humans, taunting them as she took them one by one.

What Maria couldn't believe was how Hannah was being attacked by other ghosts. There were a few trying to take her but no matter how many grouped together, they couldn't disperse Hannah; she got them all. Maria felt a chill go down her spine as she watched Hannah work. It was pure evil that had nothing to contain it. Maria felt so glad she was far away in a secure command post.

A ringing phone took everyone by surprise. Amber quickly answered before Maria had the chance to grab a receiver. Maria tried to strain to hear what was being said on the phone, but although she could hear the voice coming through the speaker, she couldn't make out any words. Amber hung up the phone and breathed a heavy sigh.

"There's a problem," Amber said. "Hannah has gotten too powerful. Doctor Tesla noticed these computers were being used and that's why he called. Maria, your objective was lost so you have new orders. The four of us are to go downtown and destroy Hannah."

"Destroy Hannah?" Maria asked.

"The controls and containments have failed," Amber said. "Doctor Tesla had some of the warriors go up against her and they have all been destroyed. Twenty warrior women lost, their souls all feeding Hannah, making her stronger."

"If twenty failed," Maria asked, "what are we to do?"

"Doctor Tesla suggested that we take flame throwers," Amber said. "A heavy flame coming from all directions should be enough to take her out."

Amber moved to the supply closet. She pulled out some clothes and quickly changed into black tights, a black tank top with the Ghost Town Labs logo on the chest, black boots, and black fingerless gloves. She moved to a bank of computers, running her hand along the side until she found the latch, opening it revealing a compartment full of flame throwers.

"We'll use these," Amber said, handing one to each of the women. "We don't have much time. Hannah's in the downtown area but there are so few people left in that area that Doctor Tesla doubts she'll be staying there much longer. We need to move quickly."

Amber made for the door, Kay and Dee following. Maria swallowed in a throat suddenly dry. She realized better than the others the risks they were about to take. Maria knew of a few safe places they could hide downtown if everything went to hell, but she had to be in control of the situation and she didn't want to let Doctor Tesla down; above all else, she couldn't let Doctor Tesla down.

Maria rushed out the door, getting to the black Hummer before the others and jumping into the driver's seat. Maria fired the truck up and got ready to activate the electric system that would keep them safe. Amber glared at Maria but quickly got into the passenger seat while Kay and Dee, assault rifles still at the ready, got into the back seat. Maria engaged the safety system before taking off.

"We need to have a plan," Amber said, looking at a map on a cellphone she'd taken from the trailer. "If we take this to Market Street, go on that until Colfax Avenue, taking the avenue past the gallery, we could double back on 8th then Settler's Road. We would be just about a block from where Hannah is at. If we dropped those two off when we turn on 8th, and sync a signal, we could attack from front and back at the same time."

"That's a good plan but there's one problem," Maria said. "The Hummer will be a block away from us and three blocks away from them. I don't think we should be that far from it, in case we have to make a quick break to regroup."

"Regroup?" Amber questioned. "These orders were from Doctor Tesla himself. There is no regrouping. We either take Hannah out or die trying. There is no retreat, Maria."

Maria nodded as she increased the speed of the large Hummer. She had figured that at some point everyone in Ghost Town Labs was nothing but an expense on the payroll, nothing but an expendable solider, but she thought she was different. She thought about calling Victor, asking what was going on, ask him to remember all the nights that they'd spent together, how she'd been a mother to Morgan when she needed it, but Maria knew that once Victor's mind was made up, nothing could change it.

Maria raced the truck down the roads Amber suggested, dodging parked cars and dead bodies, more and more the closer to downtown they got. When they entered the downtown area, it resembled a battle zone, minus the destruction of buildings. There were dead bodies littering the streets and sidewalks. Everywhere they looked there was death and destruction.

Maria dropped Kay and Dee off and gave them instructions on when to advance, all watches were synced up for an attack in five minutes. Maria raced the truck around the blocks, hoping to avoid making early contact with Hannah. As Maria was tearing around a corner, a man jumped out from behind a car, begging for help. Had Maria seen him earlier she may have been able to swerve but the man was too close, she hit him full on with the brunt of the truck. The man's body went flying and he landed on the ground, his spirit looking down at his twisted corpse.

"Sorry," Maria said, in a hushed voice.

"He would have been dead soon anyway," Amber said. "Amazing he lasted this long. Too bad you didn't see him, we could have used him as bait."

Maria smiled, realizing she'd been thinking the same thing. As she spun around a corner, the pair noticed a grouping of ghosts looking for more souls to take. Maria stopped the truck and the pair quickly got out, strapping the flame throwers on their backs, taking the wands for the throwers in their hands.

Maria and Amber wasted no time in rushing toward the group, and when they were close enough, they ignited the throwers, blasting the area with ten-foot red flames. The ghosts were instantly dispersed when the flames hit them, causing other ghosts to take pause, not going near the women.

The pair rushed back to the truck and took as many guns and ammunition as they could carry. Both the women figured that if the flame throwers ran out of fuel they would be forced to shoot their way out of this.

Maria knew from the reports she had seen that the best hiding place would be at the Genesis First Bank and Trust. Mackenzie had given detailed descriptions about the upstairs vault that was protected from ghosts because they had tried to make sure no one could use a listening device on the inside. The bank was only two blocks from where they were at, an easy run now that most of the ghosts had left the area for more plentiful grounds, and according to a report, when Doctor Tesla learned about the vault with electrified walls, he had one of the Ghost Town Labs' computer hackers go to work on it so the vault was now open, ready to be a safe haven for members of his team.

Maria and Amber came around a corner, seeing Hannah, thankful Hannah's back was to them, and they ducked backed around the corner, out of sight. There still had a little more time before they were to attack. Maria could feel her pulse quickening, beads of sweat starting to form on her head.

Maria tried to calm herself by looking around the buildings on the street. They were all nice, skyscrapers that were beautifully decorated and well maintained. Aside from the dead bodies and the stench of death, Genesis was a beautiful town. In another life, Maria could imagine herself working here, having a normal life, a good life.

Amber tapped Maria on the shoulder, indicating it was time to move. The women rushed around the corner with their flame throwers ready to go. As they cleared the corner they could see Kay and Dee rushing toward them, Hannah between the groups. When the teams were close enough, they ignited the flame throwers, filling the street with fire. Hannah barely had time to notice that someone was coming toward her, having been too busy toying with a group of people.

The women let the flame throwers run for a few seconds before they shut them off, looking around. Some of the people Hannah had been taunting were now rolling in the street, charred to a crisp, screaming in pain. Maria breathed a sigh of relief that Hannah had been dispersed so easily.

As Kay and Dee started walking toward Maria and Amber, a sinister laugh filled the air. A taunting laugh that pierced to the very soul. Maria looked around, trying to find where it was coming from but she couldn't see anything. As she scanned, Hannah materialized not fifty feet in front of Maria, completely unharmed from the fire.

"Is that the best you can do?" Hannah called out in a taunt.

Before anyone could answer, Key and Dee started firing their M16 assault rifles loaded with EPD rounds. The pair fired as fast as they could while Maria and Amber ignited the flame throwers and attempted to hit Hannah again. After a moment they stopped, looking around for Hannah. They couldn't see Hannah, but they could still hear her, hear her dark, evil laughter that filled the air.

Without a word Maria started to run toward the Hummer but Hannah took form between Maria and the truck. Maria turned quickly and took off running in a different direction.

The other three women followed Maria, Kay, and Dee shooting their guns toward Hannah. Maria ran with everything she had, not believing Hannah was as powerful as she'd just seen.

Maria didn't know where she was running when she took off but she wanted to run. She realized she was running directly toward the Genesis First Bank and Trust. Maria needed to pull out her pistol and shoot at ghosts that were milling around near the doors to the bank.

Maria and her team rushed through the doors and closed them, looking around the lobby. There were dead bodies everywhere. As the group moved further into the lobby ghosts began to appear from the alcoves behind the marble pillars that lined the lobby. The women wasted no time in opening fire. As they were making a hole toward the stairs going up, Hannah entered the bank, licking her lips.

"You're trapped," Hannah called out. "Don't fight it. There's no reason for you to kill more of my people?"

"You're people?" Maria called out. "What do you mean?"

"I have to create my coven," Maria called out. "I have many friends in the city now, creating the most powerful force on the planet. You will all bow to us before we kill you."

"You will never kill me," Maria called out as she ignited her flame thrower.

Hannah disappeared but her laughter filled the air. Maria used her thrower to clear a path, forcing the ghosts to stay back as they rushed up the stairs. Maria pushed the group as fast as they could, moving up stairs and through hallways, not pausing at all to disperse ghosts when they appeared in front of them.

Maria rounded a corner that lead to a grouping of offices. She couldn't believe that she'd led the group down a dead end. Maria was certain she was in the right hallway for the vault. Maria tried to leave the hallway but Hannah blocked the way. Maria ignited the flame thrower and pushed forward, watching Hannah disappear but not disperse.

Through a few more twists and turns Maria finally found the vault as all the flame throwers the group had were spent. They only had their guns left, and not many rounds of ammunition to feed the guns. Maria entered first, ushering the others in before closing the door and activating the electric field.

The group looked around the opulent room, Kay and Dee instantly searched for other entrances, places they would need to monitor and guard while Amber sat down on the edge of a chair, legs crossed, back up straight. Maria checked and double checked the door to make sure it was locked and the electric field was operational.

"What do we do now?" Amber asked.

"Look at this," Maria said, pointing to a monitor near the door. "This monitor is hooked to a number of cameras in the hallway. We can see what's going on outside."

Maria activated the monitor and waited while it warmed up. When it did, Maria wished she hadn't activated it. Standing in the hallway was a grouping of ghosts, about ten, from what Maria could count, led by Hannah, all trying to find their way into the vault.

"What is it?" Amber asked as Kay and Dee took up guard positions by the door.

"They are waiting in the hallway for us," Maria said. "Ladies...we're trapped here."

City Police Part I

Jake Arnold and Ryan Minot stood in the small hallway, dumbfounded at what they'd just seen. Morgan Tesla, daughter of Doctor Victor Tesla, their boss and leader, had just made the decision to turn on her father, desert him and walk away from Ghost Town Labs on their day of victory. Morgan had killed warrior women and used the mind control machines to keep people as her friends even after they knew about her involvement with the ghosts.

The pair of men, both dressed in black city police uniforms, exchanged a glance, neither knowing what to do as the daughter of the boss led her three friends out the tunnel and away from Genesis. Once they were certain Morgan was far enough in the tunnel, the men entered the main room, stepping over the bodies of the dead warriors, surveying the area.

"Now what?" Ryan asked.

"That's a tough one," Jake said. "I've known Morgan for a couple years and never thought she would do something like this. She always seemed so level headed."

"I've often warned Doctor Tesla about his mind control systems," Ryan said. "There's something that I didn't trust about them."

"Morgan's his daughter," Jake said, surprised. "When was she through the mind control program?"

"When she was younger," Ryan said. "How do you think we trained her? She's brilliant and a deadly fighter, well beyond her years...I guess we should have programmed in a childhood. I told Doctor Tesla we needed to do that with some of these people. I'm actually worried about some of the warrior women starting to break down like Morgan did. If that happens, even one or two having second thoughts or longings for better lives could break down the entire order of the warriors. There's so much that could go against us here, Doctor Tesla isn't worried about it, once this test is over, once he reaches his goals, he plans on killing all of them anyway. He is so narrowly focused that he can't see the forest from the trees on this one."

"I was just hired to be a mechanic in the shop," Jake said. "I'm good with women, always have been. Mackenzie and I had a thing going on, she brought me to Doctor Tesla's attention as someone to be brought up. I didn't know what I was getting into. I was just told to build equipment for a mission."

"We have issues though," Ryan said. "Do we tell Doctor Tesla what went on?"

"I'm not as sophisticated as you are Mr. Minot," Jake said. "Nor am I as educated as you are. I do know one thing though; you never want to deliver bad news to a man about his daughter. That's a truth that crosses every race, creed, religion and income group."

"Profound," Ryan said.

Ryan was about to continue when his police radio came alive with chatter. There were reports pouring in from the Colfax Gallery, something about an attack, but no one was sure exactly what was going on. All officers were instructed to get there as quickly as possible.

"I say we head out," Ryan said. "Away from the gallery. I'm not a coward, I just don't want to be in the way. We are to gather information, not end up dead...as for Morgan, we were on our way here when police business called us away."

"I can live with that," Jake said. "Let's roll."

Jake drove the Genesis City Police car—a brand new Dodge Charger all-wheel drive sedan, black and unmarked, lights in the grill and hidden behind the glass of the cabin, with a modified police engine. More than once Jake found himself burning rubber as he took off from stoplights, impressing and distracting the people driving around him. Jake desperately wanted to find a straight stretch of road and really open the car up, put the hammer down and see what it could do, but he knew that he didn't have time for fun today.

Jake drove through a commercial zone, two lanes of traffic on each side, divided by a grassy berm. To his north was a never ending string of box stores, home improvement stores, electronic stores and restaurants. To his south was almost the same, except where the giant Mall of Genesis was located, the building they'd just come from. The traffic was heavy that morning, like all mornings in Genesis, the past few years the city experienced a rebirth; rapid growth and renewal. Most of the people in Genesis were in the highest end of the middle class bracket, if not upper class.

Jake looked at all the people around him as they came to another red light. None of them had any idea their lives were about to be changed forever, changed so profoundly that if any of them did survive they would never recognize the life they had before. Jake noticed something out of the corner of his eye and quickly turned his head; a group of college-aged women, all very fit and healthy, all on rollerblades waiting to cross the street. Jake smiled, knowing that he had a sixth sense of sorts, if there was beautiful women around, especially if they looked like they were dressed for the beach, he could instantly sense them near him.

One of the women noticed Jake was looking at her. She smiled and waved, alerting the other women of Jake's presence. Jake lowered his mirrored police sunglasses to get a better look at the women before waving at them. Jake lit the tires of the police car as the women whistled and catcalled him, all with giant smiles on their faces. Ryan did not look amused.

"Keep your mind on the mission Jake," Ryan said, looking at his phone. "Reports are that these ghosts are vicious. You don't want to let your guard down for a second around them."

"I know," Jake said. "I saw what happened back at Whiterock. I saw how many people, good people I might add, wound up dead, bodies lying there for the animals to pick the bones. You don't need to remind me what we're up against."

"Then why are you flirting with a bunch of floozies?"

"Because I can," Jake smiled. "Hell Ryan, we're cops today. You know how women love men in uniforms. Let's use this to our advantage."

"I'm married to Erin remember," Ryan snapped.

"She's pretty hot," Jake smiled. "You're a lucky guy. She treat you right?"

"What does that have to do with anything?" Ryan asked. "Keep your mind in the game."

Jake was about to respond when he saw something stunning; a man dressed in business attire tried to race through traffic but was hit by a red sedan. Jake flipped on his lights and cut across traffic to block the road as the man twitched on the ground. The red sedan stopped and the driver, a teenaged girl heading home from a shift at a fast food joint, got out, clearly distraught from what she'd done.

"I didn't see him," the girl said, as tears started coming down her face. "He came out of nowhere."

Jake nodded and motioned for her to stay back as he and Ryan checked the man. The man's leg was clearly broken and he most likely had damage to his ribs. Ryan began to help the man as Jake went to the girl.

"It's all right miss," Jake said. "Everything's going to be okay. I need to call that man an ambulance before I take your statement." Jake reached to his radio, turning it on before speaking into the microphone clipped on his shoulder. "Car 25 requesting ambulance for a male, hit by car, on Lowery Avenue at the corner of Twenty Fifth Street."

"Negative," a flustered voice responded back. "Get to the Colfax Gallery immediately. All rescue personnel have been dispatched to that location."

"But this man could die," Jake said, into the mic.

"Get to the Gallery," the voice barked back. "That's an order."

"They're not going to help him?" the girl asked as more tears were coming down her face.

"We will help him," Jake said. "Don't worry about that. Why don't you sit in your car and wait. I want you to do something for me while you're waiting."

Jake had reservations based on the girl's age, but he flashed her that smile of his that had caused so many women to go weak in the knees. Jake wasn't thinking about doing anything with this girl, he knew what was coming, they were about to take off, leaving the scene and he didn't want anyone near them when they did. As Jake flashed his smile, he got the reaction he was looking for—she swooned.

"While you're waiting," Jake lowered his voice, in volume and tone, "I want you to think about what happened. Or think about what could happen, ya know. I'll be over in a minute for a statement, okay?"

"Okay," the girl said, taking a deep breath and going to her car.

As Jake was looking over the situation, the rollerblading women approached the scene and stopped a few feet back from where Jake was. There were four of them, all in bikini tops and short shorts, all smiling at Jake. Jake walked over to them, walking up to the tall brunette who was perfectly bronzed from the summer sun.

"Pardon me ladies," Jake said, trying to sound official. "Police scene. I'm going to have to ask you to wait here while we get this figured out."

"Is that man okay?" the brunette asked.

"Good enough," Jake smiled. "He'll last until the ambulance gets here. I don't know, with the doctors we have in this town, might as well have the morgue come and pick him up."

The girls all laughed.

"That's horrible," the brunette said.

"While we're waiting here," Jake said, with a sly-dog grin, "I'm going to have to write all of you ladies up. Don't want to, but those are the rules."

"Oh yeah?" the brunette said, glowing, grinning from ear to ear. "On what charges?"

"No protective gear," Jake said. "City ordinance, you know. You need helmets, knee pads, elbow pads, gloves and chest protectors."

"I've got enough padding there," the brunette smiled. "But you can write me up for the other charges. You gonna have to frisk us?"

"Maybe," Jake smiled as he extended his hand. "I'm Jake Arnold."

"Lizzy Mick," Lizzy said.

"Short for Elizabeth?" Jake asked.

"Maybe," Lizzy replied. "You gotta work a little harder to find out."

"JAKE!" Ryan shouted as he was kneeling next to the man. "Get over here now!"

"Police business," Jake said. "Wait here."

Lizzy smiled as Jake sauntered over to Ryan. Ryan was on his knees, next to the man, who was starting to shake. Jake could see there was a nasty bump starting to well up on the man's head, surrounded by black and blue bruises. The man didn't look good.

"What is it?" Jake asked.

"There's no way this man will make it," Ryan said. "Not unless we get him to a hospital now. We don't have time to wait for an ambulance."

"Then let's load him up in the back of our car," Jake said, moving to the man's upper body, getting ready to lift him. "Get his feet."

"Not what I had in mind," Ryan said, as he motioned to his gun.

"Are you crazy?" Jake asked. "Look at how many people are watching. You know what kind of panic and riot that would cause?"

Jake's radio burst to life with reports, people screaming for help, something about a blockade preventing emergency vehicles from getting to the Colfax Gallery. Jake turned the volume down, not wanting the people around them to hear and get into a panic. Jake was surprised, they were describing Ghost Town Labs Hummers blocking the roads, the warrior women defeating some of the police force to hold them at bay, yet he thought that Doctor Tesla would have wanted to see the police against his ghosts.

"We can't take him to the hospital," Ryan said. "And he's in extreme pain."

"I have an idea," Jake said. "Hold on."

Jake walked back to the rollerblading women who were in their own conversations. Lizzy was clearly the dominate female of the group, their leader and they were all giggling about the conversation that she'd had with Jake. Jake didn't exactly know how he was going to do this, but he had a good idea about what one of the women, a short blonde girl, had in her backpack.

"There's some strange things going on today," Jake said, as he reached out and took Lizzy's hand. "Seems like there's some kind of big goings on over at the Colfax Gallery. All the emergency responders are heading over there."

"Is that why all the cellphones are out?" the question came from the tallest girl, a thicker woman with black hair in a tight braid.

"It could be," Jake said. "I don't know. All I know is that this man on the ground is in pain, he's hurt bad and all the ambulances are heading over to the Gallery. One can swing this way, after whatever's going on has been sorted out."

"Can you take him to a hospital?" Lizzy asked.

"I wish we could," Jake said. "But we can't move him, not in our car. You've got that backpack there...you have anything in it that could help this man?"

"What are you asking for?" the tallest girl asked.

"We have a bottle of rum," Lizzy said. "We were going to the beach and gonna spike some drinks...that's not a crime is it?"

"I may have to detain you for a bit," Jake smiled, "but no, that's not a crime. Not one that I'm going to worry about anyway...but I was wondering if you had anything stronger? Maybe something a little more euphoric?"

"You're asking if we have drugs?" the tall one scoffed. "You know buddy, even if we did, we're not going to hand them over to a police officer, no matter how cute and charming you are."

"But that man could die," Jake protested. "He's in extreme pain."

"So giving him drugs in that state is the answer?" the short blonde asked.

"I don't think that's a good idea either," Lizzy said. "We don't have any drugs on us but you can have some of the rum if you think it would help him."

"I do," Jake said.

The short blonde nodded, taking her pack off her back and slowly opening the bag, making sure Jake couldn't see what else the pack contained. She brought out a pink plastic water bottle that was big, at least a half-gallon in size, with a capped straw on the top. The woman slowly handed it to Jake.

"Is this straight or mixed with something?" Jake asked.

"Straight," the blonde said.

Jake uncapped the bottle and took a sip, it was strong rum. He winked at Lizzy and took the bottle over to the man on the ground. Jake helped the man as he drank, taking three good swigs from the bottle. Jake brought the bottle back, taking a good swig from it before handing it to Lizzy who took two good pulls from the bottle. Lizzy handed it back to the blonde who put the bottle in her bag and her bag on her back.

"We should get moving," the other blonde said, speaking for the first time. "We're meeting some guys there."

"Meeting some guys there," Jake said, as he looked into Lizzy's eyes with a sly grin. "I'd better go with to make sure you aren't in any danger."

"It's not like that," Lizzy said. "We're practicing for some co-ed beach volleyball. There's a tournament this weekend. We'll play three or four games then spend the rest of the weekend getting ripped drunk...you should swing by, off duty of course."

"That sounds fun," Jake said. "You girls should be careful today. Something seems out of place. There's a lot of tension in the town for some reason."

Jake and the women looked at the traffic that was passing them. All the cars were moving faster now and it seemed that everyone was getting more aggressive. There were horns honking everywhere, a symphony of angry drivers expressing their frustrations with their car horns.

Jake was surprised to notice that three Ghost Town Labs' Hummers were racing down the street, cutting everyone off, not stopping for red lights, even going over the grassy median when they had to. Jake was dumbfounded as they rushed right past him, forcing the women and Jake to step back as they went by.

"I'm not one who likes to tell people how to do their jobs," the tallest said, "but shouldn't you go after those lunatics?"

"I can't leave my partner," Jake said, watching the Hummers disappear around a corner, "and he can't leave the guy on the road until an ambulance gets here."

Jake was about to continue when he noticed the teenaged girl who'd hit the man was getting out of her car. He'd glanced at the girl a few times, seeing that she was in the driver's seat of the red sedan, arms across the top of the steering wheel, head on the arms, tears dripping from her face. The girl looked sick, like she was ready to vomit. The teen was flushed pale, shaking, and on the verge of hysteria. She slowly approached Jake.

"I tried to call my parents," the girl said, in a choppy voice. "My phone doesn't work. I don't know what to do."

"We'll get ahold of your parent's sweetheart," Jake said, trying to sound as sympathetic as he could. "There's nothing for you to worry about. This was an accident, that's all, and accidents happen all the time. Nothing to worry about."

"But I could have killed that man," the girl sobbed.

"But you didn't," Jake said. "He's alive and well and he's going to laugh about this tomorrow, I will too. I laugh at you tomorrow, laugh that you were so worried today when I told you that everything is going to be okay."

"But…" the girl tried to continue.

"What's your name sweetie?" Lizzy asked as she approached the girl.

"Heather," Heather said.

"That's a very pretty name," Lizzy said, putting her hand on Heather's shoulder. "Look, I know what you're thinking but I have to tell you, it's not the end of the world. Life will go on and before you know it, this will be a distant memory, only coming up when you need a good laugh about something. Don't be too hard on yourself, stuff like this happens."

"How would you know?" Heather asked between sniffs.

"It happened to me," Lizzy said. "It was after school and we were goofing around in the school parking lot. My boyfriend at the time had snuck out with his father's sports car, his parents were gone and he was driving his dad's 1969 GTO Judge. I jumped in the driver's seat and took off, burning the tires as my boyfriend screamed at me to come back. I was watching him in the mirror and didn't see where I was going. I was headed for a tree and I tried to correct but the car was way too powerful, I lost control as I thought I was slamming on the brakes but I hit the gas instead."

"You put a '69 Judge into a tree?" Jake exclaimed.

"I wish," Lizzy said. "It veered off. I wasn't even strong enough to steer since the car had so much power. I motored over three members of the marching band. Put all three in the hospital for a few days. They didn't march again for months. It was pretty bad. I got in loads of trouble, my boyfriend got in loads of trouble, he broke up with me and I had to sit in jail for fifteen days. I thought the world was over for me, but hey, here I am, back at it, one year away from being a registered nurse."

"You're gonna be a nurse?" Jake asked. "Why didn't you say something? Come on, help this guy."

"There's nothing I can do," Lizzy said. "We have nothing here to work with and I'm not certified. I do something to mess him up I could be out of nursing school."

Jake was about to say something when he noticed a couple of the women looked horrified. Jake turned to look and he saw Ryan, with his gun pointed directly at the man's head. Ryan didn't shoot, he waited, waited for the spirit to return, the man had died from the accident. Ryan wasted no time in shooting the spirit, dispersing it, causing everyone watching to begin freaking out.

City Police Part II

Everyone who'd seen what just happened was in a state of shock; nothing could have prepared them to witness a man turning into a ghost. Jake unhooked the strap that held his pistol in place, knowing there would be trouble soon. Jake wasn't sure what would happen, but he knew everyone was already on edge, panic setting in.

Lizzy was breathing deeply, as if she was practicing a meditative breathing exercise to keep herself calm. Heather, who was already distraught, was crying hard, nothing to hold back the tears streaming down her face. The short blonde was in her bag, using the Rum to chase down some pills while the other girls were wide-eyed, trying to wrap their heads around what they'd just seen.

"I know I didn't see what I thought I just saw," Lizzy said, still trying the relaxing breathing exercise.

"What did you think you saw?" Jake asked.

"That man turned into a ghost," Lizzy said. "But what's more disturbing is that your partner shot the ghost. I don't understand."

"There's not much to understand," Jake said. "It's life and death here. That's what the world is all about...and right now, there's about to be a hell of a lot more death."

Heather had been listening to the words that Jake and Lizzy said but she wasn't hearing them. The only thing in her mind was that the man she'd hit was dead, nothing else registered. Perhaps if things had been going better in her life, if her boyfriend hadn't dumped her, if her parents liked her new friends, if school had been going better, Heather may have tried to fight harder, but she didn't.

The short blonde on rollerblades noticed Heather first, slowly making her way toward traffic. She tried to get to Heather, screaming out, alerting everyone as to what was about to happen, but there was nothing she could do. As the blonde got to Heather, trying to grab her around the waist, both of the girls got hit by a Ghost Town Labs Hummer that was speeding down the road.

Jake couldn't believe what he was seeing. Heather and the blonde went flying through the air, landing near each other, blood splattering in all directions as the large black Hummer, adding insult to injury, ran over both girls. There was no way either could have survived, there was barely anything left of them as the Hummer didn't even slow down as it raced away.

Jake and Lizzy stood with their jaws open, neither one knew how to respond to what they'd just seen. It didn't take more than a few seconds for the ghosts of the two girls to appear, standing near their bodies, completely clueless as to what had just occurred. Ryan was ready with his gun, firing twice, needing only one shot to take out each ghost. Once the ghosts were gone, Ryan instantly went back to looking at his phone, intensely reading the screen.

Jake turned to look at the two other rollerblading women, wanted to see how they were handling this, but they were racing away, fearful of what they'd just seen. Jake turned to Lizzy who looked to be torn, she didn't want to stick around to see who was going to die next, but something inside her told her not to run, she didn't know why, but she stayed next to Jake instead of taking off with her friends.

"We have to get to the Lowery Lift Bridge," Ryan said, as he approached Jake and Lizzy. "There's trouble there."

"There's trouble here," Lizzy said. "Those were ghosts that I just saw, three of them now and each one of them disappeared because of your gun...what's going on here?"

"You really think you saw ghosts?" Ryan scoffed. "You'd better run along now."

"Three people just died and you're going to leave them here?" Lizzy asked. "What kind of police are you?"

"The kind that follows orders," Ryan snapped. "Our superiors told us to go to the Lowery Lift Bridge so that's where I intend to go. Jake, get in the car and let's move."

"Take me with you, Jake," Lizzy said, stepping forward and grabbing his hand. "I don't want to be alone in this mess."

"We can't take you," Ryan said. "We have police business to do."

"Her friends left her," Jake protested, "and one of them is dead. I'm sorry, so sorry about that."

"I can cry for her later," Lizzy said. "Right now we need to be safe. I can't think of anywhere safer than with two cops."

Jake and Ryan exchanged a glance. Jake knew Ryan wouldn't allow it, didn't care at all about Lizzy. To him, Lizzy was just another test subject, a lab rat who didn't know she was in a lab. Jake couldn't image losing a friend like she just did and he wasn't about to leave her standing there, no matter what it might cost him.

"You were drinking in public," Jake said. "That's public intoxication. I'm placing you under arrest, for the moment." Jake moved to the police car and opened the back door. "Please get in ma'am. Don't make a scene or make me cuff you."

Lizzy smiled and moved to the door of the car. She gave Jake a quick kiss on the cheek as she sat in the back seat.

"Thank you," Lizzy said, as Jake started to close the door. "I'll return the favor as soon as I can."

"Are you out of your mind?" Ryan almost screamed. "We can't take her with us. Get her out of there."

"I'm going and she's coming with," Jake said, as he got into the driver's seat of the police car. "Are you coming with or are you staying here?"

Ryan quickly moved to the passenger side of the car and got in, glaring at Jake the entire time. Jake only smiled as he gunned the engine, spinning the tires, tearing away from the bodies and the scene of the deaths. A small crowd had gathered, all amazed at what they saw, taking pictures and video with their cellphones, yet none of them were able to upload the content to the net, no one was able to show the world what was going on.

Jake was dodging between cars, keeping his lights and sirens blaring while he raced toward the lift bridge. The traffic was getting heavier and slower the closer they got, Jake trying to get to the main road, 394, which would take him right to the bridge but as he got close to the entrance ramp, he saw the road was at a standstill.

"We're not going on 394," Jake said. "Look for a different route."

"Take Golden Valley Road," Lizzy said. "Just a few blocks up and it's always a quiet road."

"That goes through a lot of residential, right?" Jake asked.

"It does," Lizzy said. "Right past my house actually."

"Then we can drop you off there," Ryan said. "We really can't have you tagging along with us all day miss."

"She can stay with us if she wants to," Jake said.

"I want to," Lizzy said. "I couldn't imagine being alone after everything that I've witnessed today. I have to be with someone."

"Where do you think your friends went?" Jake asked.

"I'm sure they went to the house," Lizzy said. "We all rent a house together, until we finish school anyway. They were headed in this direction."

"If your friends are there then we drop you off and we go about our business," Ryan said. "End of discussion."

"No, it's not," Jake said. "We can't leave her alone like that, not after what see's seen."

"On that point," Lizzy asked, leaning forward toward Ryan, "how did you do what you did to those ghosts?"

"How do you know they were ghosts?" Ryan asked.

"They were," Lizzy said. "I know they were and so do you. Just level with me, what the hell is going on here?"

"I have no idea," Ryan said.

"Why are there Black Hummers everywhere that say Ghost Town Labs on the sides?" Lizzy asked. "I've seen them around for the past few days."

"I have no idea," Ryan said. "Have you checked the internet?"

"I did," Lizzy said. "Not much comes up about them, just some information about a government cover-up and a lot of people dying in a town called Whiterock."

Jake tried not to reveal too much with his expressions. He couldn't believe that this woman had figured out so much. Jake didn't know how much he should tell her or if he should let her in on what was going on. Jake never had trouble with the ladies before, perhaps he was able to land them too easily for all he could think about was the lust he was having for Lizzy. She was sweating from rollerblading, her abundant chest held in a black bikini top and only short black volleyball shorts beneath, exposing her long legs. Jake knew he had her dialed in and could have fun with her whenever he wanted, something he wanted to do as soon as he could.

"Never heard of Whiterock," Ryan said. "Can't believe everything you read on the internet, can you?"

"I suppose not," Lizzy said, "but I did more research into the company. It seems they infiltrate all levels of government for their own ends. You wouldn't be working with them, would you?"

"Not in the least," Ryan said.

"Here's my house," Lizzy said, pointing.

Jake looked to where she was pointing, a simple two story white house with red trim. It was a cute house, not large, but adequate with a small, well taken care of bare grass yard. Jake turned into the driveway, not bothering to check what Ryan thought. If there were more women in the house, Jake wanted to help them if for nothing else but to earn more points with Lizzy. Jake put the car in park, jumped out, and opened Lizzy's door.

"Come on," Jake said, offering a hand to help Lizzy. "Let's see if your friends came home or not."

Lizzy followed Jake to the front door while Ryan stayed in the car. Jake entered the house with Lizzy a step behind him. The house was bare, devoid of any furniture or décor, just off white walls and a hardwood floor. Jake passed through the entryway heading toward the living room. He could hear the sounds of computers and networking equipment running, but couldn't see anything.

As Jake entered the living room, he felt hands grabbing his arms, turning him around. Lizzy was poised and ready, delivering some heavy blows to Jake's stomach then head as his arms were being held by the other two women that had been with Lizzy earlier. Jake had no time to even comprehend what was going on, let alone have a chance to protect himself from the blows. As Jake doubled over in pain from a straight right to the stomach, Lizzy lifted a knee while forcing Jake's head down, driving the point of her knee into the side of his head.

Jake was seeing stars as he dropped to the ground. He was sprawled out on the floor, trying to regain his senses as he felt someone on top of him, pressing his back onto the floor, pinning him down, preventing him from moving. Jake was amazed at how powerful the blows were but he didn't feel as bad when he saw Lizzy removing the brass knuckles that were on her hands.

Jake began to become aware of what was going on in the room. The taller woman with the black braid was on top of him, holding him on the ground. Jake didn't resist, his head and upper body were still throbbing with pain from the blows. The blonde girl and Lizzy were standing near Jake's head, both holding large black Glock pistols aimed right at him. Jake was amazed that the two women had changed; both wearing black tights, military boots, and black t-shirts. On Lizzy's nod, the woman got off of Jake and the three of them hefted him into a chair, handcuffing him in place.

"I like how this is starting," Jake said, smiling at Lizzy. "I love a woman who plays rough, but you didn't need to be that harsh. The only question, which one of you is going to be first?"

The blonde cuffed Jake hard across the head while Lizzy just smiled at him. Jake knew that even though they were on opposite teams, she was thinking the same things he was.

"Don't make me kill you Jake," Lizzy said. "I don't want to do that."

"I think there's been a misunderstanding here," Jake said. "Nothing we can't get cleared up. No need to alert higher authority about this."

"Can it, Jake," Lizzy said. "We know all about Ghost Town Labs. We got to Whiterock just minutes too late. I saw the Ghost Town Labs' Warriors gunning down military and civilians like animals, not a care of concern for the lives they were destroying."

"Who are you?" Jake asked, stunned.

"Ethan Drew wasn't the only person who was sent to Whiterock to investigate," Lizzy said. "We were there. We passed through the town a number of times, posing as college girls doing a photo journal of the state. We even met the government's RAW Troops on the edge of town after the destruction had occurred. They wouldn't let us in."

"You feds like Ethan?"

"Higher than that," Lizzy said. "Doctor Tesla was right about one thing, the government cannot be trusted. They were going to turn on him, kill him, and take his research. His old country knew he survived but Tesla was protected and hidden away in Whiterock, every person there fully vetted to make sure no sleepers could get to him. A deal was made so that Victor could do his work, his old government would stop hunting him and our government would share the knowledge they learned. We never gave them anything good, but kept them away."

"So what are you doing here?" Jake asked. "What kind of team are you?"

"There are those in the government that don't want this to happen," Lizzy said. "Those who believe the dead should remain dead, that ghosts shouldn't walk the earth. Even some of those who brought Tesla to the country are regretting the decision to let his madness continue. That's why we were brought in. We're members of Quad Force and our only goal is to stop Ghost Town Labs by any means necessary."

"You got me," Jake smiled. "A lowly mechanic who got tangled up in a twist with the wrong girl."

"Seems that happens to you a lot lately," Lizzy said, with a wink. "Here's the deal, we have a mission to carry out—stop Ghost Town Labs. That's it. We're being paid to bring the corpse of Tesla to our commanders and to destroy all the information that he's developed. All of it must be destroyed. I hate to have to do this to you Jake Arnold, but you can either join us or die."

Lizzy aimed her gun right between Jake's eyes. She was so calm and steady with the gun, a trait that told Jake this wasn't the first time she'd threated someone nor would it be the first time she'd shot someone. Jake knew that he only had a moment to give them a decision, but it was a decision that he didn't need to think about.

"I'm on your side," Jake said. "No worries about that. I don't agree with what they are doing either. I was just here for a paycheck but I know what they are doing is wrong."

"I figured you'd see it our way," Lizzy said.

"I don't trust him," the tall woman with the black braid said. "He's Ghost Town Labs. We should get what information we can out of him and dispose of him."

"That would be unwise," Jake said.

"Why?"

"You kill me and my ghost will be here," Jake said. "I have a way to disperse ghosts but you don't. There would be nothing you could do."

The blonde reached to the back of her tights and unclipped something she had hanging there. Jake had noticed that she had something that looked like a tail but couldn't focus enough to see. The blonde had a shock stick in her hand. She depressed the power button and arcs of electricity jumped between the prods on the end. The cylinder shaped stick looked to hold about four 'D' sized batteries.

"I think this would handle it quite well," the blonde said. "We've tested it on ghosts in Whiterock."

"There's no need to kill me," Jake said, quickly. "I want to join you. Think about this, Doctor Tesla's daughter, his real daughter Morgan, has deserted. Even his own daughter understands this is going too far, that this is wrong. She left with a group of friends. I will follow you, help you, and guide you through this mess."

"I trust you," Lizzy said. "I can tell it in your eyes that you're being sincere."

"What's our play then?" Jake asked. "How do you guys want to work together and what information do you need?"

"We need to find some people," Lizzy said. "First off, Ethan and Michelle. We must get them out of here alive. They are the witnesses to all that has happened, plus they entered the lab beneath Whiterock. We know they made it out but we don't know what happened to them after. We also have to find Madison. She's a full-fledged warrior now but your partner out there, Ryan, was the one who put her through the training, so there's no telling what kind of surprises she might be in for."

"I think Ryan is fully behind Ghost Town Labs," Jake said. "He's loyal to Tesla to the end. His wife on the other hand..."

"Erin," Lizzy said. "She's a tossup. They're both working other angles but we don't know who is legit and who is working for Ghost Town Labs. I agree that Ryan is loyal to Tesla, I think they're playing both sides, no matter who wins they have a place in the world...a dangerous gambit."

"I know where Erin is at," Jake said. "I know she's still in the mall, working the sporting goods store. I know where the other Ghost Town Labs' people are, too. I can take you to anyone you want to find."

"That's good," Lizzy said. "See girls, I told you he could be valuable to us. One of the first things we need to do is get Jade Angels here."

"Who?" Jake asked.

"Jade Chance," Lizzy said. "Deserted RAW Troops with a number of other people. They are now trying defeat Ghost Town Labs. They have a good shot, Madison is leading them, but they are going to be late getting to the party. They should arrive sometime this evening. Once they are here they are going to be going after anyone and anything associated with Ghost Town Labs and Doctor Tesla. We are going to try and make contact with them, help them as much as we can."

"Good," Jake said. "I know some of the RAW Troops, saw what they could do in training and in action. They should do well here...we need to get moving though. Ryan isn't going to wait in that car forever."

"I will go with you," Lizzy said. "These two have other things they need to be doing. We were on our way on a mission when we bumped into you. I recognized you right away from your file, that's why I flirted you up."

"Here I thought it was my charm," Jake said.

"Your charm helped," Lizzy said, "along with your looks but that's something we can talk about when this is over. Ladies, make contact with the Angels and get them here. You know what to do."

"You sure about this?" the black haired one asked.

"I am," Lizzy said.

"How about some names?" Jake asked. "I got yours, Lizzy, but I never got you two."

"You don't need them," Lizzy said. "They can stay anonymous for a little longer."

"Hmm," Jake said. "Worried I might figure out identities if I know names?"

"No," Lizzy said. "If you're caught you can't give us up if you don't know who we are."

"Fair enough," Jake said.

Lizzy unhooked the handcuffs and Jake stood up. For a moment he wondered if he should be with these women, but he knew he didn't want to fight this alone. His mind had been made up to turn on Ghost Town Labs before he walked into the house, so them allowing him to join up was a gift. Jake knew that whether these ladies were good or evil, they couldn't be worse than Ghost Town Labs.

Lizzy kicked her rollerblades off and grabbed a pair of sneakers, quickly doing up the laces while the other two girls rushed down the stairs. Jake tried to look to see what was down there but they had all the doors closed. Lizzy checked to make sure the others were out of sight before motioning Jake to go. Jake took a step, like he was going to leave, but turned back, quickly pushed Lizzy against a wall and kissed her passionately. Lizzy had no choice but to give into the kiss, which she felt throughout her entire body.

"Couldn't leave without doing that," Jake said, as he pulled away, leaving her wanting more but swiftly, gently but firmly dropped Lizzy to the floor. "But one thing, don't ever jump me again."

"Next time," Lizzy smiled, "we'll have to agree on a time and place."

"Anytime you want," Jake said, standing and bringing Lizzy up with him. "Now, let's send these demons to hell."

City Police Part III

Jake kept glancing in his rearview mirror, catching glances with Lizzy as he slowly made his way through traffic. Even in the residential area the cars were thick, driving was slow, and motorists were mad. Horns were honking and fingers were flying out the windows. Jake kept his police lights on but most people didn't even seem to care, their minds preoccupied with everything else going on in their city.

Jake noticed Ryan was constantly on his phone, looking through pages of reports pouring in from other Ghost Town Labs' employees. Jake was certain Ryan was looking for reports from Erin, he knew the pair was deeply in love and would follow each other to the ends of the earth.

As the Lowery Lift Bridge came into sight, Jake could see that it was raised in the air, with cars and people on the bridge. In front of the bridge, in Genesis, were cars backed up everywhere, groups of people yelling and shouting, and general panic. Jake could see that some of the people yelling were holding guns, something he knew would happen, considering Genesis had a strong gun owning population.

"Lots of civilians have guns there," Jake said, matter of factly. "I wonder if that played into the decision of choosing this city."

Ryan glared at Jake, snapping his head away from his phone and burning holes into Jake for the statement he'd made. Jake made a quick decision.

"This will all go a whole lot easier," Jake said, "if you know what's going on. Ryan, Lizzy and her friends are Quad Force."

"The group the government started to internally take over Ghost Town Labs?" Ryan asked.

"Yes."

"Then what the hell is she doing with us?" Ryan asked.

"She's my prisoner," Jake said. "I couldn't let her go and I think that Doctor Tesla would very much like to question her, find out what Quad Force has planned, don't you?"

"I don't like the idea," Ryan said, "but nice work." Ryan unbuckled his seatbelt and turned around to look at Lizzy. "What's Quad Force's plans?"

"I think you have a good idea," Lizzy said. "Total destruction of Ghost Town Labs and the rotting corpse of Doctor Victor Tesla in a government lab is a good place to start. All of his high up minions also have body bags waiting for them at headquarters."

"Including us?"

"There's 'his and hers' caskets for Ryan and Erin Minot at our headquarters," Lizzy smiled. "You all will be buried in the unmarked graves in Blackstone Hollow. You all would have stayed right where your first attack took place."

"How profound," Ryan said. "The government has no idea what they are dealing with. I guarantee Ghost Town Labs has already infiltrated your little Quad Force and are already running the show. You can't hide from us, Ghost Town Labs is simply too powerful."

"You want to know what's really funny?" Lizzy asked.

"What's that?"

"Quad Force has a sleeper in Ghost Town Labs," Lizzy smiled. "One of the people you've got monitoring events today is working for us."

"Who is it?" Ryan asked, drawing his gun on Lizzy.

"That's for me to know," Lizzy said. "For now."

Ryan didn't respond. Jake could feel the tension building between the two. Jake noticed Ryan was typing on his phone. Jake tried to see what he was writing but he was too busy navigating traffic to get a good look. Traffic was at a complete stop, no one even moving for the police car with its lights and sirens going.

Jake gave up trying to maneuver the car around. The traffic was so heavy there was nothing he could do. He thought about trying to drive down the sidewalk but there were a lot of people standing around, making it too risky. The thought going through Jake's mind was that ghosts would be overtaking this area very soon—although, according to reports from the Ghost Town Labs warriors, shots had been fired around the bridge area and people had been killed.

Jake noticed there was a park a few blocks up that seemed to have some activity going on. People were screaming and fighting while other cops tried to keep the peace. Jake got out of the police car and climbed up on the roof, trying to get a better view of what was going on. He could see two bodies on the ground, near the river's edge, but he didn't see any ghosts.

Jake jumped off the roof and motioned for Ryan to get out of the car. Ryan got out and rushed over to Jake, still looking at his phone.

"There's bodies over there," Jake said. "In the park a couple blocks down. A lot of people look pretty upset but there's no ghosts."

"I'm reading a report from the warriors across the river," Ryan said. "Sounds like they shot two women who were attempting to cross the river. The women turned to ghosts but they weren't powerful enough to do anything. They only lasted for a few moments before they dispersed on their own."

"Where's the nearest separator?" Jake asked.

"A few blocks away," Ryan said. "Closer to the gallery. This could be something though, with all the activity there the separator didn't have the power to maintain the ghosts here. That's something that I will note."

As Ryan was typing on his phone, a group of people noticed Jake and Ryan standing next to their car. The group, led by a middle-aged man in khaki pants and a red polo shirt, smooth black hair and a fit body, approached. Jake noted there were three men and three women, all around the same age, mid-forties, except one woman who looked mid-twenties and they were all wearing wedding rings.

"Officer," the man said, "what is going on here? We have rights that cannot be violated. That bridge has to be lowered immediately."

"I'm sorry," Jake said, trying to sound sympathetic, "rights only extend so far when there is a threat or risky situation. The greater good, the good of society, has to be considered. That is what is going on here. I can't lower that bridge."

"Then it's true," one of the women gasped as she stepped forward and grabbed the man's hand. "There's been a viral attack at the Colfax Gallery and we're all at risk of contamination."

Jake looked at the woman. She was skinny, too skinny, with almost as much weight in gold and diamond jewelry on her fingers, wrists and neck as her total body weight. She wore a tight green cotton dress, haltered on the top, short hemmed, with sneakers. Jake thought the dress fit her nicely but it was made for a woman much younger. The woman kept running her hand through her spiked and frosted, brown pixie cut hair.

Before Jake could answer, another one of the men stepped forward. He was dressed in khaki shorts and a designer athletic blue t-shirt. His head was shaved but he sported a black goatee that was perfectly trimmed. The man was buff, his shirt fit tight, showing the broad chest and washboard abs beneath. The man moved half a step too close for comfort to Jake.

"Look *officer*," the man said, mockingly, "we've got a tee time in half an hour across the river at the Northdale Country Club. You know how hard it is for all of us to get together with enough time for a round of golf? We can only do it once or twice a week. Now, the three of us are lawyers, so I think you really want to be lowering that bridge."

"Honey," the youngest girl said, "be nice. He's just trying to do his job."

The man and Jake both turned their heads to stare at the woman. She was short and fit, lavish brown hair curled as if fell past her shoulders. The woman was wearing black yoga pants with a green and white design on the side with a matching haltered tank top. Jake guessed the woman could only be about twenty-four years old but the man she was holding hands with was at least forty five. Jake thought the wedding ring the young woman was wearing had to cost at least as much as the average four year college education – a high priced trophy wife. Jake gave her that glance and smile that started many a seduction for him.

"First off," Jake said, locking eyes with the young girl, speaking to her while ignoring the rest, "there's no attack, no viral outbreak. I believe we are having an emergency services test to make sure the city is up to code and ready if an event such as that happened. Things will be moving soon my dear, don't worry about that."

"You ever call my wife 'my dear' again," the buff man said, getting right in Jake's face, "you will have a lot of explaining to do at city hall. You value your job?"

"Possibly," Jake smiled.

"Then lower the bridge," the man barked.

"I can't," Jake said. "I don't have the authority to."

"What about what the others were saying," the third woman asked, stepping forward.

A cute but chunky blonde lady in tight khaki capris pants with a green polo shirt who seemed to be distant from the other people in the group, but most distant to her husband. She wore her short hair in a ponytail with a white visor and looked to be bored by the entire day.

"What were the other's saying?" Jake asked, still making eyes with the young girl.

"That some women turned into ghosts," the woman said.

"Ghosts?" Jake scoffed. "That's the dumbest thing I've ever heard. How is it possible for ghosts to be running around here?"

"I don't know," she replied.

"We all heard the people talking about it," the young woman said. "They said that…"

"I'll do the talking," her husband cut in. "You just keep your mouth shut. They said that two women were going to swim across the river but those people on the other side shot and killed them. The rumor is that the women returned almost instantly as ghosts."

"And you believed it?" Jake asked.

"A lot of people are saying it," the man said.

"A lot of people say a lot of things," Jake replied. "Believe none of it. You sound foolish for even asking something so stupid."

Jake smiled inside, knowing he'd gotten under the man's skin and that his young wife was smiling a sly smile. Jake looked back to the car, seeing Lizzy in the back seat while Ryan was still on his phone. Ryan noticed Jake was looking at them and he walked up and flashed his phone so Jake could see the screen, video of the destruction that had taken place at the Colfax Gallery.

"Hang on a second," the young woman said, trying to look at the screen. "All of our phones are dead. How do you have one that works?"

"Police frequency," Jake calmly replied. "With all the network devices and data usage the police found that the phones didn't work fast enough nor were they reliable enough. We put our own system up."

"Another waste of taxpayer money," the buff man said. "And what's with the broad you got in the back of your car? No cuffs yet, she's detained. What did she do?"

"That's classified," Ryan said. "And none of your business."

"I demand some answers," the man shouted, getting closer to Ryan this time. "Someone better tell me what's going on here before I get really mad. I swear I'll sue both of you and make sure you never do police work in this state again. I can, you know. Lower that bridge or I will sue you so fast you won't believe it."

"Honey," the woman said, tugging at her husband's arm, "not again. Don't embarrass me like this again. You keep pushing it and you'll have to go back to the judge. You don't want that do you? To have to tell the judge why you got into a fight with a cop."

"Don't talk to me like I'm a child," the man said, brushing his wife off. "Adults are talking here *dear*, why don't you do what you're best at and shut the hell up."

"You prick," the woman shouted as she went to slap him.

"Don't do that," Jake said, as he grabbed the woman's arm and prevented her from slapping her husband. "Then we'd have to arrest you and it would be lots of paperwork for me."

"Sorry about this," the skinny woman said. "We've warned them that if they don't start getting along they aren't coming golfing with us anymore. Jesus Steve, you want to get divorced a fourth time? Not even a year and you're already messing this one up."

Steve didn't respond. He just stood stone-statue still, looking toward the park. All the color had left his face and he was sweating, scared. The others slowly turned, realizing that the sounds of screams and panic were filling the air.

Jake took two steps back and opened the rear car door allowing Lizzy to get out. He knew something bad was about to happen and he didn't want her trapped in the back of a police car without a fighting chance to get away. Lizzy held Jake's hand as they moved closer toward the park. There had been screaming but it was louder now, something telling them it was more than just an upset crowd.

The buff man saw it first, a ghost moving in from the side streets and taking someone. There were ghosts everywhere, pouring in from all directions. The people who'd been in the park were trying to get away, some running toward the road only to get picked off by the ghosts and others trying to swim only to get snipped by the warrior women's massive rifles. The entire population was trapped in that area with nowhere to go.

Jake looked around, looked for some way to get out of the area but he didn't see a safe path. He pulled out his pistol, dropping the magazine that was in it and loading a different mag, one loaded with EPD rounds. Jake noticed that Ryan already had his gun at the ready.

"We can go to the buildings across the street," Lizzy said, grabbing Jakes arm and pointing at a row of office buildings. "We can get to the high ground."

"And be trapped there," Jake replied.

"No," Lizzy said. "We have choppers, black and unmarked, like Ghost Town Labs'. They can set up an evac for us."

"We'd better run," Jake said.

As Jake and Lizzy started to move, ghosts appeared everywhere. They were killing at an amazing rate. Jake noticed there were a number of ghosts draped all in black, with hoods to keep their faces hidden. He counted twelve of them. As he scanned the area, he noticed that Hannah, the Genesis Ghost, was directing them. The ghosts were busy taking people as well as other ghosts that were coming back.

The buff man was the first to go, getting hit by a random ghost, a girl who looked no older than twelve. He didn't even see her sneaking up from behind. The girl got two more people before she was taken by one of the ghosts in black. Jake grabbed Lizzy's hand and started running, not even bothering to call Ryan. As Jake looked back, he saw that both Ryan and the younger woman were following them.

Jake slowed down and had to shoot three ghosts to protect the younger woman, letting her get to him before they started running again. The woman had tears running down her face, near hysteria from what she was witnessing. The ghosts were destroying everything and the people around were acting crazy, some even killing others before the ghosts could get to them.

Jake reached the front revolving door to the tallest office building and ushered the others in. He followed them in and ran straight for the stairs, rushing past the guard who was clueless to what was going on outside, yelling at them to slow down in the concourse of the building.

Jake led them into the cement stairs that were hidden in the back corner of the building. Jake knew right where to run thanks to the abundance of signs hanging, indicating where stairs and elevators were located. The group ran, up and up, through many floors, Jake and Lizzy never tiring, Ryan and the young woman getting winded and sweating heavily as they got higher and higher in the building.

The group reached the top floor and Jake led them out of the stairs and into a hallway that was lined with offices. There was no one there, no indications that people were in the office. Jake pulled his pistol out, nodding to Ryan to do the same. They moved through the hallway, looking into the cubicles and offices but not seeing a person there.

"What are you doing up here?" a female voice rang out behind them.

Jake turned to see a startled woman in her thirties, fit and beautiful, wearing a tight black skirt, white button-up sleeveless blouse, with her eyes hidden behind black-rimmed glasses. Her blonde hair was in a ponytail that went past her neck and the instant she saw the guns in the men's hands, her hands went in the air.

"Don't hurt me," she blurted out.

"We're not going to hurt you," Jake said, approaching her. "There's something strange going on outside. An attack of some kind. We came here to get a better vantage point of the river to see what's going on and to possibly get an airlift out of here. Where is everyone in this office?"

"There's training this week," the woman said, hands still in the air. "All the sales reps and support staff are there. I'm just the receptionist so I have to stay here."

"Is there a room with a view to the river?" Jake asked.

"Follow me," the woman said.

Jake couldn't help but stare at the woman from behind as she walked, her tight skirt over a fit body and smile that he now had three women up here. He knew he should try to keep his mind focused on what was going on outside, but he'd always been a ladies man, always loved experimenting and meeting new women. Even with all the ghosts and destruction outside, all Jake could think of is how far he could get with all three of these women.

The lady led them in to a conference room that had a large black oblong table in the middle with sixteen black leather office chairs around it. To one end of the room was a white dry-erase board with a projection screen that could be pulled down hanging above it. A projector hung over the table with various input devices and controls in the corner. The room had floor-to-ceiling, wall-to-wall windows looking out over the park and river—an amazing view from the twenty-fifth floor of the building.

From their vantage point, they could see all the chaos occurring on the streets below. While Jake was sure people were yelling and screaming on the street level, at their level there was no sound at all. The receptionist removed her glasses as she gasped, looking at the carnage she hadn't known was going on. A tear ran down her cheek. The young woman was still fighting back fits of hysteria while Lizzy, Jake, and Ryan simply looked on.

Jake noticed some of the ghosts were starting to cross the water, walking across the river. The warrior women were firing guns but when there became too many for the women to contain, the entire river went up in flames, a circle of fire surrounding Genesis to keep ghosts and humans contained inside.

City Police Part IV

All the people in the conference room were silent, including Jake and Ryan. Jake knew there were procedures in place to contain any threat of the ghosts leaving, but as he looked at the river of fire, he never imaged it would be that extreme. A red flame, blue at the base and turning a yellow orange at the top, the flames climbed ten feet over the river. Jake could see that everything within ten feet of the river was melting from the intensity of the flames.

All the women in the group with Jake had their jaws on the ground, tears rolling down their faces. The people who'd been near the river were charbroiled, no chance of surviving the extreme heat. As they watched, a news chopper flew near the building to the south, hovering, trying to shoot video of the river. Before it could stay too long, a streak of fire tore through the air, hitting the chopper in an explosion.

Jake looked at the smoke trail and saw a warrior woman holding a rocket launcher. He knew they were going to be well armed but he didn't think they would have that level of fire power. Jake knew his decision to join Lizzy and Quad Force was the right one, now his only question was how to get away from Ryan and explain what was going on to the other two ladies with them.

"How can something like this happen?" the young woman asked, still almost hysterical.

"Why would they do something like that?" the receptionist asked.

"What are your names?" Jake asked, turning to the women.

"I'm Holly Brie," Holly said. "I've been a receptionist here since college, six years ago."

"I'm Kelly Salt," Kelly said.

"Holly, Kelly, nice to meet you," Jake said. "I'm Jake Arnold, that's Ryan Minot, and Lizzy Mick."

"Pleasure ladies," Lizzy said, smiling. "We are in a world of trouble. There were ghosts down there."

"Wait...ghosts?" Holly asked.

"There are ghosts down there," Jake said. "Genesis is the testing grounds for a new weapon developed by Ghost Town Labs. They won't let anyone leave the city, that's why they torched the river."

"I can only imagine how much pollutants that fire is putting in the water," Kelly said. "Someone needs to pay for that."

"How can you think of water pollution when you just saw your husband die and turn into a ghost?" Lizzy asked.

"I'm studying to be an environmental lawyer," Kelly said. "Both my parents are divorce lawyers. My dad represented my late husband in his third divorce, that's how we met."

"Sounds like a match made in heaven," Lizzy said.

"Judge me if you want, but it's a jungle out there," Kelly said. "Yes, I had to keep him happy, to an extent, but in return I got a powerful lawyer name. That name got me into college and graduate school. Steve practiced corporate law and was very well known at the University of Genesis."

"So your marriage was a sham?" Jake asked.

"Somewhat," Kelly said. "He was pathetic and treated me like garbage but I was planning on leaving him. I'd been accepted into the final law program so I didn't need him anymore, just his money, which I now have all of...makes this so much easier than leaving him."

"You don't care about him at all?" Lizzy asked.

"With the amount of shit I've put up with," Kelly smiled, "not in the least. I set a friend of mine on him, they were having an affair. This weekend I was going to catch them and that would have put everything in motion."

"Fine and dandy," Holly said, "but what about ghosts? What are we supposed to do?"

"Jake," Lizzy said, motioning. "Come with me."

Jake nodded and followed Lizzy out of the room to a small office just down the hall. The office was basic, a desk and chair, with pictures on the walls of a husband, wife, and three kids. The office smelled like stale cigars with a hint of old vanilla air freshener.

"There's no way we can risk a chopper," Lizzy said. "Not after what they did to the news chopper."

"What's our play then?" Jake asked.

"I don't know," Lizzy said. "I didn't have a contingency for something like this. We had boats in a harbor, cars, and a chopper...what else were we supposed to prepare?"

"I don't know," Jake said, looking at his phone. "I'm getting some strange reports here too. Someone was watching Hannah, the main ghost, she was near the fire when it went up and fire destroys those things. They don't know if it got her or not."

"How powerful is she?" Lizzy asked.

"I doubt anything can stop her," Jake said. "She's the top of the food chain when it comes to the ghosts, plus she's developed a group of ghosts, thirteen including herself. I shudder to think what they could do together if they ever left the city."

"That's something that cannot happen," Lizzy said.

"How many people do you have in the city?" Jake asked. "How many people were at that house?"

"We had ten total," Lizzy said. "You met the two in the house, one died trying to save that girl, and I'm with you, leaving six others out and about. There hasn't been a report posted for the last hour. We are using special satellite communications. I don't know what's going on."

"I think we stay up here," Jake said.

"What do you mean?"

"We're safe here. I doubt that the ghosts are going to search floor to floor looking for people, and we know how to defeat them, we can defend ourselves here."

"Good plan Jake," Lizzy said. "It will die down out there, no pun intended, and then we can get a chopper out of here. What about the other two?"

"Kelly would fit in perfectly with Ghost Town Labs," Jake said. "Anything to get to the top. Holly seems nice but I fear Ryan is loyal to the end to Ghost Town Labs. I think we'll need to get rid of him somehow."

"Kill him?"

"I was thinking of just ditching him," Jake smiled. "But if it comes to it I guess we'd have to. It could turn into a situation where it was him or us."

Just then gunshots rang out, two distinct shots. Jake and Lizzy rushed toward the conference room, Jake with his gun drawn, loading the magazine with real ammunition instead of the EPD rounds. Jake wished he had a larger gun than the 9mm but he was a good shot and knew how to handle himself.

As Jake peaked around the glass to see into the conference room, he saw Holly, in tears, holding a gun aimed at the ghosts of Ryan and Kelly. Jake quickly switched his magazine back to the EPD rounds and rushed into the room, shooting the two ghosts, each needing one shot to be taken down.

Jake pointed his gun at Holly, who dropped the gun she was holding as Lizzy rushed to her and hugged her. Jake noticed that Holly's white blouse was splattered with blood and she was trembling.

"What happened?" Lizzy asked as she embraced Holly.

"Kelly and Ryan were talking," Holly said, with a weak voice. "She was going on and on about how she really wasn't a bad person, just wanted to get ahead. Ryan looked at his phone and slowly started to pull a gun out. I backed up to the wall and pulled the office gun out."

Holly pointed to the board on the wall that was held on by a hinge on the top. Jake swung the board out and saw a small cubbyhole that was just large enough for a gun.

"Why is there a gun there?" Lizzy asked.

"Just in case someone comes to shoot the office up," Holly said. "If a sale goes bad or a customer gets angry. It's never been used and only a few people know about it."

Jake nodded as he picked up Ryan's phone and looked at the screen. There was a message saying the ghosts were overrunning the river and all Ghost Town Labs personnel were to destroy anyone they were with and return to the main compound in the downtown area. Ryan was just following his orders.

"Have you ever used a gun before?" Jake asked.

"A few years ago," Holly said. "I dated a guy who was big into target shooting. We would go to the shooting range and I got a lot of practice in with him. This was the first time I had to fire a gun that wasn't on the range. That's why they told me about it. I went to a couple of shooting competitions with him and actually placed in one of them. They figured that there might as well be a decent shot knowing about the gun."

"Here's the thing Holly," Jake said, squaring up with her, "I'm not a cop. Both Lizzy and I work for a company that's trying to bring the group that did this down. You can help us."

"What can I do?" Holly asked.

"We need people," Jake said. "I'm not sure how or what we'll do, but we can destroy this evil, the madness of Doctor Tesla before this damage falls on another group of innocent people."

"I'm with you," Holly said. "I need to change out of these bloody clothes. I have some extra stuff in a closet here, what should I wear?"

"What do you have?" Jake asked.

"Another work outfit like this," Holly said, "a black dress, a workout outfit, and some lounging clothes."

"The lounging clothes or workout stuff," Jake said. "Wear something you can run in."

Holly nodded and left the room. Jake and Lizzy exchanged a glance. Nothing needed to be said, they both were worried about what they'd gotten into. Neither knew how they were going to get out of the mess they were in. They passed the next few minutes looking at their phones, looking over the reports coming in.

Holly reentered the room, wearing a white cotton tank top and gray baggy sweatpants. Neither of the pair knew what to do yet, both were hoping the other would come up with an answer. There were no reports that helping them along. Finally, Jake broke the silence.

"We can't leave here," Jake said. "Not yet. Once things quiet down, can your people get a chopper in here Lizzy?"

"They should be able to," Lizzy said, looking out the window at the still raging fire. "Once that fire calms down and the Ghost Town Labs' women move out of the area."

"Then we wait," Jake said. "And pray."

With Ryan's corpse, a member of Quad Force, and a woman caught in a war she didn't know existed, Jake Arnold waited in the top floor of an office building, hoping some news would come that could rescue them.

Morgan Tesla, along with Isabella Corvus, Jack, and Tiffany had escaped through the tunnels. Morgan knew exactly how to lead them to get past any of Ghost Town Labs' guards. Once they were free, the group went to a nearby airport, a small single terminal port that mainly handled connecting and private flights, and bought tickets on the next flight out. By the time the river was set on fire, they were half-way to the west coast, ready to begin a new life together away from all the damage that Ghost Town Labs had caused in the Midwest.

Erin Minot, Cindy, and Donna stood guard at the tunnel, welcoming more Ghost Town Labs' Warrior Women to the city. The reinforcements cleaned out the parking ramp at the mall before heading into the city. They were stationed at the door when a strange order came in; if Jade Angels attempted to enter the city through the tunnel, they were to let them.

Maria, trapped in the bank vault with Amber and the Nancys, Kay and Dee, wondered when help would come. The hallway was crawling with ghosts and they had no way to get out.

The first day of the Genesis event was almost a complete success for Ghost Town Labs, the deaths of Ryan Minot and Mackenzie Hanson a black mark on the day. They'd seen the extent of what ghosts could do and how large populations were reacting to the threat. Although reports from the city leaked out, leading military to surround the town, waiting to get in, Ghost Town Labs couldn't have asked for a better day. As night set in, reports started coming that members of the former RAW Troops, Jade Angels, were making their way to Genesis. With them was Madison Tesla, now a cunning and brave warrior.

Although no one had seen Ethan Drew, Michelle Tesla, or Doctor Victor Tesla, people knew that as night set in on Genesis, the destruction would only continue. Ghost Town Labs was busy making extraction plans for key personnel trapped in the city when a two-part report came in that made them all very happy; part one was that Jades Angels had reached the parameter of Genesis and were in the process of entering the city, and the second part is that there were more dead than living walking the streets of Genesis.

The only concern that anyone had was that Hannah, the Genesis Ghost, and her coven hadn't been seen since they were seen leaving the park area after the river started on fire...

ABOUT LEIF J. ERICKSON

Leif Erickson was born and raised on a grain farm outside Wheaton, MN, just a stone's throw from White Rock, SD, which served as the inspiration for the Ghost Town series. From a very early age, Leif knew that he was going to be a farmer, just like his father and grandfather. As he grew up, Leif learned everything he could about farming, always riding in equipment with his dad and helping out wherever he could.

After Leif graduated high school he attended North Dakota State University in Fargo, North Dakota, where he achieved a BS in Agricultural Economics along with a minor in History. During his time in college, Leif networked with many other farmers from across North Dakota, South Dakota, and Minnesota, while advancing his knowledge in all aspects of agricultural. With a diploma in hand, Leif returned to the family farm and started his career as a farmer.

The first season was very successful and stood as a testament to the hard work and education that Leif had received. All signs pointed to a lifetime career as a farmer until a family tragedy struck and the family farm was dispersed. For the first time in his life, Leif didn't know what he wanted to pursue for a career.

Leif returned to Fargo, ND where he began his career as a stock and futures trader. It was during this time that he began to become serious about writing. With one computer watching the markets, Leif would be on the other, writing. Leif quickly realized though that Fargo wasn't the city or location that he wanted to make a home in. Less than one year since he moved there, Leif moved to Plymouth MN, in the Twins Cities area.

Continuing with the trading and writing, Leif began to learn everything that he could about writing, about storytelling, and about the hero's journey. Leif spent his spare time reading novels or books about writing. It was during his time in the Cities that Leif wrote many, many different stories, getting the outlines and first drafts finished. In the three years that Leif was in the Cities, he wrote the first draft for over fifty different stories.

Leif received information about a career opportunity that was back in his hometown of Wheaton so he returned to go to work for the local grain elevator. The work was hard and the days were long without much time for writing. Leif missed being able to write every day. He had so many more stories that he wanted to write. Being aggressive and a hard worker, Leif quickly moved up the ladder in the company and within six months he was in a management position.

Although Leif had met and dated many women when he was in the Twin Cities, it was in Wheaton where he met the new Science Teacher at his old High School and within fifteen months of meeting the pair were married at Good Shepherd Lutheran Church in Wheaton. Many have described the pair as absolutely made for each other, and they spend much of their time hiking in State Parks or canoeing the local lakes and rivers.

Being back in Wheaton, Leif used his free time to polish up and finish some of his stories. He got two stories to the point where he was satisfied to bring them to the marketplace and share them with others. Although he still works for the elevator, Leif looks forward to the day when he can write fulltime, offering more novels and screenplays to entertain and delight others.

Throughout his life, Leif was always quick to be able to tell a story. He had an uncanny ability to quickly make up a story on the spot (sometimes to the dismay of parents and teachers) and to pull people into the story with wild characters, amazing locations, and fantastical storylines. Although Leif